This Place Of Men

"Your Sweetness Is My Weakness" by Barry White
"Simply Beautiful" by Al Green

Chapter I

Sometimes he saw things when he drank. But that was only when he drank too much. He didn't drink often, but sometimes he would become careless of his burden when he sat before a glass, and the one glass would become a full bottle until his head would fill and the visions would come.

They had been happening most of his adult life, the visions. They began to occur while he was in prison. They started as reflections he would have at night; then they transformed themselves into quick momentary sightings during the day until finally turning into resonant narratives that gripped him whenever he was inebriated. He wanted to tell people who looked at him when he was drunk that once, when he was younger, he had dreams. He had had dreams like every young man, but now he saw things, no dreams. And sometimes he even wondered if calling the images visions was appropriate, so he would have told them he simply saw things. That's what he would have told them if he spoke to them, but he rarely spoke to anyone about his life.

Once he saw a man stumbling through an alley with his throat slit. It was one night while he was getting his dick sucked. At first he didn't notice the man; he was watching the kid's head going back and forth at his crotch. Probably some student from NYU whose parents didn't know they had sent him all the way to New York to suck dicks.

It was the kid who saw the man first. He fell back against the wall and gasped, 'Oh my God!', his eyes wide with terror.

He turned to see what had startled him, and there he was. A man was stumbling, his hand to his throat. It was too dark to see the wound, but he saw the blood, like searching fingers down the front of the white shirt and he knew by the position of the man's hand and by the hollow wheeze that rose through the closed hot alley what had happened.

The boy jumped up and ran from the alley, but he had stood for a second and assessed the matter. Then, realizing his own possible endangerment and the fact that the kid had run out without paying him, he too ran towards the street.

At least that's what he thinks happened. He knew there was a man who stumbled through the alley, and he knew it had startled him and the boy, but he was never sure if the man's throat had been cut. He never heard the sirens or saw the EMT racing to the alley as he stood a bit away, or the gathering of a crowd; in fact passersby moved across the entrance of the alley with no awareness of the assault. It was times like that when he would assume that what he saw had not really happened.

But all his visions were not so gruesome. Some of them would be pleasant. They would be of better times so long ago: sitting in his car, his arm around him, watching the tops of trees against the remaining light of day, neither one speaking; the soft lime glow of the radio dial against their faces. The low music, warming them in spite of the chill of a winter's eve, and how they would talk of their love for each other. . . but at that point the silence would set in; it always set in, the dark, covering silence. And he would drink more to fill that silence, the darkness and the pain.

But today he wouldn't drink much. In fact, he hadn't drunk too much in the last few weeks in anticipation of his return. He knew he would need everything in tact for his return. So now he sat and looked out the window of the bar and assessed the changes of his hometown. It had been a long time since he left home, but now he was back. He had arrived in Cincinnati two days ago but hadn't let anyone know he had returned except for his younger sister with whom he was staying. He chose to lay low because he knew he would have to account for the years away; and after all those years away people might want to know the reason for his return. The first deed wouldn't be too difficult to explain. After all, everyone knew of the circumstances that drove him away. But it was the second question that would be hard to answer because he wasn't sure why he returned.

He turned the glass that held his drink and watched as the amber liquid splashed against its sides. How many times over the years had he done that? How many times had he held the same thoughts that now crowded his head? He was tired of nursing drinks and memories. Things would be different now.

Raising the glass to his mouth he finished his drink with one swallow. Then rising from the bar, he turned and walked out onto the street. Yes. Things would be different now.

Chapter II

"Daddy, momma said you better git up an start gittin' ready!" Abassi was calling at the top of his lungs and giggling into his father's pillow that was playfully wrapped around his head. Suddenly tossing off the pillow, Terrell reached out and grabbed his son and wrestled him to the bed. Abassi screamed and kicked as he engaged in what had become a morning ritual. Terrell looked down at his son in the morning sunlight that shone through the window.

He knew he would miss them and their mother over the next few weeks. They were leaving for Atlanta for Karen's family reunion. Terrell wasn't able to leave just yet. He had to remain behind and oversee the budget for the construction of the new church.

"Daddy, when are you coming down?" Kenya asked as Terrell loaded the last piece of luggage in the car.

"In two weeks, baby."

"Well, hurry up."

Terrell laughed, "Yes ma'am."

On the way to the airport, Karen went over last minute details. Her hands moved emphatically as she recounted the number at which she and the kids could be reached, the meals he should cook to make sure he ate well, and how to do laundry without fading the clothes. Terrell just smiled and nodded his head to her instructions.

At the gate, Terrell kissed Karen and the kids. "I'm gonna miss you," he said as he held Karen to his chest.

"Me too. Just hurry up. Okay?"

"Okay." Then he kissed them again before they boarded the plane.

"Bye Daddy!" Kenya and Abassi yelled as they pulled their mother along the walkway.

"Bye," he waved.

The plane lifted to the sky as Terrell continued to wave his good-byes. After it had disappeared into the depth of the sky he stood a little longer, his face to the window, then he turned and made his way to the car.

The drive back to Mason wasn't too long so he decided to kill a little time. He expected he'd make it back in time to receive Karen's call letting him know they had made it to Atlanta. Then he would wait for the call from Bishop Abrams.

It was a hot, lazy day with a sun that sat white and high against a blue sky. He guided the car silently onto the streets of downtown Cincinnati where the sun shone bright and vigorous and heated the large buildings that seemed to push against the sky.

Next he drove to The West End where he watched a game of pick up basketball. At first he felt uneasy as he walked up to the court. He had never had the experience of playing basketball. He'd always felt he just wasn't made for it. But he had always been astounded by the sheer grace and athleticism of the guys as they moved with quick starts and stops, sudden twists and turns and then sudden leaps, their dark lean bodies, like stilettos, jabbing the rim.

But soon he gained confidence and leaned against the link fence at the edge of the court, his fingers gripping the links. He could hear the grunts and the taunts of the players, and he could hear, almost feel, the contact of their bodies as they pressed at each other. One of the young men glanced over at him before turning on the heat, driving past his opponent and slamming the ball through the rim. The rim shook under the force of the dunk and the young man came down gracefully before springing backwards and pointing his finger triumphantly at the guy who had attempted to guard him.

Terrell laughed and shook the fence, "Woo!" The suddenness of his own voice startled even himself.

The young man looked at Terrell then broke into a wide grin as his dark brown face glistened under the sun. Terrell couldn't help but grin back.

After a while, Terrell looked at his watch. He had been at the court longer than he thought, so he hurried to the car. As he got in the car he looked back at the court. The young man looked at him and raised his head slightly to bid him goodbye.

It was late when he arrived home. He pushed the key in the lock and just as he unlocked the door his cell phone rang. He answered it, "Hello?" He knew who it was.

"Where are you?"

"Home. Sorry Babe. It was such a beautiful day and all, so I just took my time getting back. Sorry."

"I called the house twice and you weren't there," Karen said. Then she clicked her tongue. It was almost two hours since she and the kids had arrived at her parents' home. "You know, you could at least be by the phone to find out if we made it okay."

"I knew you'd be okay. I mean…" He stopped short as he realized he had no excuse for his behavior.

After a short silence, Karen spoke. "Terrell, for once, try to think about others. Okay?"

"What're you talking about?"

She let out a sigh. "Never mind. Just be careful. You know there's a lot going on out there these days."

"Karen, please. Don't start it."

"Look. Let's not get into this. I love you and I just become concerned sometimes."

"I know Babe. And I love you too."

"Then you might want to show it. That and a little responsibility. Try to focus on your family just for once, okay?"

Terrell didn't respond. She always knew the right words to say to cut him short. They were words that she carried with her, words like sharp things she'd collected over their years together: pins, needles and glaring shards of glass that she would pull out at need and hold him hostage.

That said, she ended the conversation.

"Well I have to go now. Good bye." The deed was done.

"I'll call you tomorrow," Terrell said.

This time she didn't respond. She just hung up the phone.

He stood for a second with the phone in his hand. Then he laid it on the kitchen counter. Would she ever let go? This thing she held over his head. It was in the past. Way before he'd even met her. He was young and crazy then. Things change. He often wished he'd never told her about his past. But she wasn't alone. Everyone who knew him, family and friends alike still had that look in their eyes that never seemed to go away. The shame they held for him always stood somewhere in their deepest stares and in the faintest sorrow their voices carried when they spoke to him. It never seemed to end.

Sitting down to the meal he had prepared, the one marked 'Monday' in bold letters, he began to eat his dinner. Then he placed his bible alongside his plate, opened it and began reading the first passage his eyes fell upon:

'... seat two men, unprincipled men, near him, and have them testify, "You cursed God and the king," and then take him out and stone him to death.'

After a while Terrell closed his bible and sat in the fading sun that moved to the corners of his den.

It was exactly eight o'clock when the bishop called. "How are you this evening, brother Mitchell?" He spoke in his usual manner, a tone deliberate in its compassion. Sometimes, when Terrell playfully imitated the minister for his wife he imagined the years of studied compassion to which some ministers must adjust. But he never told his wife of his musings. Though he jested about Bishop Abrams' style, to demean him would be akin to heresy. After all, it was the bishop who had stood by his side and deflected Terrell's detractors years ago when it was suggested that he was less than a victim of the incident. And it was Bishop Abrams who made sure the proper party received its just reward. From that time on the bishop influenced Terrell's life, and his parents were grateful for the intervention. However, their were times when Terrell wanted to be out of the shadow of the powerful man, to remove the albatross from around his neck. But at the same time he was reminded of what he might have become if it hadn't been for the bishop. And it was this gratitude that bound him to the man.

"I'm doing fine bishop."

"How are Sister Mitchell and the kids doing? Oh yeah, they're in Atlanta now, aren't they?"

"Yes, they are. They left today. I talked with Karen this evening. She and the kids are staying at her parents' and all are doing fine."

"Give them my love. So have you straightened out the budget matter with the contractor yet?"

"Yes I have. Actually it was a trivial matter and they were more than willing to comply."

"Well I'm sure that in dealing with you they had no choice."

"We-l-l-l..."

"Come on now. Why do you think you're managing this project?"

"Because I'm a penny pincher."

"Well that too," Bishop Abrams chuckled. "So what do you think of their work? I mean really think of it. I've seen some of their work and it looks good, but is it quality stuff? You know I do want a black-owned business constructing the church, but not at the expense of shabby craftsmanship. We want to raise the roof during services, not have it come down, you know." The bishop laughed.

"I know what you mean," Terrell chuckled. "But really, they're good. They're the ones who constructed Mission Baptist. They really did a good job with that. I think they'll do us proud."

The bishop hummed in agreement. "You got the ball on this. By the way, speaking of Thurman Brothers, I might need some occasional input from you and

Karen concerning the Black Ministers Coalition and the Stanton Thurman race. It won't take much of your time. I figure with Karen's background in history and your financial background, we might just need some advice every now and then. Just to keep you two on notice in case we need you."

Much of what Terrell knew of Stanton Thurman came from the construction deal, campaign ads and from what he'd read in the papers. He did know enough about him to know he shared many of the bishop's political views. However, Terrell wasn't sure if he wanted to be part of this campaign, if not because he hadn't made up his mind whether or not he shared Thurman's views, a fact that the bishop hadn't taken into account, but of the fact that he was beginning to feel he was being pulled into a world in which he wasn't sure he belonged.

"I'm not sure what I can do. But I'll do my best."

"That's what we need. I'll get back with you later this week to check on things. Give Sister Mitchell and the kids my love. Good night Brother Mitchell."

"Good night Bishop."

Chapter III

"So do you still love him?"

His sister's question floated from the kitchen and coupled his shoulders in

search of a reply and he knew, from the sincerity with which she spoke that she

deserved an answer. He leaned forward on the railing of the balcony and watched

the perfect evening that was growing around him. The sharp white day and

stifling heat was now turning into a quiet warm sunset.

"What do you mean?" He spoke as he turned to face her.

"You know, do you love him - - at least a little?"

"Girl, don't ask me any questions like that."

"Why not?"

"Because."

"Because what?"

"Because I don't feel like talkin' 'bout that," he said as he turned back to

the balcony. It had been years since the subject had been broached and years just to get over the feelings he held for him. So that now he'd just as soon leave that part of his past in the shadows.

"Oh. So let me get this right. So you just come back here after being away for twenty years and say you don't feel like talking." Courtney put down the head of lettuce she had been shredding and walked into the living room. "Has it occurred to you that this is the first time in my life that I can recall ever seeing you in person? I was only three years old when you left. All I ever saw of you for the past twenty years were photographs. So excuse me if I ask you questions."

He stood silent for a moment before finally replying. "Yeah. You're right." He turned back around and leaned against the railing of the balcony. "And to answer your question... I really don't know, y'know? It's been twenty years. It ain't about me and him no more. It's about everything. It's about being hurt... big time and spending the last twenty years of my life trying to sort it out."

"Why didn't you just come on home?"

"To what? A father who couldn't look me in the eye? And Mama. All the time fighting to make people respect me. She couldn't force anybody to respect me. Everybody hated me. Nah," he said, shaking his head.

"Or we could've gone up to see you. Me and Mama were always trying to get you to let us come up."

"I couldn't let y'all see me that way."

"What way?"

"I had it rough when I first got to New York. No, I couldn't let y'all see me that way."

"But twenty years?" Then she sighed, "Well, whatever the case, I'm just glad you finally came home." She spoke as she walked over to her brother and hugged his tall, athletic form. "And I'm sure everybody else will be too. But you know what's scaring me about all this? The silence. It's the silence that scares me."

His dark complexion deepened even more as he stared into the space before him, "Everything'll be alright," he mumbled as he stroked his sister's hair.

* * * *

That night he lay awake and stared at the ceiling. He reflected on his conversation with his sister. She was right; there were a lot of questions to be asked. But he had survived for so long by avoiding questions that now answers didn't come easy.

She just didn't know what he'd been through, the true nature of his agony. She didn't understand that the pain hadn't ended upon his release from prison; it simply took on a new face. That was why he didn't come home after his release. He didn't know what to do with all the pain and he wasn't about to put any of it on his family. They had been through enough. So instead of returning home he headed for New York.

He recalled the day he arrived in New York City; his mix of fear and anticipation as he stepped off the bus in Port Authority. He looked around the huge terminal at all the faces that seemed to have someplace to go and he wondered what would be his next move. He knew that outside of the terminal was his chance to make things right, but he had no plans on how to make it all happen.

He took the escalator up a few flights and got off in the main lobby of the terminal. The sheer size of the building was fascinating. He looked across the lobby, past all the people and the indoor shops, at the doors that led outside and wondered which one he should walk through. He knew that one of them would lead him to a better life, while the others…

Finally, he gathered his meager belongings and took a chance. He stepped through one of the doors and found himself standing outside. The dizzying rush of people and the din of the mid-town traffic immediately overwhelmed him, so he stood for a moment and gathered his senses. He didn't know which way to go, so he took a deep breath and stepped into the currents and became washed along the shores.

No, Courtney couldn't know of these things. He would never let her know. She would never know how it felt to sleep on benches, to go for days on paltry handouts of food, to feel so much grime on your skin until it cut through the flesh. She would never know how it felt to hide with shame from condescending glances, to hear the cries of the insane or to fall into the scope of predators.

"… You must work out…"

"…I used to…"

"…You ever play football?…"

"…Mm hm…"

(A tug at the waist. The sound of a belt buckle.)

"…Nah man. I don't wanna get undressed…"

"…Just a little bit. Come on…"

(The sound of a zipper. He closes his eyes)

Those were memories he'd rather forget. He didn't need any answers. He just needed to forget.

The next morning he sat in the living room and looked out the balcony window. Courtney had left for work but not before stopping by his room to check on him. He had told her everything was all right; and now he sat with the phone book in his lap. He knew time was running out, that soon he would have to return to New York.

His hand moved with slight hesitation as he fingered the light sheets of the phone book, each page creating a soft swishing sound as they passed his view. Then the name came to him. It rose lightly from the page of the phone book and floated, airily, before his eyes causing the mists of memory to lift. A breath of relief escaped his mouth as he realized he had taken that step into the past, that he was going even deeper along the journey he dreaded most.

"Terrell." He whispered with disbelief as if he'd never expected to see the name again. Then he stared off into the distant morning. He wasn't sure how he felt about seeing Terrell's name. At times he despised him, and at times he still cared for him.

Picking up the tablet and a pen, he scribbled down the information. Then, laying the instruments aside, he stood and walked across the living room to a point far from where he had been sitting. There he stood in the cool shadow of the room as if the glare of his past was too much to bear.

Sometimes he frightened himself with his attachment to his past. He wanted to leave it alone, but like a wounded animal it always returned to its home in search of nurturing. Yet unlike an animal, mortally wounded, it never died. He was often unsure about how he would treat the elements of his past if he ever came in contact with them again. That is what frightened him most. But that fear wasn't enough to overshadow his need for resolution, and that need to end his nightmares is what now took him from the shadows back to the phone book as he whisked through another set of pages. Another name:

Abrams, Walter, Bishop

Chapter IV

"So while the cat's away the mice will play."

"What?" Terrell looked at Harlan who had come into his office and had securely closed the door.

"You know. You are a single man. Well at least for the next couple of weeks."

"Harlan, I'm not a single man; my wife's out of town. That's all."

"Well call it what you want. But look, you gotta make the best of it while you can."

Terrell smiled and shook his head.

Harlan looked around Terrell's office, "What? She got spies lurking around here?"

"Man, whatever."

"So you gonna go out with us for a few drinks after work?"

"On a Wednesday?"

"On a Wednesday?" Harlan mocked as he walked across the office. He was short and had a dark complexion; and with his shaved head and bowed legs, he looked like a panther cub. "Hell yeah. Who says we have to wait until Friday to go out for a couple of drinks. Come on, bruh," he said as he punched Terrell's chest.

"I can't. I got a meeting tonight."

"Oh yeah." Harlan spoke incredulously.

"No, really."

"What time?"

"Seven-thirty."

"Man you can still make that. Now say yeah so I can win this bet."

Terrell laughed, "That figures. Yeah. Tell the Nubians yeah, I'll step out with them tonight. But only for a moment."

"Cool." Harlan turned and headed for the door.

"And since you just won a bet, the drinks are on you," Terrell advised.

"Damn. Me and my big mouth. See you at five."

Terrell and his colleagues arrived at Donny's where they took a table out on the patio.

"I got first round," Melvin said as he waved his large hand in a sweeping motion. "Whatcha havin'?"

"CC and seven." Jasper was quick to order as he loosened his tie from his skinny neck.

"Damn boy. Slow down," Harlan jokingly reprimanded. "I'll have a gin and tonic," he said.

"Terrell?" Melvin asked.

"A coke."

They all looked at Terrell with exasperation.

"I have a meeting. What can I say?"

"He'll make up for it on Friday. Right?" Harlan looked at Terrell for agreement.

"Yeah. I guess so."

The other three rolled their eyes and laughed.

Melvin leaned slightly over the table and tapped his pointer finger on its top, "She got you on a chain my brotha."

"Let's not start that again," Terrell moaned.

"She does," Melvin persisted.

"How do you know it's Karen? Maybe it's just that I like spending time with my family."

"Oh, oh, oh," the other three called out.

"So now you're trying to say we don't like to spend time with our families." Jasper cocked his head a bit as he spoke.

"Nah, nah. I'm just saying I tend to do most of my socializing with my family and my church. I never did do much hangin'."

"Not even as a young buck?" Harlan asked.

"Nope."

"Now you know we don't believe that."

"So just how did you live your buck years? I never hear you talk about nobody but Karen. I mean she's a down sister. Don't get me wrong. But she's not the first one is she?" Melvin grinned.

"Wait, wait. This ain't no high school truth or dare. I came out tonight to hang with y'all and you givin' me the tenth degree. Now what's up with that?"

The other three men looked at each other.

"You're just so sneaky, man; but not in the bad way." Jasper said.

"Private." Melvin corrected.

Terrell turned his head from Melvin to Jasper, then back again. "Privacy's good. Or haven't the two of you learned that?"

"You're right," Harlan spoke up. "Ain't none of our damn business. I mean, why do I wanna know about his younger years anyway? I got mine on. That's all that matters to me."

"And that *is* all that matters," Terrell chuckled.

Melvin and Jasper looked at each other.

"Hey. It's cool with us- - that you used to sleep with dogs." Melvin kidded. Then they all burst into laughter.

"So look, you know they're asking where we go when we hang out." Jasper said, changing the subject.

"Like who?" Terrell asked.

"Matt, Leonard."

"Yeah. Even Mr. Bartlett made some comment last week," Melvin said.

"What did he say?" Harlan asked.

"You guys going to hang out again this evening?"

"I told him 'yeah'. I wanted to say, 'why'? Nat Turner's dead. We ain't gonna burn this firm down. Relax. Shit."

They all laughed.

"So that means we really gotta go out Friday. Drive 'em crazy," Terrell said.

"It's on." They all laughed and hit their fists together.

In a while, Terrell looked at his watch. "Hey look y'all. I gotta make it.

Got that meeting."

"Yeah, I gotta head on out too," Melvin said as he glanced at his watch.

"Got you on that chain, huh?" Terrell laughed.

"Ahhh…" Harlan and Jasper laughed as they pointed at Melvin.

"Yeahh," Melvin sighed.

* * * *

Terrell arrived a bit early at the church. He tapped on the bishop's office door. "Hold on," he heard the bishop say to someone.

"Come on in," the bishop called through the door.

Terrell stuck his head in the office and saw that the bishop was on the phone. "I'll just sit out here until you're finished," he whispered.

The bishop winked and nodded his head.

Then Terrell walked back into the sanctuary. It was quiet. Charles, the janitor, had finished for the evening and had taken off. Soon choir members would be arriving for Wednesday practice. Terrell never understood why Charles cleaned the church before choir rehearsal instead of afterwards. He assumed it was because rehearsal ended so late; but with Charles there was no telling. He looked at the rows of empty pews, and in his mind's eye he saw the faces of the congregation: Mother Abrams, Deacon Morliss, his own parents, and many others. He also saw the years he'd spent at Savior's Temple. This church, this place of worship, was all he'd ever known. It was home and the faces that had come and gone over the years would always be his family. Then, for reasons he couldn't explain, his mind began to drift back until it settled on a particular evening twenty years ago when he had stood in the same spot; only that time the feelings were different.

Savior's Temple had always seemed like a large church to him, full of love and warmth; and of laughter and fiery sermons meant to extol the spirit. But it had never seemed so cold as it had that evening as Terrell sat alone in the sanctuary waiting to be summoned to the bishop's office. He looked around at the stained glass windows that radiated from the pristine walls of off white and he breathed in the warm scent of the wooden pews that shone dark and polished. All the years of his life had been spent in there, from his christening through his baptism and he'd always had fond memories of being a part of the church family until now. Now his place in the family was being called into question and his standing in the eyes of God suspect. He had been told that he was an abomination, though he didn't feel like one. All he knew was he was in love. He remembered how he had just wanted everyone to leave him alone. He recalled looking up at the painting of a compassionate Christ that looked at him from a radiant nimbus, and wondered why God made him if He knew it would be like this?

His thoughts were interrupted by the bishop. "Brother Mitchell, come on into the office." He spoke just the way he had at that moment twenty years ago.

"You were a bit early."

"I know. I called myself beating the traffic and must have beat myself as well."

Bishop Abrams laughed. Then he looked at the clock on his desk. "Actually, you're still a little early because Stanton called and said he'd be running a bit late." Then he motioned for Terrell to sit.

"Oh. Okay."

"I was talking to Bishop Clemmons up in Detroit. We were thinking of holding a convention here sometime this year."

"Where?"

"Hopefully the convention center."

"That's cutting it kind of close bishop. I'm sure it's going to take at least six months to get everything moving."

"That's what I was telling Bishop Clemmons, but he's persistent."

"Next year, maybe spring or summer, would be more feasible."

"I agree. By then we'll have the new church finished and can host some of the convention there."

Terrell nodded his head.

"I would like to telecast portions to those members of the organization that might not be able to make it," the bishop continued.

Again, Terrell nodded in agreement, "That's an idea. We'll have to start making arrangements to do that."

"I know. And that's part of the reason you, me and Stanton are meeting tonight. You see, I would like to build a production and telecasting facility in the new church."

Terrell raised his eyebrows which caused Bishop Abrams to grin, his hazel eyes sparkling. "It can be done."

"Yessir. But so late in the game..."

"It's never too late. I've already run it past Stanton and he says it can be done."

"So I just have to go over the budget to see where to get the money."

The bishop smiled and nodded his head. "We'll be the talk of the town. Probably the talk of the nation with an on site state-of-the-art production and telecasting facility. Some white churches have things like that; but I don't know of any black churches that have that."

Terrell rubbed his chin, "We got a lot of planning to do."

"I'll say." Again, the bishop grinned.

The sound of a door opening came from the sanctuary.

"That must be Stanton."

Stanton came up the steps and walked briskly into the office. He was a tall husky man with a striking face and unusually smooth skin for someone who was in his mid-fifties.

"Hi bishop, Terrell." He spoke from gleaming white teeth.

"Hi Stanton." They both spoke as they shook his hand.

"I was just telling Terrell about our conversation about the production and telecast facility."

"Yeah. It can happen. No problem," Stanton spoke in his baritone voice as he settled in the chair next to Terrell.

"So how much is all this going to cost?" Terrell asked.

"I'm not gonna lie. A lot."

"But it's an investment. We can recoup the money sooner than you think." The bishop joined in.

Stanton measured Terrell's response, which was one of silence. Then he pulled out the paper work. "I've already started checking into possible suppliers. Surprisingly, there's quite a few here in town."

"But are they the best?" The bishop inquired.

"Now that's what I'll have to find out. I've already enlisted the services of someone who knows a lot about that stuff. We'll go over each respondent with a fine tooth comb." He shuffled through the papers and laid a folder on top of the pile. "Now here is a rough draft of the RFP." He said this while distributing copies to the bishop and Terrell. "I figure we can start looking it over and Terrell, you can make notations regarding cost… and anything else you might see."

"Bishop, you don't think we're moving a little too fast, do you?"

The bishop took off his glasses and gave Terrell a stern look. "If you're talking about running it past the board, it's no problem. You know they'll see it my way. Anyway, who in the world would deny that this is what we need to expand our reach," he said as he put his glasses back on his nose. "Now let's get going with this fellas."

It was nine-o'clock when they finished the meeting.

"Look, you two go ahead," the bishop said. "I have to make one other phone call to L.A. I have to get all my work out the way before I leave here. Mother Abrams becomes quite bothered when I take work home," he chuckled.

Terrell and Stanton bade the bishop good night and headed outside.

"You can probably tell the bishop is adamant about this project." Stanton said. They stood by Terrell's car.

"Yeah."

"There's a reason for that, you know. You see, Bishop Abrams is getting old. And he knows it's just a matter of time before some young minister, standing in the wings, will replace him. I mean, hell, I'm sure you've probably heard the rumblings yourself. 'He's too old,' We need somebody who can reach out to the younger crowd'. Hell they're probably even complaining about the type of music he prefers to have played. But Mahalia's gone. And so is James Cleveland. It's a brand new day. Everybody knows that- - even Bishop Abrams. So he just wants to do this one last thing, to leave his mark."

"Yeah. And I guess what happened at Zion doesn't make the bishop feel too comfortable," Terrell agreed.

"Yeah. Had the sheriff's department come in and move ol' Reverend Smallwood from the church. His own congregation. Now you know that's sad."

"Yeah. So I guess we gotta make this happen, huh?"

"I think so, man," Stanton said as he nodded his head. Then he looked at his gold watch, "Well look, I better get goin'. Let's try not to let the bishop down, okay?" He shook Terrell's shoulder, then walked to his car. "Oh, and Terrell, I hear you might be interested in helping with my run for city council."

"Well, I said I'd think about it."

"Well, I hope you decide to. We could use your talents. Talk at you later." Then he disappeared into the large black sedan and drove off into the night.

Chapter V

The sight of The Crutchfield Motel was a forewarning of what he would see upon his return home. The abandoned motel, with its modern angles, rose like a ghost ship out of a sea of abandoned cars that covered the lot; a bleak greeting to visitors as they crossed the city limits. He remembered when the motel was a place of constant activity, dubious, but alive. But now it sat quiet and served as an echo of its former self.

Turning off Shepherd Lane, he headed for Steffens Street, which was once the center of town, and saw that it too had fallen. He remembered when he used to sit along the curbs or on top of cars with his buddies and drink sodas while watching the busy traffic there and coming on to the girls who passed by in tight bell bottoms and sporting large afros that shimmered in the sun from an abundance of Afro Sheen, and a smile traveled across his face because he knew that regardless of the changes that had taken place over the twenty years he was away, Lincoln Heights would always be home.

He was never quite sure of the history of Lincoln Heights. He knew when it came to be, around nineteen forty-seven, but he wasn't sure how it came to be or why. He'd heard that it had started as a company town for the defense plant just east of the city and that when the war ended the black folks who had settled there to work in the plant remained. But he was never sure. All he was sure of was the memories of growing up in a town with all black faces; and that was special enough for him.

The sky was gray and hung low the day Otis returned home; so low that it seemed to rest on top of the small houses that lined Jackson Street. He pulled into the driveway of the one floor house he grew up in and sat for a moment in the car. He didn't remember the house being as small as it now appeared. A new roof and fresh siding covered the outside and thermal windows had replaced the old ones; but other than that, little had changed. Even one of his father's dump trucks was parked to one side of the narrow driveway the way he used to park years ago. It was as if his parents had been holding everything at bay until he returned.

As he walked up to the door he heard his mother's voice come from inside, "Lord, Jesus!" then the front door swung open and she grabbed him round the neck and began to sob uncontrollably, "Thank you Lord, Thank you Lord!"

Otis was overcome by his mother's tears and began to cry as well; and for the first time since he left he felt a real sense of guilt.

After a while, his mother loosened her embrace and took him by the hand where she led him into the living room. She turned on a lamp and looked at him, her eyes moving over his face, "Sometimes I wondered if I

would ever see my child again, Lord. But you knew, you knew." Then she
began to cry again.

Otis put his long arms around her shoulders, "It's alright Ma. It's
alright." He rocked her and rubbed her shoulders. The plumpness of her
body brought back memories of her warmth and the guilt in him rose even
more.

Finally his mother looked up at him and smiled. Then she shook her
head. "When you called me last night and told me you were here I almost
fainted. I just couldn't believe it. But Lord, here you are. My child is
home." She stood there for a while longer and assessed him. He wanted to
hide his face, unsure of what damage the years had done. Then she hooked
her arm in his, "Come on. Let me get you somethin' to eat" and led him to
the kitchen.

Otis watched his mother as she sat a plate in front of him. "Where is
everybody?"

"It's just me, your daddy and Munny. Jun lives in Paddock Hills."

"Paddock Hills?"

"Mm hm. Got a nice home there. And Dana lives in Pleasant
Ridge."

"Well alright." He spoke in a lukewarm tone.

"Daddy ain't in yet?" Though he asked about his father, his
anticipation of him was lessened by memories of how his father had treated
him while he was going through his ordeal. When the accusations arose and
the incident came to light, his father had hardened like the after-thought of a
transgression, never looking his son in the eye, even rarely standing in the
same room as him. Conversation with his son had diminished; terse replies,

done only in passing, and grunts of disapproval became common. For any needful communication he employed his beleaguered wife as emissary. Even during the sentencing his father had fixed his eyes straight ahead and did not look at him.

The years had softened his anger towards his father, but the darkness remained.

"No. Munny ain't either," his mother added. "They usually come in around the same time. Munny works at Ford. Been there seventeen years."

"And still living at home, huh? She just won't leave y'all's side, will she?"

His mother poured some punch into the glass in front of him and then into one that sat alongside her own plate. "No. Munny is still Munny. Gonna be no matter what happens," she said as she seated herself. "She and your father should be comin' in soon."

She looked in Otis' face once again. Then she smiled and put her hand on top of his, "You really look good. I know you sent pictures over the years, but seeing you is better than pictures any ol' day. A mother's got to see her child grow."

Otis gave a weak smile, "Yes ma'am."

"Sometimes I would take all the pictures you sent me over the years; and I would lay them out across the table here, and I would just look at them trying to keep up with you. And I would see the changes," she grinned as she waved a finger, "but I needed to see you."

"I wanted to see you too." He looked at his mother's expression and saw the questions behind her eyes. "I just had too much going on."

"But ain't that what life's all about, Otis? Things going on?"

"Yeah. But I didn't know what to do about it. There was so much
happening in my mind that I just wanted to get away." He paused, and
looked down at his plate, "To tell you the truth, I was ashamed."

"Ashamed? Look I know what you did… what happened back then
was on everybody's lips, but so what? Wasn't any of them gonna live your
life for you, so why should you care what people think?"

"Ma, that's easy to say until the shoe's on the other foot."

"Mm, mm, mm. Boy, you act like you the only one with problems."
Then she waved her hand towards him, "Eat."

A slight smile came to Otis' lips as he watched his mother. She had
always been easy to talk to. She was perceptive and wise beyond words;
and she had always been one to limit judgment because she realized that no
one could possibly know everything. She had always been that way. She
had even been that way that night years ago when she questioned him about
Terrell.

The two of them had been sitting on the patio. It was a warm night
and the air was still; the sound of crickets rose from the grass and mixed
with the sound of the radio that drifted from the kitchen. He wasn't sure
why he had come to the patio at that time, but something seemed to
summon him. He found his mother strangely silent that night as she sat and
gently rocked in one of the patio chairs. She was so quiet that it made him
uncomfortable. Suddenly she spoke, "Your friend ain't called here in a
while."

Her words startled him. "Ma'am?"

"Your friend," she repeated, "That boy who's always callin' here."

Otis' eyes widened. He had no idea his mother paid any attention to Terrell's phone calls. He stared at her for a bit; her profile, dark in the night, framed by the light from the back door, the light that spilled out onto the patio, and he licked his lips, "We… we ain't that close no more."

"Why not?"

"We kinda had a fallin' out."

"Mmh. That's too bad. Seems like y'all were close," she said as she continued to look past him.

Otis lowered his eyes to the ground.

For a while, neither of them spoke. Then his mother moved her large, sturdy hands across her full thighs, smoothing the soft fabric of her dress. "Is that the reason you been so moody lately?"

He remained silent.

Finally her hands came to rest in her lap, one covering the other.

"Then she lifted her dark face a bit and looked out into the night, "He's special to you, ain't he?"

Still, Otis couldn't reply. His eyes continued to stare at the ground. He moved his mouth, but nothing came out. He gave one more attempt. This time a sound came, "Ma?" And again his voice left him.

"He's special to you in that way. I can tell. How long y'all been knowin' each other?"

"Ma…"

"Otis."

"Eight months."

His mother expelled a short breath and clasped her hands.

Otis looked at her, "I'm sorry, Ma."

"Well, sorry ain't gonna help nothin' is it?" Then she turned to him, "And you might as well hold that head up. 'cause looks like you gonna have to do that a lot."

Otis raised his head slightly, but he still couldn't bring himself to look at her.

Then she continued, "Is he the only one?"

"Ma..."

"Boy will you stop callin' me? Now I asked you a question. Is he the only one?"

"Yes ma'am."

"Then why, Otis? Why you wanna start actin' that way?"

Otis blew a sharp breath as he moved his head side to side, "Ma I ain't startin' to act that way. I always been this way."

"No you haven't. I know my child."

"Yes I have, Ma. I just ain't never told nobody." Then he calmed his breath, 'It's true. I always been that way. When I was the little bad ass kid on the block I was that way. When I was hangin' with my cats." Then his voice softened, "Even when I was with Tangey." Then he fixed his eyes on his mother, "And all the times we laughed and talked, Ma... I was that way."

His mother closed her eyes as if she needed a respite from the truth. Then after a short while she slowly opened them. "Your father never wanted me to work. Always said I should stay home with the kids. But I wanted somethin' more for the family."

"Ma that ain't got nothin' to do with it."

His mother just shook her head. Then she loosened her hands and placed them palms down on her thighs. She looked out into the night. "I done been around. And I've known some people like that. Homosexual. They all said they didn't choose to be that way. And I kinda believe 'em. Ain't nobody in they right mind would choose such a hard life. Everybody hatin' 'em and all." Finally she sighed, "But I never thought the Lord would visit this on my family."

Otis sat back hard in his chair. It seemed despondency was becoming his attendant in life.

His mother continued, "You know, a part of me wanna say I wish this wasn't happenin'. But if I do that, then it's like wishin' you away. And I don't wanna do that. You're my child and I love you. That's all I know. That's all I'm supposed to know. But baby, I can tell you, you have some rough times ahead of you. You know that don't you?"

Otis didn't answer.

"Now I ain't tellin' you to live that kind of life. That's between you and the Lord. Who knows? Maybe it is okay bein' that way. I don't know. Only He knows. But all I can tell you is you gotta keep livin' the best you can. Keep your head up and your eyes on the Lord. Listen to Him. And you know that you can always count on me to be there for you. 'cause I know my child. And I know he's a good person."

Otis sat for a while and took in his mother's blessing. Then he leaned forward and folded his hands, "Yes ma'am. Ma? I know you probably don't wanna hear this, but Terrell is a nice guy. We been good to each other."

"I believe that. He seems like a nice boy."

"And what I'm sayin' is- - Ma, I love him."

"I believe that too." Then she got up and started towards the house. "And I love you too."

She had always been there for him, and now he felt as if he had betrayed her. How could he have hurt her all those years?

Suddenly, the sound of a car was heard.

"That must be your father. I can tell his car anywhere. He said he was goin' to let Big John take over for the rest of the day."

His father came through the door, "Where my boy! Where my boy!" He was laughing as he made his way through the living room.

"Right here, Daddy!"

The two of them rushed into each other's arms and held one another tight. At first the contact of his father's body frightened him; it frightened him because the years of anger had warned against ever getting close to him again. But he calmed himself and held onto the man.

His father stood there in silence, but Otis could hear him through his body and his embrace.

"What took you so long?" his father finally whispered, he tightened his embrace. When he finally let go he stood back and shook his head. His eyes were moist, "Boy…"

Otis looked in his father's face and saw the subtle changes that had come over the years. The pictures his mother would send him were descriptions of the family; but they weren't able to speak of feelings, ever so slight, almost unnoticeable.

"I'm just glad to be home," Otis smiled.

"You?" His father laughed as he slapped his son heavily across the shoulder.

"Clarence. Look at all that dirt you trackin' across my floor." Otis' mother interrupted as she went over to the utility closet and retrieved a mop.

"See? Some things just never change," Otis' father laughed.

"Yup."

"Let me go and wash up. You stayin' for dinner?"

"Not tonight. I told Courtney I would pick her up when she got off from work. But I'm gonna come over tomorrow and spend the night."

"Well stick around for a little bit." With that, his father left the kitchen and headed down the hall to clean up.

"This is the happiest I seen your father in years," Otis' mother said, glancing uneasily at him as she splashed a little water from a glass onto the floor.

"Here, let me do that Ma." Otis took the glass and mop from his mother and began mopping the floor. He didn't have an answer for her. It wasn't that he refused to give her an answer, he simply had none.

At that moment the back door opened and his sister walked in. She stood in the doorway of the kitchen holding her lunch box and looked at Otis.

With her caramel complexion, short hair and strong jaw, she looked very much like her mother's father in some of the family photos Otis had seen.

"Munny." Otis greeted through the years that had gone before them.

She smiled and walked over to her brother and put her arms around him. "Good to see you." Her embrace was lax and her voice lukewarm.

"You too. It's been a long time little sis."

"Yeah."

"Otis is comin' over for dinner tomorrow and he's gonna spend the night."

Their mother spoke after a quick second of assessing the mood.

"That's good. How long you here?" Munny asked. She seemed to have posed her question more in search of an agreement than an extension of an invitation.

"For a few weeks."

"That's good. Give us time to do some catchin' up."

"Yeah."

"You stayin' for supper?"

"No. Like I was tellin' Daddy, I have to pick Courtney up from work."

"Oh. Well I'll see you tomorrow then."

"Oh yeah."

"Well I gotta make a phone call. Glad you're back," she said as she patted him on his arm, then exited down the hall to her room.

A silence fell over the kitchen as Otis and his mother searched for words to resume the afternoon.

"So Big John is still with Daddy, huh?"

"Oh yeah. He ain't goin' nowhere. He wouldn't make that kind of money if he left your father, and he knows that. Although I don't think he'd leave Clarence anyway. Your father's been too good to him."

"Who dat callin' my name?" his father joked as he returned to the kitchen. The bright fragrance of soap rose from his skin.

"Ma was just telling me that Big John is still with you."

"Oh yeah. He ain't goin' nowhere. Want a beer?"

"Yessir."

His father went over to the refrigerator. "And let me kiss my ol' lady before she hit me with that frying pan," he laughed as he kissed his wife on the cheek.

Then he took out two bottles of beer and held them by the neck in his large hand. "Let's go on into the living room. Get outta your mother's way here. You gotta tell me about New York. I ain't been there since God knows when."

It was a while before Otis rose to leave. "Ma, I better get on outta here so I can pick Courtney up." He walked back into the kitchen and kissed his mother.

"You goin' so soon? You got a little while before Courtney gets off from work."

"You know how traffic can be. But we'll be back over tomorrow." The smell of chicken frying filled his nostrils. "Yep, we sure will."

"Okay baby." And give that child of mine my love.

"I will."

His father walked him to the front door.

"Well Daddy, I'll see you tomorrow. Oh and tell Munny I'll see her too."

"Okay. Look, you better hurry and beat that traffic before it starts rainin'" his father said as he looked at the sky.

"Yeah. You're right."

Otis made it to the car just as the clouds opened. Large drops of rain splashed against the windshield forming great sunflower shapes, then ran down the pane forming liquid stems.

"Whose house is this?" Terrell stood in front of the French doors that opened up onto the balcony. Outside the rain fell with a steady rhythm.

"Don't worry about it. Now c'mon and sit down," Otis said as he patted the sofa. The bottle of wine sat on the table in front of him. It was warm, and so was the room.

"Otis- -"

"Look, you blockin' my view, man. I didn't open those doors for nothin'. Now c'mon."

Terrell walked over to the sofa and Otis took his hand and gently pulled him down.

"Look, you said you like rainy days, and I said I do too. So let's just groove with this."

He pulled Terrell to his chest. "A'ight?"

Terrell looked at him for a second before laying his head on Otis' chest. *"Alright." Then he looked back up at Otis, "You crazy. You know that?"*

"Yeah. That's what they say."

Then they laid back and listened to the falling rain.

Chapter VI

"Really? It's raining up here too." Terrell spoke as he glanced out the patio door. It was dark, so he couldn't see the rain, but he could hear its steady patter. "So I guess Brooke Benton was right, huh? It really is a rainy night in Georgia."

"You couldn't resist that could you?" Karen laughed.

"Well, hey. What can I say?" He moved the receiver to his other ear. "I hope it doesn't rain down there tomorrow. It'll mess up your plans with the kids."

"It's not supposed to. But oh, Babe, you should've seen them when we visited Martin Luther King's home. They were so excited, especially Kenya, because she studied him in her class. It was so beautiful the way her eyes lit up. It was like she was living the history."

"That's good. We need to let our children live our history. So what did knucklehead do?"

Karen gave an exaggerated sigh, "You know that boy of yours. Talkin' loud. Runnin' everywhere."

"That's my boy."

"Well when you get here, you can take him for yourself... everywhere."

"Now let's not go that far."

"Cousin Leon's just crazy over him. He seems to spend more time with him than with anybody else."

"Well you know how infectious Abassi's personality is. So has your brother made it down there yet?"

"Yeah. He arrived this evening. He's staying with Ernestine and Jeffrey."

"Tell him what's up. It's been a while since I've seen him."

"I will. So how's everything going up there? You been eating right?"

"Yes Karen," he smiled.

"Well, I just want to make sure. You know how you can get. Get so wrapped up in your projects that you forget to eat. Speaking of which, how is the construction going?"

"Yeah, I was going to tell you about that. Guess what? Bishop wants to add an entire broadcasting facility onto the new church."

"What?"

"Yep."

"It's kind of late to come up with that kind of change isn't it?"

"That's what I said. But he said he wants it done. Frankly, I think Stanton Thurman had something to do with it. He said it's Bishop's swan song, but I think he planted the seed."

"So where are we going to get the money to do something like that?" Karen inquired. "That's expensive."

"I asked the same question, but he said we can find it. And then he looked at me like I'm supposed to pull a rabbit out of the hat."

"Hm. Well I guess that's because you and I usually do."

"Yeah," Terrell agreed.

"So what does that mean about your coming on down?"

"Nothing. I'm not letting this mess up my vacation. We've put too much into this and you've put too much into planning your family reunion. I'm going to go over the books, do the best I can, then I'll put it right back in Bishop's lap."

"Oh. I was just wondering because I know you." There was a slight pause as if she was searching for something. "So has Stanton brought up our joining his camp?"

"Just briefly. He was busy hustling Bishop's idea for the new facility. But I'm sure he'll get around to it."

"You know, maybe that facility isn't such a bad idea. I mean we can always use it to branch out."

"And spread the Word, right?" Terrell asked.

"Well, yeah."

"I don't know, I don't think God really needs broadcast capability to get His message across."

"Oh, you know what I mean. But whatever the need, it doesn't hurt to have things like that as long as they serve a good purpose."

Terrell sighed, "Yeah. I guess you're right."

"Well look, I don't want to run up the phone bill. Let me get the kids on the line."

Terrell listened as Karen called out for Kenya and Abassi. In a second he heard them running to the phone.

"Hi Daddy!" It was Kenya who picked up the phone first. In the background Abassi was also calling out his greeting.

"Hey baby. How're you doin'?"

"Fine. We've been doing a lot of sightseeing. Man, I am too tired."

"You sound like an old woman."

"Nah. It's just that we walk everywhere. I don't know why Momma won't let us ride around more."

"It's good for you."

"But we did ride the subway. The one here ain't like the one in New York, though. It's smaller."

"Yeah. Well remember how big New York is though."

"I know. I tol' cousin Tamika Atlanta ain't as big as New York."

"Oh no. Tell her it's nowhere the size of New York. Did you tell her you've been there?"

"Yeah. But she still don't believe me when I tell her it ain't as big as New York. Not even Chicago."

"Well, sometimes people only know what they've experienced first hand."

"But she should know that."

"Wellll... I hear you had a nice time at Martin Luther King's birthplace?"

"Yeah. It was so neat. Just think, to stand there in the place where greatness was born."

Terrell smiled. *She is so bright.*

After a while of talking to Kenya he asked to speak with Abassi who was pitching a hissy fit in the background.

" 'ey man. What's up?"

"Nothin'. Ooo, Daddy! Yesterday we went up to this tall mountain, Stone Mountain, and we had fun. You can look around at everywhere from there. At the whole world- - you can too!"

"Tell Kenya to mind her own business."

"Daddy said mind your own business." Then he turned his attention back to his father. "And then we went to Martin Loofer King's house."

"Martin Luther King. What did I tell you about that 't h' sound."

"Martin Luther King."

"There you go."

"Man, his house is old."

"Well that's the house he was born in. That's why."

"Oh. Well he musta been old when he died then."

"Well, no. Actually he was still pretty young. He was my age."

"Oh. Then that's sad."

"Yep. So what else did you do?"

"Then we went to The Underground. Man they got a lot of stuff down there."

"You didn't spend all your money down there, did you?"

"No. Mommy wouldn't let us."

"That's good, because you have to save some so when I make it on down there we can do some things, too."

"When you comin' down?"

"I got about two more weeks. I'll be down as soon as I finish some work up here. Then we can all do our thing. Okay?"

"Okay."

"Well, I love you."

"I love you too."

"And tell Kenya I love her."

Abassi turned from the phone, "Daddy said he hates you."

"Abassi!" Terrell scolded while at the same time smiling as he heard Kenya's reply, *"No he didn't. You said that. My daddy loves me."* "She knows I love her. Now go get Mommy. Love you both."

"See what I have to put up with?" Karen said.

"I'll be there soon to help you whip 'em into shape."

Karen chuckled.

"You know, it's lonely around here," Terrell continued, "I never realized just how much I miss all the noise.

"Well you'll have it when you come down here. That's for sure."

"And I miss you too, babe."

"... I miss you too..."

"Well, I guess I'd better go, huh?"

"Okay. We'll see you in a few weeks."

After he hung up the phone he sat for a second and measured the silence. He recalled how he had never liked silence; it had too many openings, too many possibilities. He stood for a while and looked around the den. There was nothing to do or anyone to talk to; it was just the silence. So he went over and turned off the light and went to bed.

In a little while the phone rang. He reached over and picked up the receiver. "Hello?"

"Terrell?"

"...Yeah...Who is this?"

"Stanton."

"Stanton? How did you get my home number?"

"We're working together, remember? Bishop gave it to me. Don't be so damned paranoid."

"What's up?"

"I was in your neck of the woods and thought maybe we could meet up to talk about the addition to the church. You weren't in bed, were you?"

"Actually, I was. So you know where I live too."

Stanton laughed. "Man, it's nine o'clock on a Friday night."

"I know. But hey, I didn't have anything else to do, so I just went on to bed."

"Well how about I come by, pick you up and we can go out and talk over drinks."

Terrell paused for a moment. "Nah, I think I'll just call it a night. And anyway, it's raining."

"So what's a little rain? Look I'm just a few minutes away. I'll drop by. In the meantime start getting ready."

"Look, how about tomorrow?"

"Tomorrow's fine. What time?"

"Noon is fine. We can do lunch," Terrell suggested.

"Mmm... can't. Got something planned. How about tomorrow night? Round eight? We can go to the 267 House for dinner. I know the owner."

"Okay. Eight it is."

"Later."

"Later."

Terrell hung up the phone and rolled back over in bed.

The rain outside tapped against the house with a penetrating, calming rhythm. He got up and opened the windows and the sound of the rain rushed in; then he lay back down and felt drops of water splash, every now and then through the open window, against his face. If Karen was there she would look at him as if he was crazy; but he had always loved the rain.

Then they laid back and listened to the falling rain.

* * *

Otis stepped out of the rain and into the bar. Somehow he had navigated his way from the car to the door without getting too wet; and now he sought to spend a few hours out, his first time since his return.

He had decided to check out PJ's since he had passed by it earlier in the week and had noticed the faces of rhythm and blues artists painted on the façade of the building. He wasn't sure how the place would be, but if anything he figured he would at least hear some old school there.

Having paid the charge, he walked further into the club and stood a second as he checked out the scene. The interior was a far cry from the way he remembered it twenty years ago when the building served as an auto parts store with dull lighting and an equally dull gray paint job; now it shimmered from reds and golds and a dance floor that moved under swirling lights. The bright colors and lights made the building seem much larger than years ago.

In the middle of the floor was a number of tables at which sat mostly women and the few men who attempted to woo them. The men made large, strong gestures, their heads raring back as their throats let out gruff laughter in an attempt to make their presence known while the women sat by coyly and stirred their drinks with measured grace.

Otis observed this scene, then shook his head as he realized how little things change. He walked over to the bar and took a seat near the end of it, just off from an area that held two pool tables.

"What'll you have?" A bartender approached him.

The bartender had a face, dark and bearded, that reminded Otis of Teddy Pendergrass. "CC and Seven."

The bartender prepared the drink and as he did so Otis noticed how nice his ass looked in his slacks.

"Three seventy-five," the bartender said as he set the drink in front of him.

Otis paid him and slid a tip.

"Thanks."

To the side, some of the patrons were engaged in games of pool at the two tables. On one table were two men; at the other were a man and a woman. The man and woman seemed pretty well matched as they both had the same number of balls on the table. But suddenly out of nowhere the man came from behind and overtook the woman, going from one side of the table to the other tapping its top to indicate his shots until finally he sent the eight ball racing into the corner pocket. Then he grinned and yelled "next!" as the woman hit him playfully on the arm.

The woman returned to her seat, which was right next to Otis.

"Don't feel bad. You handled yourself pretty well out there," Otis complimented.

"Oh I don't feel bad. Me and him go at it all the time. Sometimes he wins, sometimes I win."

"Oh, so y'all are old foes, huh?"

"Oh yeah. For as far back as I can remember. We grew up together out in Winton Terrace. We always did try and see who could outdo each other."

Otis thought how strange it was for a man and a woman to compete to that extent.

The woman continued, "But if you had to sum it all up, I guess I'm the best man." Then she broke out laughing.

They continued to talk and Otis found out her name was Shirley. He assumed her to be around his age, but he wasn't sure. At times she seemed older, while at other times she seemed a bit younger. She had a round face and a light complexion that reminded him of one of those smiley buttons from years ago; only this smiley face had large red glasses that sat firmly on its nose and that never seemed to slip down even though the face constantly moved its head as it spoke. She was full of information: about the bar, its owner and everyone who was there. It wasn't so much gossip that she engaged in, it was all just matter of fact.

In a bit, her partner came over. He had finally lost a game.

"Charles," this is Otis. Otis, Charles."

"What's up?" Charles said as he shook Otis' hand.

"What's up?" Otis replied. "I see you finally gave the table up."

Charles grinned, "Yeah. I figured I better let somebody else get a game in."

"Yeah. Right. Yo' ass just lost." Shirley said this as she waved her hand through the air.

"Girl, be quiet," Charles grinned. Then he raised a finger and the bartender began to make his drink.

"Otis is from New York," Shirley said.

"Oh?" Charles replied.

"Yeah," she answered.

The bartender set the drink before Charles.

"What part you from?" Charles continued.

"Brooklyn. But I'm from here originally."

"Oh. Brooklyn."

"Charles goes up there a lot."

"I try to get her to go with me, but she won't. She always says she's too afraid."

Otis raised his eyebrows as he looked at Shirley. "Afraid? I didn't think you would be afraid of anything."

"Shit, I would be afraid as hell in New York. With all the shit that goes on up there." Shirley shifted in her seat.

"It ain't like that," Otis gushed.

"Man, I keep telling her that."

"Shit, I don't know," she said as she pulled her fingers through her jheri curl. "But who knows? Maybe one day I'll go up there with Charles."

Otis tried to pick up on whether the two of them were romantically involved. It didn't seem as if they were, but he wondered if they were possibly sometime bed partners. He was just curious.

"So how long has it been since you been back here?" Charles asked before sipping his drink.

"Twenty years."

Shirley and Charles looked over at Otis.

"Twenty years?" Shirley asked in surprise.

"Yeah."

"You got family here?" Charles asked.

"Yeah."

Charles saw the cloaked expression that came to Otis' face. He cut his eye at Shirley and they both shied away from further discussion on the subject.

"Well welcome back, man," Charles said as he patted Otis' shoulder.

"Yeah. Welcome home," Shirley spoke in a gentle voice.

"Thanks."

It was almost two o'clock when Charles looked at his watch. "Damn, the bar'll be closing soon. Better get that last drink on before we hit the road," he said to Shirley. "You want a last one for the road?" he asked, turning to Otis.

Otis was about to reply when Charles stopped him. "Hey. Better yet, how 'bout we just go on over to my place and finish talkin'? I got something to drink over there."

Otis looked at him for a second. He wanted to feel insulted by the offer as he usually did when he was propositioned. In such instances he would give a scowl, perfected over the years to turn away unwanted advances or to change the mind of anyone who might even *think* about fucking with him, and he would walk away. That was what he did when he was sober and responding to an unfamiliar face.

He would feel equally insulted when he was drunk, however, but it would be just before he would leave with the person.

But tonight he wasn't drunk, and the man and woman standing in front of him weren't propositioning him, nor did they seem like strangers. In fact, they seemed like the type of people he'd longed to see, to once again become familiar with during his trip home.

He looked at Shirley then hunched his shoulders, "It's alright with me."

"Me too," Shirley joined in.

"Where're you parked?" Charles asked as he raised his umbrella over Shirley's head.

"I'm just around the corner" Otis replied.

"How far? We can give you a lift."

"Nah, it's not far."

"Well look, you get your car and you can follow us," Charles suggested.

"Cool."

Then the three of them dashed out into the rain.

Charles lived in Mt. Auburn in one of the row houses that lined one of the many steep hills that overlooked downtown Cincinnati.

Otis gasped as they stepped into the vestibule. "Awww. Man, this is too nice." He said this as he eyed a small chandelier in the entryway that swung lightly creating the sound of glass chimes as the breeze from outside rushed in.

"Thanks. You should see Shirley's. Her's is in Mt. Adams. She got a view of the river and of downtown."

"It's okay. I like it." Shirley spoke with modesty.

"Y'know, that's what I miss about Cincinnati, man; all the hills and the river front," Otis clicked his mouth.

"Well, like we said, welcome back." Shirley smiled as she entered the living room with Otis and Charles following. "I'm going to fix us something to eat. Charles, you fix us something to drink; and Otis you just relax." With that, she disappeared into the dining room, on her way to the kitchen.

"It's her home, too," Charles joked. "So what'll it be?" he asked as he went over to an armoir.

"CC and seven. That's my favorite."

"Comin' up."

The room was large and silent. There was expensive period furniture in the room but none of it seemed to have been used much. It seemed as if very little activity took place in the room, as if it's only purpose was to pass one through to other rooms, nothing else.

After he fixed the drinks, Charles handed Otis his. "C'mon. Let's go into the kitchen. See what that woman's up to."

They entered the kitchen and found Shirley moving hurriedly about.

"Get the margarine out. Otis you put some bread in the toaster." She directed the two men who immediately followed her orders.

"How many slices?" Otis asked.

"Six."

Soon the microwave chimed and Shirley removed the dish. "Charles, I hope you seasoned this spaghetti and meatballs right."

"It's leftover, so it'll taste good."

"Well I hope so, because I may be hungry, but I want food that tastes good."

The three of them settled down to the kitchen table with their meals and drinks.

"Mmm. This is good," Otis said.

"Oh, thanks. I do pretty good," Charles replied.

"Yeah, he had to. Maria wasn't gonna let him just hang around while she did all the cooking. She knew what time it was." Shirley said.

"Yeah. You got that right," Charles grinned.

"That your wife?" Otis asked.

"Ex," Charles corrected.

"You married?" Shirley inquired of Otis.

"Nah. Never have been. Why? You wanna marry me?"

"Baby, I've had my share. I enjoy my independence too much."

"Right on," Charles agreed.

"And evidently you do too," Shirley continued.

Otis smiled, "I don't know. Sometimes I think I've had too much freedom."

Charles leaned forward, "You can never have too much freedom, man."

"I don't know about that."

Shirley waved her fork at Otis, "Maybe it's responsibility that you're talking about. Maybe you want someone to be responsible for. I think everybody needs some degree of responsibility, even if it's for another person. I mean, think about it. It gives us purpose."

Charles set his fork down. "Look, I know some brothers out there in the streets who ain't never took responsibility for nobody and no thing," he defended.

"Yeah. And look at 'em. I bet they're just as lost as I don't know what," Shirley countered.

"And I bet even they had some type of responsibility some time in their lives. They just probably lost it. And who knows? Maybe that's why they're out there lost now," Otis heard himself say.

"True." Charles had to agree. "But I done done my time."

"Brother, there's a lot more to do. Just get ready," Otis smiled as he lifted his fork to his mouth.

"Anybody for seconds?" Shirley asked. "I warmed enough."

"Not me. I'm stuffed," Otis said.

"Me too. Want another drink?" Charles asked Shirley and Otis.

"Yeah." Shirley flashed a grin.

"I'll have another one too."

"And turn some music on. It's too quiet in here," Shirley demanded.

"You know where the stereo is," Charles said as he got up to fix the drinks.

"No, I mean the good one. Upstairs." She turned to Otis, "You should see his AV room up there. The man has everything there is."

"Take him up there. I'll join y'all in a second," Charles said as he handed the drinks to his guests.

Shirley and Otis entered the room on the second floor where she turned on the lights with great showmanship. "Ta da."

"Damn." Otis' eyes widened as the room opened before him. "He got everything."

"Told you." Shirley went over to the music library and pulled out some CD's. "And I know exactly where all my favorites are."

"He must have over five hundred CD's." Otis was amazed.

"Probably more than that." She went over to the stereo system, loaded the music and picked up the remote. "It took him almost two years to let me touch this damn thing."

"Well he probably spent a lot of money on it."

Shirley clicked her mouth. "Of course he did. That's Charles." Then she pushed a button and soft music filled the room. "You know I just love me some Luther."

"Who don't?"

At that moment Charles came into the room. In one hand he held three glasses by their stems and in the other a bottle of wine. "Yeah. Now that's music."

"Charles. Man, you got it laid out here."

"Thanks. It's home. But like I said, you gotta see her place." He nodded his head towards Shirley as he set the wine and the glasses on the coffee table.

"Yeah. But I ain't got all this electronic stuff."

"Okay, so who copied off who?" Otis asked with a wry grin. "I know all about this competition thang."

"He did," Shirley immediately replied.

"She used to live right up the street from me. She lived up here first, then I saw how nice it was and I decided to do the same. But she just had to get one up on me by moving to Mt. Adams."

"Nah, nah. That ain't the reason I moved there." Shirley shook her head loosely about and Otis wondered if she needed any more wine. "I got tired of his ass always beggin' for sugar." She laughed and tapped Otis' hand. "No, but really, I had always wanted to live in Mt. Adams and one day I saw some property for sell and, hey, I just jumped on it."

"I bet you paid a pretty penny for that," Otis said.

"No. I got a bargain. You see, I found out that the property had gone through foreclosure, so I snapped it up."

"That's the way to go. That's how I got my place."

"And I know that would've cost you some bucks up there if you hadn't," Charles assured. He handed the glasses of wine to them.

"Hell yeah. But mine is an apartment."

"You bought a whole apartment building?" Shirley's eyes widened.

Otis and Charles laughed.

"I wish. Nah, that's just what they call apartment condos."

"Oh. They tried to give me the runaround when I went up for my house," she continued before taking a sip of the wine.

"That's because it's in Mt. Adams. You know they just ain't used to us being up there," Charles added.

Shirley shook her glass. "I even had to threaten to sue their ass if they played me one minute longer."

"You have to," Otis agreed.

"Then they wanna say how aggressive we're being." Charles took a sip of his drink.

"But hey, I got it; and that's all that matters." She took a swallow.

"You got that right," Otis concurred. He wasn't sure if he should take another drink because there would be consequences he might have to own up to if he had too much. Besides he wasn't sure where this evening was going. Was *supposed* to go.

They became quiet for a moment and listened to the music; it was Luther and Cheryl Lynn singing "If This World Were Mine". They moved their heads to the song, their lips mouthing the words.

Finally, "That's the man," Charles said as the song faded.

"Oh yeah," Otis smiled, "Oh yeah. Marvin and Tammi gave it gold; and you know you ain't suppose to dis Marvin, but Luther and Cheryl Lynn gave it shit, baby." He finally took a swallow. Then he looked at the CD player. " 'ey, how many CD's does that thing hold anyhow?"

"Five hundred," Charles replied.

Otis got up and took a closer look at the player. "Oh yeah, I see. Man you got the whole layout," he said as he leaned closer to the system. He could feel the sudden rush of wine to his head. The lights and meters blurred momentarily as he moved his head from one unit of the system to the other. "Shit, I wouldn't even know what to do with all this. Mine is just a plain ol' stereo."

"You learn. It's like anything else, if you love it, you learn it."

"Yeah, you're right." Suddenly, Otis noticed how quiet Shirley had become. He turned and looked at her. "Man, Shirley's gone." He grinned as he looked at her sleeping form.

"She sure is," Charles laughed. Then he called out to her, "Shirley! Shirley!"

Shirley awoke to find the two men laughing at her. "Child I was sleep," she said as she pulled her hand through her hair.

"No shit," Charles laughed. "Why don't you go on to bed? You're too tired to drive home."

"I'm not drunk. I don't believe in that."

"I didn't say you were drunk. I said you're too tired. Now go on to bed. Get you some rest."

She sat for a second as she got her bearings. "Yeah." Then she got up, "Well Otis. In spite of the fact that I fell asleep on you, it really was a pleasure meeting you. And I hope to see you again the next time you visit. And next time I'll stay awake."

Otis stood and gave her a hug. "It was nice to meet you, too. And if you're ever in New York, drop on by. I'll give Charles my information. And I really mean that, because I really feel like I made some new friends, here."

Shirley gave him a kiss on the cheek. "Me too." Then she turned and left the room.

"She's really cool people," Otis said as he looked after her.

"Yeah, she's special to me," Charles agreed. "We done seen each other through childhood, good times, bad times, marriages and everything. I don't even have a male friend that I feel as close to as I do to her."

"You're lucky."

"Yeah. I am," he smiled wistfully. Then he looked up at Otis. "Hey, you like jazz?"

"Real jazz? Not that Kenny G shit?"

"Real jazz. Miles, M J Q, Ron Carter, Winton Marsalis."

Otis grinned with appreciation as he sat down on the sofa, "Yeah, man. Now you talkin'."

In a minute the muted strains of Miles Davis' "Kinda Blue" rose from invisible places in the room and floated like mist through the air. "Time for a refill," Charles said as he began to fix Otis another drink. Then he handed the drink to Otis and sat down on the sofa beside him. "And I done found a brother who listens to jazz. That's alright," he smiled. "Most people think they do, but they don't."

"I know. They keep talkin' that instrumental pop, shit, thinking it's jazz."

Charles moved his hands emphatically through the air, "And it's our music; our classical music."

Otis nodded his head in agreement. "Yup. You know what I like about jazz though, man? It captures the moment," he snapped his fingers, "like that! The moment."

"It's what they felt at the moment they hit the note," Charles agreed.

"Yeah. The moment." Then he shook his finger at the stereo, "And that was the master, right there. Love me some Miles."

"Sketches of Spain..."

"Hell yeah." Otis and Charles slapped palms, "That was classic Miles," Otis grinned as he put his drink to his lips.

"You want me to put it on?"

Otis took a sip and lowered his glass. "Nah. That's cool. This what you got on here is just perfect. The rain and the night, y'know?" he said as he looked towards the French doors across the room.

"Yeah, you're right. Let me open 'em up."

Charles got up and walked over to the French doors and pushed them open letting the cool breeze and vagrant drops of rain come in. "You're right," he repeated and walked back to the sofa.

The two men sat in silence for a moment sipping their drinks as they relished the music and the atmosphere. Then Otis spoke, "Y'all really have to come up and visit me, man. It ain't nothing like listening to jazz on a cool New York night. It's just something about it. New York was made for jazz."

"Oh yeah. Now you know I know what its all about. And I promise, me and Shirley will come and visit you."

Then they retired into a long silence. The music continued to fill the air along with the cool breeze and the sound of the rain as Charles and Otis relaxed in the late hours of the night.

Suddenly Charles spoke, "Where's your head?" He spoke in a slight whisper.

Otis' mind seemed to ride the mist. "It's already there." He replied with an equal tone.

Then they both went back into the silence.

Suddenly, out of the silence, out of the space between them, Charles put his knee gently against Otis'.

Otis remained still, relaxed. "Mmmh," he breathed.

Charles looked over at him, at his profile, and slightly smiled. Then he put his hand lightly on Otis' knee.

This time Otis reached down and placed his hand on top of Charles' hand and rubbed it, feeling the hair and prominence of veins on the back of his hand.

They sat like that for a while longer before Charles spoke. "Otis."

Otis turned his head to look at him, "Hmm?"

And Charles kissed him lightly on the lips.

Otis smiled and kissed him back.

Then they quietly looked at each other, their eyes searching for permission; and, finding it in each other, they moved closer as they kissed again, this time longer, this time with reason.

Charles moved his head down to Otis' dark, muscular chest and, with one hand unbuttoning his shirt, began to kiss Otis' chest.

"Charles..." Otis spoke as he put his hand on Charles' face, halting his movements, "Shirley."

Charles smiled, "She's cool." Then he raised his head and looked into Otis' eyes, "Come on," he said as he took Otis' hand.

And they went to Charles' bedroom.

Chapter VII

"I had a dream about Otis." Terrell and his sister, Charmaine, sat on a
bench surrounded by plants and shrubbery at a gardening center.

Charmaine looked at her brother for a quick second. "Who?" Then she
suddenly realized who he was talking about. "Otis?"

Terrell looked at her, "Yeah."

"What brought this on? Do you always dream about him?"

"No. I mean, he crosses my mind every once in a while, you know, and I
wonder whatever happened to him. And once or twice he's appeared in a dream.
But that was long ago."

Charmaine glanced over to where their mother stood. She was busy
checking out some shrubbery for the yard. "You haven't told Momma this, have
you?"

"No." Terrell shook his head. "Why would I do that?"

"Because you have a tendency to do things like that."

"Well I would never bring all that back up."

"Good. Because I don't think that's something she should ever have to hear about again."

Terrell nodded his head, "I know."

"So what was the dream about?"

"I was downtown and I hailed a cab. And when I got in the cab, the driver turned out to be Otis. And before I knew it I was sitting up front with him and we were talking."

"About what?"

"Just everyday stuff. But I kept noticing something on the side of his face. At first it was barely visible, then the more we talked I could see it. It was a long scar."

Charmaine raised her eyebrows.

Terrell continued, "I was too embarrassed to ask him about it... but somehow I knew it was my fault that he had it."

"Did he ever mention the scar to you?"

"No. He just kept talking like it was nothing. No matter how much I stared."

"Hm. That is interesting." Then she turned half way around to face him, "What was his attitude like in your dream? I mean did he seem angry?"

"No. He was just as cool as he used to be. As if nothing happened." Then he shook his head, "But it was the scar. It was so clear. And I knew I had put it there."

Charmaine sighed, "Terrell, you need to forget about all that. What's done is done."

Terrell shook his head and stared at his sister, "I know, but… Charmaine, you know me and you could always talk. You're the first one I told about the feelings I had for Otis. And, well, I just wish I could see him, just to find out if he's okay."

"Terrell, I'm sure he's okay. If something bad… worse had happened to him I'm sure we would've heard about it by now."

"How? I haven't spoken to his family in twenty years."

"We would know. Believe me. Frankly, I didn't think you still held onto all that."

"Why wouldn't I? I had something to do with it. Why would you think I could just walk away from what happened without any guilt and…" He paused.

"And pain?" Charmaine said, finishing his statement. Then she reached over and put her hand on her brother's thigh, "Terrell. You have to let it go. You have a better life now. You have Karen and the kids. They should be on your mind. Only them. Them and God."

"What are you saying? That Otis is competing with Karen and the kids? Charmaine, that's not what I'm saying at all. I'm simply saying I feel bad about something that hurt somebody who was good. That's all."

"I guess so…" Charmaine said as she looked out at the plants. Then she spoke without looking at Terrell, "Terrell, can I ask you a question?"

"Yeah."

"Do you still think about him in *those* ways?"

Terrell shook his head vigorously, "No."

At that moment, their mother waved for them.

Charmaine called out, "Okay, Ma." Then she turned back to her brother, "Look, like I said, the only ones who should be on your mind are your family and

God." Then she stood to leave.

Terrell also stood; and he looked at his sister as he rose, "Maybe God is on my mind."

* * * *

That evening, Terrell replayed the conversation he'd had with his sister. He didn't think the conversation would have bothered him so much, but it had. It was the way she was so quick to request he forget what had happened to Otis. Would she have made such a request if Otis had been a young lady; if the relationship had been heterosexual? Her cavalier treatment of the matter bothered him, but he knew there was nothing he could do to change her attitude.

But what bothered him even more than the conversation was the dream. Not just the content of it, but the fact that he had it.

The dreams were far and in between now, having become less frequent with the passing of the years. Still, every once in a while he would see evidence of Otis in other dreams; maybe in the eyes of one of the characters in his dreams, the deep knowing of the eyes; or it might just be a familiar phrase from long ago. He had come to accept these patches of memories as evidence of his being. Nothing more, he would tell himself.

But this dream had come at him in a way that was more powerful than any he'd had in years; vivid, it had embellished itself firm in his mind. And that was what concerned him even more than the conversation.

Experience, though, had taught him to keep moving as he had done so for twenty years and the concern would diminish with the passing of the dreams.

So now he watched himself in the mirror as he buttoned his shirt. Stanton said he would be by at eight, and if what he'd heard about Stanton was true, he would be there exactly at eight. He still couldn't understand why Stanton insisted on picking him up instead of the two of them meeting at the restaurant. It made him feel strange, almost as if the two of them were going on a date. He smiled at such a ridiculous thought as he sat on the side of the bed and slid on his loafers. Maybe Otis did still have an effect on him; even if only a little.

Eight o'clock. The doorbell rang. Terrell got up and walked through the foyer to answer it.

"So it's true what they say about you, that you're exact. Come on in."

Stanton grinned, his teeth appearing like porcelain against his dark complexion and even darker beard. "Yep, it's true. That's how I make my business," he said as stepped through the door.

"Then I see I got my hands full with you and this contract."

"Yeah. You do." Stanton looked around the foyer. "Man, this is nice," he said, nodding his head. "How long you been living here?"

"Thanks. About nine years, now."

He nodded again, "Okay. Real nice. Well, you ready?"

"Yeah. Just let me get my notebook and set the alarm. I'll meet you at the car."

"Okay."

"Change of venue," Stanton said as Terrell got in the car. "Instead of going to The 267 House, let's go to Jeff Ruby's."

"Jeff Ruby's? Why? That's so expensive."

"I like it. And it's my treat? Okay?"

Terrell looked at him. "No, no. I'll pay half. But I don't want to go to Jeff

Ruby's. You done got my mouth ready for some good soul food and Nubian class. I haven't had a good meal since Karen left."

"Don't you have family members who cook?"

"Yeah. I just haven't gotten around to going around for dinner yet."

"Why? Man I always have time to get a good meal," Stanton laughed.

"Yeah, well me too. I'm not developing this belly on imagination."

Stanton reached over and patted Terrell's stomach. "Man, it ain't so bad. You act like you got a gut."

"It'll be getting there if I don't watch it."

"So no Jeff Ruby's."

"If it's okay with you."

"Yeah. It's cool with me. So 267 House it is."

"And anyway, didn't you set a reservation at The 267?" Terrell inquired.

"Yep," Stanton said as he pulled away from the curb.

They arrived at The 267 House and was immediately greeted by the maitre'd who knew Stanton by name. "The usual spot?" the maitre'd asked.

"You know it, Calvin."

"You must come here a lot," Terrell said as he followed Stanton's lead.

"I do."

Once they were seated and had placed drinks, Stanton smiled. "So you do drink."

"Of course I drink. What made you think I didn't?"

"I don't know. You just seem so... good."

"Good?"

"Yeah. You know, like all you do is work, go home to the wife and kids and then to church. I guess you being Bishop's right hand man and all, it just seems that way."

"I'm not Bishop's right hand man."

"Oh yes you are. Trust me. You would think Pastor Calloway would be his right hand man since he's assistant pastor; and he is- - on paper. But not in fact. You are."

"Well it's nice to hear that. I think."

"What do you mean, you think? That should make you feel good."

"I guess I don't really look to be his right hand man. I don't want to be anybody's right hand, except my family's."

"Really?"

"Yeah. I don't like being in the spot light."

"Or is it the responsibility?"

"That could be it too. I've got enough responsibility just trying to live my own life."

"Hey, leaders rise only when they're needed. And you should never try to escape your time when it comes."

"Yeah, yeah. I know."

Then Stanton leaned forward. "So tell me. If you don't want to be Bishop's right hand man, then why do you take on all those tasks he asks you to?"

Terrell looked at him. "He's been a part of my life for a long time. That's why," he said as he smiled and nodded his head.

Stanton stared at Terrell for minute. "Yeah, he's been there for a lot of people," he finally spoke.

The waiter came to the table with appetizers.

Terrell and Stanton thanked the waiter and began to eat.

"So what do you really think about building the broadcast facility?" Stanton asked.

"You know my take. I still feel the same way I did at the meeting. I think it's a bit much, and frankly, I can't see how we can recoup the cost anytime soon. He's about to put the church into a bind that it won't be able to recover financially for a helluva long time. Long after he's gone."

"Hmm. That makes him sound a little selfish."

Terrell just looked at Stanton without saying a word.

Stanton continued, "Well like I said, Terrell, this is his swan song."

"Yeah, but at whose expense? I would think the new church would stand as his legacy."

"Look, maybe the whole thing won't cost as much as you think. I mean, you haven't seen my figures yet."

"Well that's why we're here."

Stanton grinned, "Yep." Then he pulled a folder out of his clutch and laid it on the table. "I knew I would have to sell you."

Terrell pulled the folder over to him.

Stanton continued, "Why don't you take that home with you and look it over. Tell me what you think. You'll see that most of the elements are already in place to make this work; just a little expanding of the resources, that's all."

"That's what concerns me," Terrell said as he shifted through the pages. "You have to remember, this whole broadcast thing is someone's dream," then he looked up at Stanton, "someone's pipedream. And you know how some people are, out there looking to take advantage of people like that."

"What're you saying? That I'm out to take advantage of Bishop?"

"No, not you. Some of the businesses you might contract."

The waiter brought their food to the table and Terrell and Stanton removed their paper work.

"You gotta admit, when you find out someone wants to build a production facility it must be a part of a pipedream; especially if it's here in Cincinnati. I mean, were not the television capital of the world, you know. And there are people who are out to carpetbag."

Stanton continued to look at Terrell as he cut into his food.

Terrell continued, "After all, isn't that what business is about; to cash in on people's wants and needs, to cash in on desire?"

"I guess you could say that; but not necessarily. Some of us use business to make a living. And many of us even give back to the community."

"Still it's something to watch out for when presenting this whole project. I don't want Bishop to get stung- - nor the church," Terrell warned.

"Look, you don't have to worry about that. I have Bishop's interest at heart. He and I go a long way back; even to when you were just a young kid." Stanton spoke with a warm spark in his eyes.

"Well, I hope so."

"But like I said, look over the proposal and let me know what you think. It's important that you're in on this because in spite of what you think, Bishop takes your views on matters like this to heart."

"I will."

Suddenly, Stanton began to chuckle, "You know, that's what I like about you. On the one hand you have this bright, warm side; but on the other you're aware of the darkness. You're not as naïve as I thought," he said, raising his fork and pointing it at Terrell. Then, leaning over the table, fork still raised, "And I bet there's a darker side to you that you're aware of, too." He sat back and grinned.

Terrell stopped eating long enough to peer at him. "Okay. I don't see what any of that has to do with our meeting."

Stanton smiled, "Actually it does. A man's character, his personality, is always a part of the equation when you're doing business." He put down his fork, "Let me explain something to you, little brother. Always get to know the person you're dealing with. Because at the start, it's the person you're after. After that, everything else will fall into place."

"This is beginning to sound scary," Terrell said as he turned his attention back to his meal.

"Well I wish you didn't see it that way, because I'm trying to make a segue here."

"To what?" Terrell asked as he raised his glass to his mouth.

"I want you on my team. What else? I really could use a man like you on my campaign for city council."

Terrell picked up his fork.

"Look, I know you're not interested," Stanton went on, "at least it seems as though you're not, but just hear me out on this. Now, we just had a brief conversation on taking and giving back, right? I didn't just say all that to win you over for the production deal; I really believe in what I said. I believe in altruism. I really do like to give back to the community, especially our community because it needs people to give back to it. And you know there ain't a damn soul on that council who cares anything about anybody in the black community. All you have to do is look around; downtown is being pumped up, and that's cool because it presents a large tax base. But some of that money will have to eventually be spread out to the people, and not just affluent white people. And that's where I come in. And you can help me."

Terrell set his fork down, "I know I told you I would think about it, but to be honest, I really have no interest in the political scene."

"Hnh," Stanton breathed. "And just what do you have an interest in, Terrell? I'm just curious."

"Like I told you before, my family, my church and God."

"You do understand, m'man, that in the real world, as it exists here on earth," Stanton said as he poked the table with his finger, "that with the exception of God, politics affect all those things that you hold dear. It's inescapable. It's a fact of life. And there are people who stand to make a difference in how those things are affected, and then there are those who just stand by and take what's tossed their way. And don't tell me about your voting record, because that's not the final answer to politics. Come on, you should know that by now." Then he sat back in his chair, "All I'm saying is, we need to make a change, a change that will affect your life whether you like it or not; and I think you're somebody who can help this brother do that."

Terrell paused as he looked at Stanton. "I can't make any promises right now."

"That's cool. But give it consideration."

It was late as the two men walked back to the car. They were the last ones to leave the restaurant, a fact that would normally put the restaurant's staff on edge if not for the hefty gratuity Stanton left, "To be shared by the entire staff for being so cool tonight."

"You know man, we should get together more often," Stanton spoke as he put his hand in his pocket to retrieve the keys to his car. "I had a nice time. I never thought we'd have so much to talk about. Not that we particularly agree on everything, but who does? But at least we challenge each other."

"Yep, that's true. I gotta admit, we do interact with our ideas a lot," Terrell smiled.

"Why don't you go to the gym with me sometime? You said you were concerned about your gut, so why not join me?" Then Stanton laughed, "I'm not one of those Bally men, but I do hold my own pretty well. I'm in pretty good shape. I mean, look, I got you by what, ten years or so?"

"I don't know."

"Well I know I was in my late twenties or early thirties when you were a teenager."

Terrell looked questioningly at him, "You know, this is the second time you mentioned knowing me when I was a younger. I don't ever remember meeting you. How is it you know so much about me?"

"I never said I knew so much about you. I never even said I knew you at all. I just knew who you were. I had been to your church a few times and had seen you."

"I was just wondering."

"Just wondering," Stanton mocked.

"Look, you're Stanton Thurman, celebrity, sometime creator of cause celebre. It's not often someone like you would know someone like me."

"What? A person? What do you think makes all this happen?" Stanton pressed the car alarm on his key chain. "So I'll see you at the gym sometime this week, right?"

Terrell laughed, "Right."

* * * *

Otis looked around the bedroom. It was the role of the stranger that caused his eyes to move along the walls to the corners of the room; along the ceiling, stopping at the ceiling fan; and along the floor where their clothes lay. Then he looked at Charles who slept soundly beside him. The sun filled the bedroom and played across the sleeping man who lay on his back with one arm across his eyes. Otis looked at his handsome face with its reddish brown complexion, his moustache and the hair that covered his chest and stomach, and he thought about how the hair had felt the night before when they made love. From below he could hear movement; the sound of feet moving across the floor; the warm creak of wood; then the light clang of pans being settled and the clack of plates. He figured it must be Shirley starting to prepare breakfast. He wondered if she knew he had spent the night; though something told him she did.

It was times like this when he felt uncomfortable, unsure of how to respond to someone whom he barely knew yet had lain naked beside for the night. When, sober and with a late sun covering the room, he would have to look into a face that wondered if the right thing had been done the night before and he would wonder the same.

The rustle of the sheets interrupted his thoughts as Charles stirred in the bed; he moved his arm from his eyes and cuddled closer to Otis. Obviously he wasn't awake. But in a second he would be.

Then, with a slight breath, he awoke. He looked at Otis with still sleepy eyes. "Aww man. I didn't keep you awake, did I?"

"No." Otis smiled. Although to him it felt like a foolish grin.

"I know I can sleep rough," Charles continued.

"No, you didn't."

"Oh. So did you get any sleep?"

"Yeah."

Charles smacked his mouth and closed his eyes once again. The two of them lay in silence for a while before Charles spoke, his eyes once again weak with sleep.

" 'ey. You know I had a nice time last night. At the bar, and just sitting around here talking. We got a lot in common."

"Yeah."

Then Charles put one hand behind his head, "Feel a bit more comfortable now?" he smiled.

Otis looked at him in surprise, then he began to laugh. "Yeah man, yeah, I'm beginning to feel comfortable."

"Good. Because I think we got the makings of a friendship here. What do you think?"

Otis grinned, "Yeah. I would say that. I never thought I would make friends here."

Charles rose up on his elbow, "Why? This is your home isn't it?"

"Yeah. But, well, it's a long story." Otis pulled back from the conversation. It was a subject held only for the initiated.

Charles smiled to dispel the matter, "Yeah, well I ain't got time for no long stories right now." He spoke as he looked into Otis' eyes.

Otis smiled, reached up and stroked the hair on Charles' chest, "Nah, no long stories right now."

" 'bout time you two got up." Shirley sat at the table with a cup of coffee in front of her and the morning paper. She had on a flowered silk robe that was

opened enough at the top to show the lace across her nightgown. It was obvious
to Otis that she spent many mornings there. "I made this big breakfast and I just
knew y'all weren't going to let it get cold."

Charles came into the kitchen with Otis close behind. "Why did you make
all this food anyway? It's just the three of us."

"We got guest. Hello?" She moved her head before taking another sip of
coffee. She set the cup back on the saucer. "For as long as I've known him, he's
never had much class," she shook her head towards Otis.

Otis grinned and patted Charles' shoulder. He felt a bit uncomfortable
standing there in front of Shirley now that she was aware of his sexuality. He
glanced at her, then at Charles, and at the kitchen. Funny how things change in
the light of day.

"Well, you sure made enough," Charles continued. "I hope you left some
food in the refrigerator."

Shirley looked at Otis, "When I saw your car was still here, I decided to fix
you a big breakfast. You know, to show you how hospitable we can be. Because
child, if it was left up to Charles, you'd have a bowl of cereal and a cup of coffee.
And you probably wouldn't have any cream for your coffee."

"Now, he can't be all that bad, can he?" Otis said as he took the plate
Charles had handed him and began to put food onto it.

"Shoot!" Shirley responded. "Baby, you just don't know."

The three of them sat down to eat, Charles having fixed Shirley a plate as
well.

"This is good," Otis complimented.

"Thanks."

"She's a good cook. I don't know why she doesn't just open up a restaurant or something." Charles said this as he raised his fork to his mouth.

"I'm not interested in running a restaurant. Seems like too much trouble. And besides, we got enough restaurants in Cincinnati."

"You can never have enough restaurants if there's something unique about each one of them," Otis advised.

"And how many restaurants do you know in Cincinnati that serves good home breakfasts?" Charles added. "New York got a lot of them," he said, looking at Otis for agreement.

"Yep."

"I tell you Shirl, you really need to think about it." Charles persisted.

"I got enough on my hands right now. I don't need anything else going on. Maybe when I'm older and don't have anything to do."

"What do you do now?" Otis inquired.

"A lot of work," she laughed.

"She's head of records at the court house," Charles offered.

Otis raised his eyebrows, "I bet that's interesting." He wondered if she had ever come across his record. Suddenly he felt betrayed.

"Like I said, it's a lot of work," she smiled.

Charles reached over and picked up a remote and turned on the TV

Otis continued, "How long have you been there?"

"Oh about fifteen years. I've been records manager for only three years, though."

"I bet you know everybody's business." Otis gave a wry smile.

"I could. Well, at least all the criminals, if I wanted to. But shit, I don't give a damn. It's all a set up anyway."

"There you go..." Charles said as he looked at the TV screen.

"We won't even get started," she said as she looked at her friend who continued to stare at the TV "So what line of work are you in?" she asked of Otis.

"Warehousing. I used to work for Time-Warner. But I'm in between jobs right now."

"Oh. Then you can make that move back here."

Charles turned and looked at Shirley. "Be serious."

Otis laughed. "Charles is right. Nah, I could never come back here," he said as he shook his head. "But I'll start looking for another job when I get back there."

Shirley lifted a slice of toast, "Yeah. Because you don't want to lose that apartment," she said before taking a bite.

"I know. I got too good of a deal on it."

Suddenly Charles called out, "Look. Ol' Stanton Thurman formally announced his run for council yesterday." He aimed the remote at the TV and raised the volume. From the TV the three of them heard the newscaster give details of the event, while on the screen stood Stanton surrounded by a half moon of African American men and women, all of whom were well dressed and stood, the men with their hands behind their backs and the women, with their hands clasped in front of their bellies, with collective pride.

"And as usual, the old guard is there," Shirley commented.

Charles nodded his head, "And I see Bishop Abrams is still hanging with Stanton."

At that moment Otis' eyes widened. "Which one is Bishop Abrams?"

"The older light skinned man. He heads up the Black Ministers Conference."

Otis stared at the bishop. There he stood, the man who had haunted him for the last twenty years. He wasn't sure if he'd ever seen him, but during the trial he'd heard his name whispered. And now he stood before the cameras tall and confident; probably the same confidence with which he pursued him twenty years ago. And it was this confidence, this standing proud and righteous that made Otis' blood rise.

"People just don't know..." Charles lamented as he continued to stare at the screen.

"What?" Otis was curious about the secrets of these proud people.

"You know how you told me you had a long story? Well I got mine," Charles said. Then he dropped his voice and narrowed his eyes, "But that's neither here nor there right now."

In a little while Otis made his way to his sister's apartment, having promised Shirley and Charles that he'd see them again later in the week. But for now he wanted to go home, kick it with his sister and to think about a few things before heading out to Mason.

Chapter VIII

It was a large transitional home that stood along a cul de sac, not unlike many of the homes in Mason. Its deep red brick and many windows dimmed in the evening sun as Otis sat parked a bit down the street at the entrance of the circle. He looked at the house, at the shape of the windows; the size of the front door, double ones with intricate ornamentation; the run of the lawn to the front door; the light drapes that seemed to float at the windows; and he tried to connect the image before him to his memory of Terrell, but he couldn't. Terrell was small and insignificant; not large and imposing like the house suggested.

After a while he started up his car and was about to approach the house when a car passed by and pulled into Terrell's driveway. It was a large black sedan. At first Otis thought it might be Terrell, but it wasn't. Instead, a husky dark-skinned man with a beard climbed out and walked up to the door. He rang the doorbell, and when it opened there stood Terrell.

Otis' mouth parted slightly as he looked at the figure in the doorway. From where he sat he could only make out a slight recognition, but it was enough to tell him that it was Terrell. His feelings were just that sure. Now the figure that stood in the distance, the figure he thought he would never see again, held him transfixed like a deep rich color that draws the eye and holds it captive; he couldn't look away, couldn't turn away; he just stared at the man, the boy, the lover, the betrayer. Yes, it was Terrell. Then slowly, the figure disappeared behind the door, once again shutting Otis out.

After sitting a bit longer, nursing the rush of thoughts in his head and emotions in his heart, he started the car and slowly drove away into the deepening Saturday eve.

* * * *

"You got everything?" Courtney asked as Otis zipped up the overnight bag.

"Yeah." He spoke in a remote tone.

Courtney looked at him. She stood in the doorway of the bedroom. "Otis? You okay? Is something wrong?"

Otis hunched his shoulders. "I don't know... it's just that I saw Terrell today, and...

"What?" Courtney rushed to her brother's side, "Oh Otis. You sure you okay?" she asked as she put her hand on his back.

"To be honest with you, I don't know."

Courtney put her hands on Otis' shoulders and the two of them sat on the bed. "You wanna talk about it? I mean, it's okay if you don't."

"I don't mind."

"So when did you see him?"

"This evening."

"What did he say?"

"He didn't see me. I was sitting outside his house and I saw him answer his door." Then he sighed, heaving his large shoulders, "It was strange, Court. It was like I went back in time, and I saw him the way he looked twenty years ago. The way he used to smile at me and all the fun we used to have." Then he shook his head. "It was so weird."

"Why didn't you go up to the house? I mean, you came all this distance, all this time to see him didn't you?"

"Yeah. At least I think so. Shit. I don't even know. I came here to do something; to close the book, but I'm not even sure how to do that."

Courtney clasped her hands, "Well only you can do it. Nobody can do it for you." Then she turned to him, "I just hope you don't do anything crazy when you meet him. I know he hurt you, but, Otis, just don't do anything crazy. It wouldn't be worth it."

"Aw, nah. I ain't gonna do anything like that. But I have to admit, I don't know what to do. All those years and you'd think I'd have a plan, but I don't. I guess I spent most of those years trying not to think about what happened."

"I guess that's what you had to do to get through. And now it's time to confront him."

"Not just him. He really wasn't a part of the shit. It's just that- - it's just that he didn't speak up. He didn't do shit to help me out."

"Maybe he couldn't."

"Yes he could. He just didn't."

Courtney put her hand on Otis', "Look, don't jump to any conclusions."

"You don't jump to conclusions after twenty years, Court."

"Well you don't know the whole story. At least find out his side of it."

Otis didn't say anything. He just looked past her.

"Look, you'll take care of it when it's time. But, again, don't do anything stupid."

"I'm not. But you know, it just ain't right. He's sitting up there living the good life while I've been suffering all these years. It just ain't right."

"I know. But you have to move on. And looking at it that way isn't going to help you move forward. There is nothing you can do about how he turned out. You just have to make sure you turn out okay from all this."

Otis sat silently while his sister held his hand. Then he spoke softly as he looked down at her hand on his, "I don't know Court. A part of me feels like there has to be something done to rectify all this."

Courtney's eyes widened then blinked. "I don't think I like the sound of that."

Otis smiled suddenly, "Don't worry. It ain't gonna be anything stupid."

"Then what? What are you going to do?"

"I don't know... Look, Momma and Daddy're waiting for me. You know they'll bug out if I don't spend the night over there like I promised." Then he stood up and retrieved his bag and he and Courtney walked towards the door. "I'll see you tomorrow."

"Okay." Then Courtney called out down the hallway. "And Otis, it'll all be okay. I can feel it."

"I hope you're right," he smiled.

"Come on in. Come on in." Otis' father met him at the door and took the bag from him.

"Hey Daddy," Otis said as he stepped through the door.

"Your mother's been waiting for you. Got something on the table for you."

"Okay."

"I'll take this to your room." And with that, his father turned and went down the hall that led from the living room to the bedrooms. He moved quick and light like a fighter trying to dodge a blow. It was all he could do to distance himself from the history he lived everyday.

Otis' mother was in the kitchen at the stove when he walked in. "Hey Ma," he called out.

"Boy where you been?" his mother grinned as the two of them hugged. "I was wonderin' if you were gonna make it."

"Now Ma, you know I was gonna make it. I said I was, didn't I?"

His mother turned and began to fix a plate for him. "You hungry?"

"Yes ma'am."

She sat the plate on the table. It was a special recipe of hers, hickory joes. It was a favorite of the family's that was served on Friday or Saturday nights.

"I thought I smelled hickory joes. Aw Ma, you didn't have to do that."

"Oh hush. You know we always did eat hickory joes on the weekends."

Otis grinned, "I didn't know y'all still did that."

"Yeah. Everybody still likes it, so why change?"

"Yeah, y'right."

After he finished his meal he joined his parents and his sister in the living room. Walking through the entranceway he wondered how many times had he stood in the doorway that separated the living room from the dining room and watched his family as they watched T.V.

It was the same doorway in which he'd stood, years ago, a young man of seventeen and wondered where his life was headed because of the shift that was occurring. The way, once set and unobstructed, had begun to turn and course through unfamiliar lands then, and he was the lone navigator, unsure of the final spill.

Simple was what his life had once been. His family had planned it that way. He went to school, worked and played football. It was what his family wanted. It was what his brother did, and it was what he did.

But much of that would change.

Like most people, he had his share of secrets. And though most of his secrets were negotiable if he had ever been pressed to divulge them, one was not.

It was the secret that was unlike the others. It didn't lie dormant in wait of the right moment to reveal itself; it was as alive as he was, each and every step he took and for many of the thoughts he held.

Different from the other secrets, it was independent of conspiracy and commitment. It was a secret he loved and loathed, brandished and cherished.

So abundant was the care with which he protected this secret that he ended up nurturing it so that it had become a living entity in and of itself. It rose and settled without regard to his want and pressed itself upon him without regard to his comfort.

But what he could not understand was why the secret needed him? He had never done anything to summon it and could not, in all his naivete, have predicted it. He didn't know the answer to that question, but he knew of the need to continue to protect it. The secret had become him and he had become the secret.

The whole matter was crazy as far as he was concerned, this thing of loving another guy. But no matter how crazy he saw it, it was real. This secret had been with him for as long as he could remember. He had never laid claim to it, but it showed it didn't need naming. It had conveniently laid claim to him.

For many years he had realized it as insignificant; and it had been. That is, until the party.

He had been asked to attend a party with his girlfriend, Tangey. It was a birthday party for her hairdresser, Tuscan.

Otis had not wanted to go to the party. Tuscan, with his flailing hands and honest tongue had always frightened him, and he had been advised by Tangey that there would be others like Tuscan there, but under pressure from Tangey he begrudgingly got dressed and accompanied her.

There were many people at the party filling the rooms of the townhouse and spilling out onto the back yard. At first Otis had kept close to Tangey since he didn't know anyone there except Tuscan, and wasn't sure if he really wanted to know anyone there.

Finally, tired of trailing behind his girlfriend who seemed to know just about everyone, he took a place on a chair in the living room. He was careful not to take a chair in a corner because he felt it might call attention. *'Why are you sitting in the corner?'* a stranger might ask. So his space was chosen to appear conspicuous, but not to be seen.

He watched the party-goers, and wondered why they were not so different as he had always heard. There were some who stood out, but he found them more interesting than repulsive. Repulsion was what he had prepared himself to feel, but as he watched from his perch, he found it hard to acknowledge.

Instead, during the course of the evening he began to feel a release. Gradual, almost imperceptible, constricting feelings lifted and notions, heavy and burdensome, began to recede until in their places was a knowing. It was a knowledge of belonging, a knowing of place.

He looked around the room expecting to see someone smile and give an affirmative nod, however no one did, but there were smiles and warm laughter.

In a short while he stood and walked into the crowd. The warm, inviting sea. And he became submerged.

His life would not be the same after that night.

After a while of catching up on the family, friends and the neighborhood Otis excused himself and called it a night; then he retired to his bedroom.

He looked around the room as he closed the door behind him and was moved to memories of the years he'd shared the room with Jun. He'd slept in the bed just to the left of the window while Jun slept in the one on the right; and whenever the two of them would have a fight they would forbid each other to cross over to the other's side of the room, the window serving as the line of demarcation. But as the years went on the fights subsided and were replaced by deep conversations and lessons about life. Jun would confide in Otis of his coming of age, of wild times and wild girls. He would show Otis the condoms he kept hidden in his closet and the weed he carried around in his sock. And Otis would look at him with wide eyes and dream of the time when he could be like his brother; and that time did come, and he did. But soon those times began to change, and he found that he was not like his brother. He was his own man and so he staked his own ground. But the ground gave way and he fell under.

Now he lay in his bed, still his bed, and with his hands behind his head looked up at the ceiling the way he'd done so many times before. In the room next to his he could hear Munny moving about just as she had for so many years, her world a secret that everyone in the family had come to respect since it never posed a threat to structure. They accepted her personality as simply being her, just as outsiders had always referred to her as 'that quiet one'.

Otis had just lain back on the bed when there was a knock on the door. "Come on in."

His father stuck his head into the darkened room. "Just stopped in to see if everything's all right."

"Yeah. I'm fine. But, Daddy, an air conditioner?" Otis joked as he pointed towards the box in the window. "Me and Jun never had an air conditioner."

"Yep. It was your mother's idea," his father chuckled as he stepped further into the room. "She kept sayin' 'we gotta put an air conditioner in that room', like she just knew you would be comin' home soon."

Otis scooted over as his father seated himself on the bed. He had closed the door behind him, and now the room stood in compliance with quiet conversation. A soft cast of moonlight spilled through the window and over the two men, then softly onto the floor, and there was nothing heard but the soft breath of the air conditioner.

"I thought maybe Jun had been using the room," Otis continued.

"Nah, only so often when he and Kenne come down that they stay in here. But that's usually when it's colder outside. So there was no need for an air conditioner then. Your mother only bought this a month ago. You know how your mother is. It's like she just knew you were comin'."

Then his father folded his hands and looked at Otis. "You know, I'm glad she was right."

"I'm glad too."

His father continued, "I guess there was a lot of bad blood between us."

Otis didn't answer.

"Otis, I know I shoulda been there for you more than I was. I mean, I know I was there for you through all the proceedings and things, and I went through a lot gettin' you a good lawyer. But all the time I just couldn't help but think that you brought all of it on yourself." He turned away from his son as if he wanted his words to fall into the non-judgmental darkness of the room. "And when they found you guilty... I don't know," he said, turning back to his son, "I just got angry that you could've done somethin' like that. To hurt us like that. And all over a boy. It was wrong."

"I don't know, Daddy," Otis said as he raised himself on his elbow, "I think you're wrong. I didn't do it for 'a boy'. I did it because I was in love; just like anybody would do."

"Nah," his father said as he shook his head, "it ain't the same."

"Daddy, I didn't come here to argue points with you. I'm not that kid of twenty years ago. I got a life. *My* life. And I don't feel like I gotta always go around apologizing to anybody for who I am. If Momma can deal with it, why can't you?"

"Boy, I ain't got nothin' to do with all that." His father continued to talk in a calm voice. "All I'm sayin' is I'm sorry I wasn't there more for you back then. I don't know what I coulda done differently, but I would have if I knew what to do." Then he paused before putting his hand on Otis' arm. "Look, I'm just glad you're home. That's all." Then he raised himself from the bed and crossed the room.

"Daddy?"

His father stopped at the door. "Hm?"

"What about the people who sent me up?"

His father stood for a moment. Then, "I think it was unnecessary. I think it was *all* unnecessary."

* * * * * *

If it were left up to his imagination, the day he returned to his family wouldn't be in the middle of summer. It would be in winter, early winter, around January; and it would be in the evening, a dark, cold evening. Everyone would be gathered around the dining room table of his parents' home, clumsily handling their silverware as they averted their eyes from him and searched for the right words to say. And he would sit somewhere along the side of the table, perhaps in the middle, and he would hold them, every one of them except his mother and Courtney, hostage to their guilt.

For twenty years he had held that image; sometimes he even longed for it to become a reality. But he had learned long ago not to search for reality; after all, it had a funny way of asserting itself when it was good and ready. But he knew he wanted some measure of atonement.

Now, after a stroll through the neighborhood, he walked up to his parents' house and noticed a car parked in the driveway behind his rental. It was a large sedan, and it shone proud in the bright sunlight reflecting glints of sun from its smooth sheath. He could've sworn he saw the car wink at him. He tried to place the car to its owner, when suddenly he saw a tall young man come out of the house and walk over to the car. He appeared to be around seventeen or eighteen. "What's up?" Otis mumbled as he walked up the driveway. He looked questioningly at the young man.

" 'sup," the young man answered back with equal question. "You uncle Otis?"

Otis smiled, "Yeah. Who are you?"

"I'm Jamil," he smiled, "Your nephew." And with that he extended his hand.

"Jamil," Otis grinned as he shook his nephew's hand. With the young man's height, he was easily six-one, his full well formed lips, and eyes, those long almond shaped eyes, Otis knew he had to be family.

"Are you Jun's son?"

"Yessir," he grinned.

"I'll be damned. Yeah, I'm your uncle Otis."

Otis helped his nephew retrieve some packages from the car. From the backyard he could hear the sound of kids playing. Then they went into the house.

"Jamil, now why didn't you just go through the kitchen with that ice?" Jun called out from the dining room where he stood talking to his father.

"I don't know. I started talkin' to uncle Otis and we just came this way," he protested as he stepped through the door first.

Then Otis came in behind him. "Don't kill him. I just met him," he laughed.

Jun's face lit up, "Aaaah! Man, where you been?" Then he rushed to greet his younger brother.

"Workin'," Otis grinned.

"Well you got a lotta overtime."

Otis set the bag down and hugged his brother.

"You should've punched that clock long time ago," Jun said as he embraced Otis.

Again, like when his father had hugged him, Otis felt a bit uncomfortable being embraced. But love won out, and he squeezed his brother's broad back. "Yeah," he said against his brother's neck. At that point he looked over his brother's shoulder and saw a woman standing just a bit away.

"And you must be Kenne," he said as he unfolded his arms from his brother.

"Yes," she said as she walked towards him and extended her hand. She was tall and had that same bronze complexion as her son.

"I've heard some good things about you," Otis said as he shook her hand.

"And I've heard some good things about you too." She smiled with porcelain white teeth.

"Girl, boy, y'all sister and brother-in-law. Give each other a hug," Otis' father said.

The two of them hugged each other. Otis looked down, "And who is this?" he said, referring to the little boy who clung to Kenne's leg.

"That's Jun Jun," big Jun called out.

"Hey little fella."

Jun Jun clung even tighter to his mother's leg.

"Aww, now he's trying to play shy," Otis' father laughed. "Don't let him fool you."

"Daddy's right," Kenne laughed. "Say hi to your uncle Otis," she said as she tried to pry his arms loose. He clung as tight as before, but this time he smiled.

"Ol' knucklehead," Jun teased.

"Here. Let me take this bag into the kitchen," Kenne said as she took the bag from the dining table. "We have to get this dinner going. Honey, why don't you take Otis outside to meet the rest of our rug rats," she said to Jun.

"Okay. C'mon."

" 'ey, look. I'm gonna be watchin' that track and field thing on TV," their father said as he headed for the living room.

"Okay," Otis and Jun answered as they moved through the kitchen.

Once out on the patio, Jun called out to the rest of the kids who were running around the back yard. "Line up." Then he turned to Otis, "They're pagans, I tell you," he teased as his kids rushed over to where he and Otis stood. "This is your uncle Otis."

"Hi," "What's up?" They answered.

"What's up?" Otis laughed.

Jun pointed to the girls at front, "This is Sharice and Shawna." They're next to Jamil.

"How old are you?" Otis asked.

They answered in tandem, "Fourteen."

"But goin' on fifteen," Shawna informed.

"And this is Monty." Jun put his hand behind his son's head and pushed him forward.

"What's up, Monty."

"You."

Otis laughed. "There always has to be one in the bunch, huh?"

"Yup. And Monty is it," Jun laughed.

"And Cassandra- -"

"You didn't tell him how old I am," Monty interrupted.

"He doesn't want to know how old you are," Jun teased.

"Yes he does!"

"Yeah, I do," Otis smiled.

"I'm eleven."

"Man, you look older than eleven."

Monty beamed at his uncle's compliment.

"So now, Cassandra," Jun continued.

"Hey baby." Otis rubbed Cassandra's head which caused her to blush.

"And how old are you?"

"Seven." She continued to blush.

"And you met Jamil and Jun Jun," Jun continued. "Okay, y'all can go back now." And with that the kids ran back to their games.

"Man, you are so lucky," Otis said to his brother as he watched his nieces and nephews frolic in the back yard.

"Well yeah. I guess I am. But don't take that to mean you haven't had any luck either."

"It's hard to tell," Otis said as he looked out at the kids. "So I guess that just leaves me and Munny to grow old without any kids. 'Cause I'm sure Courtney will have some one day," he continued.

"Now you don't know that."

"It seems pretty clear to me. I mean, look at me. I'm almost forty years old. And come on, let's be real; you know my situation." He looked over at his brother as he measured his reaction.

Jun looked at him, "Well... things are different nowadays. You can still have a child. Adoption, artificial insemination. But you gotta have your life in order. 'Cause no agency's gonna give up a child to someone who might not have his shit together. And no woman's gonna have a child by someone who doesn't have his shit in order, either."

"What makes you think I don't have my shit squared away?"

"Do you?"

"My life ain't perfect, but it's pretty much copasetic."

"Then go for it. Have yourself that child." Then Jun hunched his shoulders, "But you know, you shouldn't have a child just because everybody thinks that's the only way to have a happy life. I mean, like, families come in all kinds of packages. And that's what you just might need most, people to call your family. He paused. His eyes dropped towards the ground, then back up to Otis. "Everybody needs to have a sense of family."

Otis bit his bottom lip slightly before giving a smile that seemed more like a wince than an actual smile. He weighed his words before continuing in a voice that was low and controlled. "Yeah, well I guess that ended long ago for me."

Jun looked at him in silence for a second. "No it didn't," Jun said.

"Funny. I didn't see any of you when I was locked up. Except for Ma."

"But I wrote you, several times."

"I guess that was convenient." Otis' words came out so heavy that they caused Jun to glance back at the house, as if the impact of the words could be felt there.

"Look, let's not go into all that," Jun said as he dropped his head slightly.

"Get into what? Man..." This time Otis' voice rose a bit. The kids stopped playing and looked over at them.

Jun looked at the house again. "Come on."

They walked over to the chairs on the patio and seated themselves in the ones that would give them a bit of privacy.

"You gotta live for now, Otis." Jun leaned forward, his hands swiping the air. "Forget the past."

"Jun, your past and mine ain't nothing alike," Otis said. He looked at Jun's kids. "That's the result of your past."

"And this is the result of yours," Jun said, pointing his thumb over his shoulder towards the house.

Otis sat in silence for a moment. Then he draped his arms across the sides of the chair. "You know, this is the same place me and Ma sat years ago when she told me my life might be rough. She was right." He raised his eyebrows and shook his head. "She was right," he repeated.

After a while Jun continued. "So do you have someone up there?"

Otis thought about the people he knew in New York. He knew a lot of people, but he had never let any of them get close to him. Alone was what he'd chosen to be, sometimes anonymous, the anonymity giving him a certain power over others, power he knew he could never have if he was to become close to someone. It was the power he had chosen because it was the power he knew would keep him from becoming the victim he had once been. "No."

"Don't do that to yourself. And don't do that others, either." Jun reached haltingly, his hand finally resting on his brother's knee. "Life ain't meant to be that way."

Otis looked at him with no words to speak.

Jun patted his knee. "C'mon. Let's go in and check out this track and field event with Daddy."

Set against the background of the sounds of the kids at play in the backyard, Jun's words rang clear in Otis' head. *"Don't do that to yourself."*

He couldn't deny that he sometimes felt that he was his own worst enemy. Even when he would look into a mirror sometimes, or catch a glimpse of his image in a window while walking down the street he would see his figure composed of nothing more than angles. Individual expression had disappeared long ago.

But he knew that his arrival at this state of existence had not been wholly dependent upon his actions alone, but of the will of others as well. And to deny that would be a lie. Each seam that held him together in his tragic state had been stitched by hands that had bid him less than fare well. And though he didn't think of these people each and every day of his life, he carried their marks, like a brand, deep in his heart.

The calls and the laughter of the children fell to the background, replaced by the conversation of the women as he came through the back door following Jun's lead. He saw their faces, the creases at their eyes and the smiles at their lips. Jun made a passing comment to which his wife immediately responded, followed by Otis' mother bringing up the rear. Then they all broke out laughing, their hands waving in the full warmth of a Sunday kitchen. He watched them and assured himself that this was one of the reasons he had returned.

"Man y'all should see these black girls runnin'," their father said as he motioned to his two sons as they came into the living room.

"I been watchin' 'em, granpa." Jamil grinned up from the floor where he had been lying on his stomach in front of the T.V.

"Yeah, I bet you have," his grandfather grinned. "Come on and sit down," he continued as he patted the sofa.

Otis sat beside his father and Jun.

"Man, I used to be able to run like that." Their father waved his hand at the screen.

"You used to run track granpa?" Jamil asked.

"Yeah. I was good at it too."

"You win any trophies?"

"Oh yeah."

"You still got 'em?"

"No. It's been a long time. I don't know where any of 'em are." Then he turned to Otis, "You used to run track too."

"Yep."

"And football too," his father continued, bearing an uncomfortable grin.

"...Yeah..." Otis studied his father's face. He wanted to know if his father was grasping for better days or simply rambling. He needed to know such things because knowing them would determine his own behavior. For the time he had spent with his father over the past few days, he had not seen any sign of remorse; maybe, he thought, that the old man's reminiscence was a sign of the guilt he felt. Maybe.

"I run too." Jamil sat up, smiling at his uncle.

"Yeah? What's your event?" Otis asked.

"Hundred, two hundred and relay."

"Man. That's what mine was."

"Nah!"

"Yeah."

There was something restorative in his conversation with his nephew; a certain allowance that he had not felt from others. Even with his mother and Courtney, both of whom had been very supportive of him, their motives were different. In his mother he had come to know the relentless desire to hold a family together; and Courtney's strident demands of atonement of the attitudes of his detractors sometimes bordered on activism.

But in Jamil he sensed something more profound, something immeasurable. Grace.

The conversation continued during which Otis discovered shared likes and dislikes with his nephew. Some of their ways were shown to be so similar that they drew cautious looks from his father and Jun.

"You know, Uncle Otis, you should move on back here. Maybe Daddy can make you his assistant coach."

Otis' father spoke up, "He ain't gonna move back here from no New York, boy." He looked at Otis for a reply.

Just then, from outside, the sound of a car arriving was heard.

"That must be either aunt Courtney or aunt Dana. Probably aunt Courtney, because you know how late aunt Dana always is," Jamil said.

But then there came the sound of another car.

"Oops. Maybe I'm wrong." He got up from the floor and walked to the door and opened it to greet Courtney. "Hi aunt Courtney."

"Hi baby." Courtney entered carrying a large covered dish. She went over to where her father sat and kissed him on the cheek. "Hi Daddy."

"Hey baby girl."

Then she greeted Otis and Jun before turning to Jamil. "Dana and Boz are going to need some help Jamil," to which Jamil went out to help.

Soon Dana came through the door. "Heyyyy. There's my big brother!" she said as she hurried over to Otis who stood and hugged her. "You're looking good," she said as she stood back and looked at him.

"You do too." He thought about how long it had been since he'd seen his sister, all his sisters. They were all so young when he'd left. None of them had yet taken on the bodies of a woman. And now they were fully realized.

"Well, I've put on a little weight in the last few years. But I'm going to get it all off in a few months, just wait."

At that moment a man came through the door.

"Otis this is my husband Boswell. Boz, this is Otis."

Boz grinned as he and Otis shook hands. "Man, seems like I already know you. But it's good to finally meet you."

"Yeah man, me too."

"And this is Chris," Courtney said of a laughing young man being propelled through the door by Jamil's knee to his backside.

"Oh, I didn't expect you to have a young man," Otis laughed as he extended his hand.

"He's fourteen," Courtney added.

Chris shook his uncle's hand.

"Stop Jamil!" Dana and Boz's daughter called out to her cousin who was pushing her through the door by her head.

"And this has to be your daughter," Otis laughed.

"Yep. Always fussin' like her mama," Jun called out.

"Hi," she said to her uncle.

"Hi. What's your name?"

"Angie."

"Her real name's Angelica," Dana corrected as she brushed her daughter's hair.

After greeting their father and Jun, Dana and her family moved to the kitchen.

The dinner started with Otis' mother expressing her joy at finally having all her family at the table. It was something that was long overdue. The faces at the table smiled and heads nodded in agreement as everyone looked at Otis.

All the attention caused him to drop his head slightly, an imperceptible smile on his lips. He was glad to be home, but he didn't know what to do about the space that separated him from his family. For so long he had not been with them; and they hadn't been with him. They hadn't witnessed his pain; they hadn't witnessed the years of indigence and the search for the love of himself he was no longer able to touch; the dim alleys, desperate with fluids that slipped beneath the soles of his shoes as he wandered through the streets too frightened of what was to become, but too humiliated to look back. He knew he was the only one at that table who had seen utter despair and now must once again confront light. Yet he realized that the people sitting before him, and alongside him had also, in their own way, experienced his history; and that was why he glanced at the faces and tried to see their stories; it was why he now looked at their mouths and tried to hear their words, and it was why he watched their hands and tried to gather their expressions. They were reaching out with those hands, trying to grasp at that space between them to shorten it, that ugly space. But at the moment no one was sure how to do it.

"So what did you think when you walked around Lincoln Heights today? Changed didn't it?" Dana looked at Otis, her elbow resting on the table.

"Yeah. It looks kind of- - forgotten. You know, I kept remembering how much used to go on. All the fun we used to have. But now... I don't know. And all the businesses... they're all gone. Steffens Street is like its own little ghost town."

"Nothin' but thugs hangin' on the corners," his father interjected.

"I noticed that."

"But I guess you're used to that up there in New York," Munny said.

Otis thought for a second. "Not really. I guess it's because there's so much going on that you don't get too caught up in noticing that kind of stuff."

"Really?"

"Yeah. It's not all thugs in New York, you know."

"Hm. I always thought New York was a dangerous place to live," she continued as she set her fork on her plate.

Otis noticed how calloused her small hands were. "Not anymore. That was years ago."

"I've been there plenty of times, and Otis is right. It's not so bad,"

Kenne said before continuing, "What part do you live in?"

"Brooklyn."

Then Dana looked at him, and with a smile, "Well I guess it's going to be a big change readjusting to Cincinnati, huh?"

"What do you mean?" Otis asked as he looked at her.

Dana stared at him. "I thought you were moving back." She turned her head towards her mother with a questioning look in her eyes. "I mean, I thought..."

"Girl didn't nobody tell you that." Jun came to Otis' aid.

"I guess I just thought it was time," she mumbled as she lifted her fork to her mouth. "I mean, none of us are getting any younger," she said as she glanced at her mother and father.

"Oh, me and your father don't mind," their mother quickly interjected, "as long as he keeps in touch and comes down when he can." She looked at their father who nodded in agreement.

"Hmph. Then I guess patience is a virtue," Dana mumbled again.

Jamil glanced nervously at her.

"Maybe it's understanding, babe," Boz offered as he looked closely at his wife.

"I guess..."

After dinner Otis helped Courtney, Munny and Kenne clean up the kitchen. From the kitchen window he could see Dana and Jun, both of whom went outside to smoke, engaged in deep conversation as they sat on the patio. At times it appeared as if Jun was scolding Dana, but he wasn't sure; but one thing Otis was sure of was that they were probably discussing him and the incident at dinner.

"You should be there out back with Jun and Dana," Courtney said as she walked up behind her brother.

He looked over his shoulder, "I ain't even pressed."

"Otis, you have to be concerned. We all have to be."

Munny overheard Courtney's statement and paused as she was putting some food in the refrigerator, "Courtney…"

Courtney turned to her older sister, "It's true. I mean, how long does it have to be before we all get over this mess?"

"Things'll work themselves out. I don't think you have to keep trying to draw blood," Munny said as she placed the food on the refrigerator shelf.

"It's not about blood."

Just then Kenne spoke up, "You know, I think Courtney's right." She waved her hand, "Now I know I'm just the sister-in-law, but you're my family too. And I think it's time to wrestle with all this so you… *we* can bring about some closure."

Otis continued to look out the window. Finally he spoke, his eyes still trained on the scene out on the patio, "I did come a thousand miles and twenty years to be here, didn't I?" And with that, he dried his hands and walked out the back door.

As he approached Dana and Jun he called out, "Is it safe for us non-smokers to come on out?"

Jun and Dana laughed as they snuffed out their cigarettes.

"Yeah," Jun said as he slid over to make room on the picnic table. "We were just talking about dinner."

"I'll sit here," Otis said as he pulled up another patio chair and sat near Dana." Then he continued, "Looked like y'all were talking about more than just the food."

Dana and Jun remained quiet for a second before Dana spoke up. "Well, yeah," she admitted as she looked over from the chair in which she sat. "Actually, Jun was chewing my head off for the comment I made at dinner." She looked at Otis with apologetic eyes. "I guess my timing was off."

"Well, that's you Dana," Otis responded as he hunched his shoulders. "You never had good timing," he chuckled.

"I know, I know."

"But the question still stands, though, don't it?" Otis pressed.

Dana nodded her head. "It's a legitimate one, don't you think?"

Jun interceded, "It's not about legitimacy. I don't know why you're tryin' to make it more than what it should be."

Dana looked at her oldest brother, "And what should that be?"

"It sure ain't about legitimacy."

"And anyway, Dana, that's what I came home to explore," Otis said. Then he clasped his hands in front of him, his arms resting on his thighs. "I came home to see where things stand."

"Why? If you don't know where things stand by now, then..." her voice trailed off.

"Dana, there's a lot that happened that I don't think you're lookin' at."

"I know what happened."

"Nah, you only know half the story. You're lookin' at the obvious.

You don't know what went on inside me. Now I know you can't sit there and tell me that. You ain't lookin' at what I went through with all this."

"That's what I've been tryin' to tell her," Jun said as he opened his palms upward.

"Well I don't think you're being fair about all this either. Otis, we're talking about your parents. I mean, you were gone for almost twenty years. And you never thought about coming home to see your own parents?" She looked incredulously at him.

Otis raised his hand, "Whoa, whoa, whoa! Dana, you actually think I never thought about seeing Mama and Daddy? Come on now, let's be real."

"You never came to see them."

"Look, me and Mama kept in touch a lot. We talked almost once a month."

Dana looked at him and shook her head, "Otis, you know how strange that sounds? You kept in touch with your mother once a month for twenty years. Otis...?"

Otis looked over at Jun and saw by the expression on his face that, for a moment, he agreed with Dana.

"Mama understood," Otis defended.

"Yeah. She probably felt she had no choice. It was the only way she could keep up with you. You know if she had a choice she would've chosen to see you instead of having a phone call a month- - for twenty years."

"But still, you can't say that Mama didn't understand where he was coming from, Dana," Jun added. "You're getting so caught up in one perspective that you're overlooking everything else."

"I think I'm looking at the most important thing."

Otis sat back in his chair and crossed his leg, "Oh, so forget about me, huh? Or is that part of what's behind your feelings, that I got what I deserve."

Dana shook her head, "That's not what I'm saying, and you know that."

Otis dropped his voice to almost a whisper, "Look, I'm about to tell you something that I haven't shared with nobody but Mama." He licked his lips. "Dana, I had to fight my way through those years in lockup." He clasped his hands and laid them in his lap, "They don't like child molesters in prison. They hate them more than anything." He twiddled his thumbs and watched them move against each other to release the shame he now felt, "I got into fights almost everyday. Almost everyday," he repeated. "That's why I had to stay an extra year there, because I got into so many fights. I used to call Mama and I used to cry sometimes because I couldn't believe what was happening to me. I just couldn't believe that I was in that place."

"But Terrell wasn't a child," Dana spoke with wide eyes.

"They didn't know that. Word got back from the streets that I had molested a little boy."

"Damn." Jun dropped his head.

"Dana, my jaw was broken twice while I was there. I had my mouth wired shut twice." Now he was leaning forward pointing at his jaw. "And through it all nobody seemed to care except Mama. I didn't want to tell her what I was going through, but I had to because she was the only who cared. And when Courtney got older she started to write me. And that really hurt because she was so young when I got sent up that she barely even knew me." He sat back once again, this time his voice cracking, "She barely knew me; my own little sister was trying so hard to reach out to a brother she barely knew. But she knew I was her brother, and she told me that was all that mattered."

The three of them sat in silence for a while.

Finally Otis stood up, "And when I got out I told Mama that I wasn't coming back for a long time. My body was broken. I felt ashamed to come back here. And most of all, I felt my family had turned its back on me." He put his hands in his pockets and turned to walk back to the house. Then he paused, turned back around to face Dana, "New York is my home now." And he turned and walked towards the house.

Chapter IX

"You were pretty focused today. Man, I thought you were never gonna get off that track." Stanton spoke as he punched Terrell lightly on the arm.

Terrell laughed as he tugged his gym bag onto his shoulder. "Yeah. I guess I'm getting the hang of this working out thing."

The two men stepped out of the Central Parkway Y onto Elm Street and made their way back into downtown. The evening was warm and still, and was lighted by an orange sun that had begun to turn its way over the horizon. To the left of them men and women, most of whom were indigent, lounged in Washington Park. In the shadows of the trees, they looked like souls that had been cast into some dark netherworld as punishment for their impotence.

"You're not feeling sore from yesterday, are you?" Stanton asked.

"A little bit. But that's supposed to be a good sign, isn't it?"

"Yeah. It shows the exercises are working." Then Stanton raised a finger, "But it's supposed to be soreness, not pain. That stuff about no pain, no gain is bullshit."

"You don't have to worry about that. I'm not one to put myself through any type of pain," Terrell said as they crossed Central Parkway. Some of the drivers eyed them as they walked along the cross walk as if they still hadn't come to terms with two black men in executive attire. Terrell continued, "But you weren't doing so bad yourself with those weights. How much were you pressing when I came in?"

"Two fifty."

"Man."

"That's my forte, though, lifting weights. I used to play mad football when I was young; used to crush muthafuckahs like paper cups."

"I can see that," Terrell said as he looked over at Stanton.

Stanton grinned. Then, "Yeah, but those days are over. Now I should be concentrating on losing some of this weight, especially some of this belly. That's why I should be running more," he said as he lightly patted his stomach.

"Man you're stomach isn't so bad," Terrell said. The image of Stanton standing naked in front of him, earlier, came to his mind. He had looked like a powerful bull as he had stood there, dark and husky, powerful, with his large firm belly protruding, not hanging, above his thick dick. It was the fattest dick Terrell had ever seen. "You carry it well," Terrell said.

Stanton laughed, "Thanks. But I'm the one who has to live with it."

As they turned a corner Terrell looked over at the brownstones that lined Ninth Street; their Italianate design appeared graceful and timeless as they extended both sides of the avenue. "These are some beautiful buildings," he gushed.

"Yeah, they are. You haven't seen mine. It's up on Liberty Hill overlooking downtown."

"Liberty Hill?"

Stanton looked at him in mild surprise. "Yeah, off East Liberty Hill-- going up to Mt. Auburn."

"Oh. I always thought it was just Mt. Auburn," Terrell said as he hunched his shoulders.

Stanton smiled, "I can tell you don't come into the city much."

Terrell turned to Stanton and replied with raised brow, "I work here. Remember?"

"Then I guess I should say you don't get *around* the city much," Stanton corrected.

"Now that much is true."

"So you're one of them suburbanites who rarely venture past the lawnscapes and malls, huh?" Stanton chided.

Terrell smiled, "Truth be known, yeah."

"Well you should come on down here more often. It's beautiful living."

"I had thought about moving down here years ago, when me and Karen first got married. But she said no way. So, well..."

Stanton stared at him for a bit. "Well she's not here now, so let's hang for a bit, alright?"

Terrell looked over at him with a slightly confused expression. "Yeah, I guess I can do that."

"Have you checked out Café Cin Cin yet?" Stanton inquired.

"Yeah. It's nice."

"Then let's go."

And with that, they turned down Race Street, then through Piatt Park. As they walked past the water sculpture, then through the archways of the narrow park they passed a couple of brothers sitting on one of the benches. One of them, a man in his early thirties, and lean, sat with his shirt unbuttoned exposing a tight six pack. His face lighted as he recognized Stanton.

" 'ey, Stanton," the man beamed as he stood and extended his hand.

Stanton's face darkened as he eyed the man. "What's up?" Then he returned a brief shake of the hand before continuing on.

Terrell noticed the expression on the man's face. The smile had quickly become replaced with a look of indignity.

"Oh. So it's like that, huh?" the man called out as he nodded his head and gave Stanton a scornful look.

But Stanton didn't break his stride as he and Terrell continued on their way.

It took them a while to make it to the café because enroute, Stanton stopped a few times to chat with a few acquaintances. By the appearance of these well-wishers' bearing and dress, it was obvious they were people of stature.

Finally, they arrived at Café Cin Cin. They took a seat at one of the tables near the window.

"I figured we could eat a little something as well," Stanton replied as a sly smile came to his lips.

"Hey. You're the one who has to live with it," Terrell laughed as he looked at Stanton's belly.

The sun had disappeared behind the hills that rim the city leaving only a faint orange glow as Stanton and Terrell ate their meals.

"Now see, this is what we need more of- - more minority owned businesses downtown," Stanton remarked as he waved a hand through the air.

Terrell politely nodded his head.

Stanton noticed Terrell's response. "You're not very political, are you?"

"Well, no, I'm not. Politics has its place, but, no, I'm not very political."

Stanton grinned, "I bet you're very religious though."

Terrell looked up from his meal, "What's with the inquisition?"

"I'm just trying to see where you're coming from."

"Why's that? I haven't signed on with your campaign."

"It's just conversation, that's all. So which are you most, political or religious?" Stanton continued his inquiry before taking a bite of salad.

"There're some things I don't go around discussing; and religion and politics are two of them."

"You can with me. I mean, I'm not trying to make an assessment or anything like that."

Terrell waved his fork in front of him, "You know, there's something going on here. I don't know what it is, but..."

"Okay, okay," Stanton laughed. "I guess I do like to engage in argument for the sake of argument."

"So you're a polemicist; as if I didn't know," Terrell smiled.

The two of them laughed at Terrell's comment. Then Terrell looked over at Stanton, "So what was your argument?"

"Ah, so you're more interested in the conversation than I thought. Well," he said folding his napkin and laying it on the table, "I've always found it interesting that some people can embrace religion, but will try to steer clear of politics when, in fact, the two are almost inseparable." Then he put his elbows on the table and cupped his hands in front of him, "You see, there's only two conditions that drives all humans: pain and pleasure. And in between those two ends is our fear; fear of pain, and our search; search for the release from pain. And as a result we seek power because power gives us authority over our fear, and, subsequently, authority over our pain."

Terrell, who had been transfixed by Stanton's supposition, picked up his fork and toyed absentmindedly with his food. "I see where you're going with all this. So you see both politics and religion as forms of gaining control over destiny, of sorts."

"Yeah. Politics, to gain control here on earth and religion to gain God's favor, therefore, control over one's ultimate destiny."

"Well, you might have a point there; but only to an extent. Because I don't think you can say *all* human beings function that way."

"Show me one that doesn't."

"I don't believe Martin Luther King did what he did to gain anybody's favor- - or God's, for that matter. And neither did Mahatma Ghandi. I really do believe they did what they did because they simply thought that what they were doing was right... and that's all. Some people do still believe in doing what's right, you know."

"Do you?" Stanton asked with a suspicious look.

"I try to. I'm always asking God to show me what's right and then give me the strength to carry it out. And guess what? I don't always go by my religious beliefs when I make some of my decisions."

Stanton sat back in his chair, "What? You?" he laughed. Then, "But you know that's far and in between to be like that. The average person isn't like that. I bet your wife isn't."

Terrell laughed as he shook his head, "Man, you have a dark soul, you know that?"

"No I don't. I'm just a realist."

"Oh, like you're the master of reality," Terrell smirked. After a second or so, he looked up from his plate, "So how is it that you've been friends with bishop all this time, I mean, with those views?"

Stanton had resumed eating his food. Then, taking a sip from his drink, he answered. "The bishop you know and the bishop I know aren't the same." Suddenly he caught himself, "Um, we just have a different friendship, y'know?" he said as he cut into his meal. "We go way back. I met him when I first moved here."

Terrell looked at him for a second before speaking. "Oh. You're not from here."

"No."

"Where're you from?"

"Milwaukee."

"How long have you been in Cincinnati?"

"Man, about thirty years, off and on. I came here to attend UC."

"That's where you played football?"

"Yep. Like I said, I used to crush 'em." He said this with a sudden large grin.

Terrell sat back in his seat and looked curiously at him. "So, about your friendship with Bishop, you didn't answer my question."

Stanton gave a stern look, "Yes I did." And with that he turned his attention back to his plate.

The evening ended with the two of them standing in front of the café. The amber light from the café shone through the window and encircled them as they stood on the sidewalk and shook hands.

"As usual, I had a nice time. A bit challenging, but nice," Terrell chuckled.

" 'ey, you know me," Stanton conceded with a hunch of the shoulders.

"I'm beginning to." Then Terrell looked at his watch, "Well I'd better be cuttin' out. Oh, and don't forget about the meeting with bishop tomorrow."

"I haven't. We're supposed to take a site visit, so bring your hard hat," Stanton reminded.

"Alright. Later."

"Later."

The two of them clasped hands.

Stanton turned to go on his way, when he stopped and turned back to Terrell. " 'ey," he said as he stepped back up to where Terrell stood. "You know me and a couple of the fellas get together every now and then and just sit around shootin' the breeze. You should join us sometime."

"Oh. Well..."

Stanton smiled and shook his head. "Always paranoid. The world outside your doorstep ain't gonna eat you up."

"Man, I know that."

"And I'm sure your wife will allow you out the house every now and then."

"See? There you go."

"We're gonna meet Thursday over one of the brothers' house. Me and you can meet up and you can ride with me or you can follow me over there. He lives in Mt. Airy. After all, your wife is out of town, remember?"

Terrell thought for a second before replying, "Okay. I'll take you up on that."

"Bet," Stanton said. "Oh, and some of them are married too. So y'all can sit around and compare notes on how to get out of the house."

"Good night, Stanton." Terrell shook his hand.

"Alright," Stanton laughed.

Terrell walked down the street towards the garage where he'd parked his car. He thought about the expression on Stanton's face upon realizing how close he was to betraying a secret that he and the bishop held; and now Terrell wondered what the secret was. He was sure the secret couldn't be that bad, after all, everyone had skeletons in their closets; that was something he, Terrell, understood very well.

He stopped in front of a store window as his mind continued to wander. Then, a smile came to his face, a lazy, elliptical smile caused by the alcohol and the irony that Bishop Abrams could have skeletons in his closet.

Continuing on his way, he looked down the avenue at The Tyler Davidson Fountain that stood in the middle of Fifth and Vine. The sight of the figure of the woman, her arms spread, splaying water that danced in the lights of the fountain, and the streams of water that jettisoned up from the base of the fountain brought back memories of the first time Otis had taken him to see Fountain Square at night:

"Man. This is beautiful."

"Yeah, it is," Otis said.

Terrell looked up at the dark handsome face and saw the lights and the shimmer of the water reflect in Otis' eyes and off his skin. It was as if his face, the lights, and the water were speaking to him. They told him how much love was there.

As he neared the fountain he slowed a bit as a melancholy came over him. Then, gathering strength, he continued across the plaza and to the garage. But at the entrance to the garage, he paused. He looked back at the city, and all the lights; then he slowly walked back from the garage and up the street. There was something enchanting about the city at night.

He turned and walked down to Main Street, away from where he had left Stanton. He knew Stanton would be on his way home, and that they might encounter each other, at which point, Stanton might inquire as to why he was not on his way home. He didn't need that type of questioning right now. He walked slowly with his hands in his pockets. Every once in a while he stopped and looked in a store window; he noticed how different some of the styles of clothing were compared to what he was used to. It bothered him that he felt as if he was a stranger in a distant land unfamiliar with the ways of a people. It was different from the world in which he lived. The clothes he saw in the windows that night were bright and bold, they were daring and arrogant, they weren't safe like the clothes he was used to. Even this world wasn't safe like the world he was used to. Then he moved on, wondering how much of life he was missing, and of how much safety had become too much.

After a while, he decided to head on home. Turning down Vine Street, he walked back towards the garage. As he neared one of the stores he saw a man leaning against the building, a bit in the doorway.

He noticed the man eyeing him as he neared where the man stood; it made Terrell a bit apprehensive, yet, at the same time he was drawn to the figure, a matter that caused him slight confusion.

"What's up?" the man spoke as Terrell walked past.

"Nothing much."

He was a younger man. A bit younger than Terrell, about in his late twenties or early thirties. He was a bit taller than Terrell, but he was leaner, so lean, in fact, that his bronze skin seemed almost translucent; but he was by far not skinny.

He looked at Terrell as if he knew his deepest feelings, his eyes speaking to those feelings.

It was a look that caused Terrell to slow his pace until he came to a complete halt and awaited the man's next move. It was as if the man held answers that he, Terrell, knew he needed.

"What'chou you up to?" the man went on as he continued to lean against the building.

Terrell felt himself begin to tremor deep inside. He hoped it didn't show. "Nothing," he mumbled. He realized how weak he must sound, so he gathered his resolve and continued, "So what's up with you?" He couldn't believe his words.

The man's eyes danced slightly behind the hard glint, and a smirk caused his closely trimmed beard to widen across his face. Terrell couldn't help but notice the nice full lips that parted exposing strong white teeth.

"Where you on yo' way to?"

"Home."

"Can I go?" This time the man gave a mischievous grin.

Terrell was at a loss for words.

"So what's up?" The man said, as he lifted his shirt and rubbed his hard stomach that had a mat of hair that went down to the top of his exposed boxers. "I can make it good."

Terrell felt nervous and embarrassed as his eyes drifted to the crotch of the man's baggy khakis.

"It's all there," the man grinned as he squeezed at his crotch causing the large imprint of his dick to become suddenly exposed.

Terrell's mouth filled with saliva as he looked at the imprint. The tremors, which had been secure in the pit of his stomach came to the surface and he found he could barely contain himself. But he knew he had to. "N- - no", he stammered. "I have to go."

The man seemed a bit confused. "A'ight," he conceded, "I ain't got time for all that." Then he removed his hand from his crotch and lowered his shirt and disappeared back into the shadow of the doorway.

Terrell turned and walked away.

It was late when he arrived home. His street was silent; the homes, like sentries, dark and vigilant as he pulled into his driveway. He entered the kitchen

from his garage and turned on the lights filling the room with brightness. The jar
of peanut butter he'd left from that morning sat on the counter, and a glass with a
ring of dried milk at its bottom sat in the sink. He walked through the dining
room, turning out the lights behind him and headed upstairs. Having showered, he
lay awake in bed and watched the blinking light of the display unit on the
nightstand. He was in no mood to check the messages. His mind was still
downtown in front of the man in the doorway. The man was still with him; he
could feel the man's presence, he could feel his warmth as it covered him; he
could smell the brownness of the man's fragrance and see the texture of the wooly
hair that ran down his belly into his pants. The way the eyes appeared, like dark
corridors inviting him to enter the place he'd shut out for so long, the place that
stayed with him for so long. He would not return there. No, never again.
Turning on his side, he pulled the sheets up over his shoulders and went to sleep.

* * * *

"So what do you think about the new church?" Terrell had invited his
mother to tour the construction site with he, Bishop and Stanton; and now he and
his mother walked through Hyde Park Square eating ice cream. Along the
sidewalks people sat at the cafes and enjoyed the cool evening breeze.

"It looks nice. It's bigger than I thought," his mother said as she raised a
spoon of caramel praline pecan to her mouth.

"Really?"

She swallowed the ice cream. "Yeah. I didn't think it would be that large."

"Well, Bishop said he wanted to go all out."

"Yeah, he did. And I see he meant it."

Terrell turned to his mother as the two of them stood at a cross walk. "What do you think about the broadcasting studio?"

His mother smiled, "Bishop told me you were having problems with that."

"Yes ma'am, I do," Terrell answered.

"Why?"

"It's too expensive."

"Too expensive like, we don't have it? Or are you being your regular self… penny pinching." His mother chuckled as they started across the street.

"Somebody has to pinch pennies."

"Yeah, but sometimes you have to let go. Sometimes you have to see the fruit of all your work; and you know Bishop has been working for that church for decades now."

"Even though we have the money, we need to set some aside for reserves," Terrell protested. "You never know what might come up. And at the rate he's going he's going to bankrupt our reserve." They had stopped at a store window and his mother looked at some of the fabrics that were draped across various expensive traditional chairs and tables.

"Oh stop worrying so much," she said without turning to look at her son. "I'm sure you won't let all the reserve dry up. That's your job isn't it?" She turned back to her son. "And besides, hasn't it occurred to you that with a church like that it'll bring in more people?"

Terrell looked at his mother, his eyes blinking.

His mother smiled, "C'mon, you know how it goes, the bigger the cathedral, the larger the congregation. People like grand churches. It makes them feel like they're in the midst of God's power."

"Ma…" Terrell was surprised at his mother's disclosure.

His mother laughed and waved her hand. "Oh grow up. You know how it works by now."

"You make it seem like a con or something."

His mother hunched her shoulders. "It works doesn't it? Sometimes that's what some people need to get on the path. It's better than not coming to church at all isn't it?"

"So we'll always get more money, is that what you're saying?"

"How many churches do you know that don't make it? Especially if they have grand cathedrals."

Terrell smiled and shook his head as he looked at his mother.

"Now, I want to go in here and check out some of these fabrics," she said as she started into the store. "Hold my ice cream."

Terrell stood outside and watched his mother as she walked around the store with the sales person. She seemed to have come into her own in the three years since his father passed. Her eyes were clear of the indecisiveness that once clouded them and her laughter and conversations were more genuine than they once were, less measured. At times he felt bothered by the way his mother seemed to be enjoying her life now that his father was gone; but he understood.

"I placed some fabric on order," his mother said as she came back out. "The sales lady said it should be in sometime next week. She beamed as she took the cup of ice cream from her son. Yes, she was coming into her own.

They walked along, stopping every now and then to look in shop windows. Then they crossed over to the other side of the street and sauntered back to where the car was parked.

"When are you leaving for Atlanta?" His mother asked.

"Week after next."

"That's good. Me and Mother Abrams were talking about that; about how Bishop shouldn't have you spending so much time on that church when your family is a thousand miles away. She said she would talk to Bishop about that."

"It's okay. Karen understands."

"But what about the kids? Do they really understand why their father isn't on vacation with them?"

Terrell blew a slight breath. "It's only been a little over a week. Then when I get down there we'll have the rest of summer. I'm also taking them to Orlando. And anyway, they're used to it. They know how I sometimes have to put in a lot of hours on some projects. We usually make up for it on the weekends. And it's not like I do this often."

His mother continued to walk beside him, her eyes trained ahead. "Do you hear how you sound? They're children, Terrell; they have the emotions of kids, not adults. They might understand, but it don't mean they're not hurting inside. And what about Karen? Don't you think she misses you?" This time she looked at her son. "You and Karen are okay, aren't you?"

"Yes ma'am. We're okay."

By this time they were at the car.

"Hurry up and join your family," his mother said as she slid into the seat.

"Yes ma'am." Terrell spoke as he closed the car door.

Terrell decided to spend some time in the city after he dropped off his mother. He needed to get away from home; Mason, with its manicured lawns and sidewalks that its citizens rarely used. Now he sat in Eden Park on one of the benches that sat high on a hill overlooking the Ohio River; he watched as the river snaked along the valley, wandering until it disappeared behind some trees, only to return before launching itself over the horizon.

It had been some time since he had been to the park, about fifteen years since he and Karen had climbed its many hills and sauntered along the walkways that rolled through the trees past the ponds, the art museum, the theatres and the conservatory. Karen had just moved to Cincinnati, and she had fallen in love with the park and had commented on how she wanted to live near it when they got married. But they never did. There had even been a time when he thought he and Otis would move in together near the park. That was almost twenty-one years ago. But that never happened either.

Those were just some of the dreams that had never come true for him. But then again, he had become used to that. He told himself that they were simply missed chances, but he knew that wasn't true; he often took chances, but usually they were based on the wishes of others. The first time he took a chance on a wish of his own, the only time, was the year he spent with Otis; and after his father and the bishop took that away from him he resigned to making no more wishes, he chose never to dream again. But what no one realized was that you can't take away something that's real; because to attempt to do so only leaves a gaping wound that readily fills itself.

Sitting in the park, Terrell thought about his mother's eyes earlier that evening, and the way she looked at him when he told her that he and Karen were doing fine.

It was obvious she had questions about his reply, but she chose not to pursue the matter at that time.

He knew there were issues between Karen and him; ones that weren't loud or strident, but were relentless; and others that lingered nameless like a child lost at birth. And yet they had rarely talked about these issues because there were no answers to them.

The issues weren't always at the front of their life, but they were always there, somewhere. Even the night before the trip to Atlanta Terrell awoke to find Karen looking at him. When he had asked her what was the matter she had whispered "Nothing," and had rolled over on her side, her back to him. But there was nothing he could do. He had left it all in the hands of The Lord years ago. Now it was only a matter of time.

Chapter X

Four forty-two. Otis looked at his watch. It was four forty-two and Charles hadn't arrived; he said he'd be home by four. Otis decided to give him twenty more minutes before he would pull off. Yet he did want to see him today. He needed someone to kick around with, to laugh and just shoot the breeze; and from the other night he discovered that Charles and Shirley provided the distraction he needed from his thoughts.

The image of Terrell from the other day replayed itself in his mind. He still found it difficult to believe that he saw the man who was once his boyfriend, who embodied the last years of his youth and who encompassed all his passing years. He still wasn't sure what he wanted to do while in Cincinnati; he had no plan before he arrived and he had none now. All he knew was he had to return. His life depended on it.

Just then a car pulled up alongside him. It was Charles.

"Make this run with me," he called out from behind a pair of aviator glasses.

Having locked up his car, Otis climbed in beside Charles. "You're late."

"Yeah, I'm sorry about that. We had a call right before quittin' time."

Otis noticed Charles' attire: aviator glasses, white tee stretched tight across his chest and shoulders, the navy blue polyester dress slacks and the corafram shoes. "You a police or EMT?"

Charles smiled, "EMT." Then he laughed, "Just kidding. I'm a cop."

"C'mon now, which one is it?"

"A cop," Charles affirmed with a large grin. "And don't give me all that shit everybody always give me when they find out a brother is a cop."

"Like- - pig?"

Charles laughed, "Man they don't use that anymore."

The rush hour had just begun and Otis could see the lines of automobiles beginning to fill the streets below Mt. Auburn, their metal glinting in the late afternoon sun. The DJ on the radio was talking to some lady who was just beginning her commute, going on about some tickets she'd just won. *'What station just made you a winner?' '100.9, WIZF, the Wiiiizzzz!'*

"So I slept with a police officer," Otis said, turning back to Charles.

Charles grinned.

In return, Otis gave a wry smile and nodded his head, then turned his attention back to the gathering traffic.

In a while they were winding along Madison Road past large Italianate and Tudor homes whose lawns seemed to roll like vast seas of green rushing towards their doorsteps.

"Withrow High School," Otis beamed suddenly as they came upon the stately campus.

"That's my alma mater," Charles said.

"Yeah? What year?"

"Seventy-five."

"You got me by a year."

"Where did you go?" Charles asked, keeping his eyes on the traffic.

"Lincoln Heights, well, Princeton."

"Oh that's right. They merged, didn't they?"

"Yeah."

"I guess they had to since we used to kick y'all's ass all the time."

"In what?"

"Well not sports, but in just plain ass kickin'" Charles laughed.

"Man, you fulla shit. Y'all couldn't beat our ass if you wanted to. We used to come out here, take y'all's women, because all the girls in Cincinnati wanted to hook up with The Heights, and then kick y'all's ass if y'all said something about it."

"Now I don't remember all that."

"That's because you probably got all the memory kicked out of you." Otis threw his head back and laughed at his own wit.

"Yeah, yeah, yeah. Whatever," Charles said as he turned off the winding boulevard.

The traffic had tamed itself by the time Charles and Otis returned to Charles' house. Otis squinted, then pulled down the Explorer's visor as they started up the steep hill that led to Mt. Auburn.

"Man I can't wait to relax," Charles sighed. "We had one of those crazy days." He pulled up to the curb in front of his house and turned off the engine. "You gonna spend the night?" He turned to Otis.

"Yep. Got my stuff in the car. I'll get it."

The two of them hauled the groceries into the kitchen and set them on the tiled counter.

"You can run your stuff on upstairs, if you want," Charles said.

Otis picked up his overnight bag and clothes and started from the kitchen. Then he stopped and turned back to Charles. Hoping to avoid presumption, he asked, "Which room?"

"I was hoping mine," Charles said as he looked at Otis.

Otis turned and walked up the stairs.

Charles' bedroom was dim and cool, and the high ceiling rose above it like a distant sky that stretched across a large plain. Otis placed his belongings on the white spread that covered the king sized bed and could smell the airiness of freshly laundered linen. He stood at the side of the bed, the side on which he'd slept the night the two of them met, and measured the silence, the comfort, the just knowing that something was there for him; then he picked up his clothes and hung them in the closet before walking back downstairs.

"I make a bomb salad, and it'll be finished before the pizza gets cold," Charles said as he stood at the kitchen sink.

"Let me put it in the oven so it'll keep warm for sure." Otis picked up the pizza and walked across the large kitchen. "Now this is a kitchen," Otis said as he looked around the expansive room. "That's what I like about old houses. Lots of feel for space."

"Oh yeah," Charles was busy chopping a bell pepper.

"How old is this house?"

"A hundred and two". How old is the building you live in?"

"A hundred and seventeen," Otis said as he lifted two glasses from the cabinet. "What'cha got to drink?"

"Got some wine in the fridge. But a hundred and seventeen, man, that's alright," Charles continued.

"Yeah, but I don't know how long I'm gonna keep my apartment, though." He took the bottle of wine from the refrigerator.

"How come?"

"I'm in between jobs right now. So..." Otis poured a glass for Charles and moved it within his reach. Then he began to pour one for himself.

"Then shouldn't you be back there looking for another job?"

Otis opened the door of the refrigerator and placed the wine back on the shelf. "Yeah. I should. But I had to come back here first. I have a lot of things I have to get out of the way."

Charles turned and looked at Otis who now sat at the kitchen table, "I've been hearing a lot of that from you," he said as he tossed the salad. "I hope you at least know what you're supposed to be getting out of the way."

"What do you mean?"

"I don't know man. It seems to me like you haven't been doing nothing but wandering around." He placed the bowl on the table and watched Otis who went over to the cabinet and gathered up the plates and silverware. "I mean, I don't want to get in your business or nothing," Charles continued, "but whatever it is you came back here to take care of you need to do it. Make it meaningful, give it some purpose, because if you don't then you ain't doing nothing but running." Then he pointed to the salad, "Now is this a bomb salad or what?"

Otis paused with the plates in his hands. His mind mulled over Charles' words. Then he spoke. "As long as it tastes good."

"It will. I'm a master chef," Charles smiled.

They ate in the living room. The room was warm with filtered sunlight and wood tones that created a relaxed mood. The click of the T.V. and then the voice of a newscaster were just as warm.

"So how long you been a policeman?" Otis asked as he cut a slice of pizza.

"Fourteen years." Charles reached for the salad dressing, his eyes fixed on the screen.

"That's a long time. What's it like?"

"It's not so bad. A lot of knuckleheads on the streets. But you know it's not just the knuckleheads on the streets that trip me out, it's some of the ones I work with, too. You know you still got those John Wayne types."

Otis nodded his head.

"Yep. It's like in their minds black equals bad," Charles continued as he leveled both of his palms like a scale. "I'll be the first to say the criminal justice system is racist. But that's part of why I got into it, to work it from the inside."

Otis didn't respond. He knew from his own history of run ins with the law that he held no love for the police. But there was something about this situation that was different; it was both beautiful and profane. Beautiful in that for the first time he saw a human face behind the uniform, and he wanted to connect with that human form, that which had previously been unapproachable. Then too a part of him wanted to destroy what the man beside him stood for. But he could not do it at the sake of destroying the man himself. The man sitting beside him was warm. He was human. Complex. Still, Otis wondered how he could dismantle even a bit of Charles' beliefs.

"So what's it like being a gay cop?"

Charles smiled and shook his head. "Well first of all I don't see myself as being gay; and secondly, I'm just a policeman."

"How you figure?" Otis questioned as he leaned back against the couch. The deconstruction had begun.

Charles looked defensively at Otis, "I'm not saying I don't, you know, deal with brothers every now and then. It's just that- - I don't see myself as being gay."

"To each his own," Otis said. Though he hoped his remark would provoke more on the subject. He took a bite of his pizza.

"So, you consider yourself gay?" Charles had picked up the glass of wine and rolled it between his palms.

It took Otis a beat before he answered, "Yeah. I do," he spoke slowly as he nodded his head. "I didn't always, but, yeah, I do now."

Charles shook his head, "I don't know, I just never saw any reason for me to label myself."

Otis looked down at the table, his hand unconsciously twisting at the stem of his wine glass, "When you got people gunnin' for you, you have to call yourself something." Then he looked over at Charles, "I mean, the people who're gunnin' for you already are, right? I mean, they already got you labeled so they can come after you."

"Yeah, but you're just playin' into their hands by calling yourself what they call you."

"Nah. You see, I ain't calling myself what they call me. I'm calling myself what I call me. Look, it wasn't until a few years after I got to New York that I realized I needed someplace to go and be with people who knew me. Up until then all I got was a lot of grief. Now I belong somewhere. It's called a community, man, no matter how solid or shaky it might be; it's still a place to live." Then he looked deeply at Charles, "And I mean live, man, not just going from one humiliation to another."

"Well, I do okay without it."

"Again, to each his own. But I bet you consider yourself a black policeman."

Charles didn't reply. He looked at Otis with a mild awareness.

Otis grinned. Then he picked up a slice of pizza, "Do any of the other policemen know that you, 'deal', every once in a while?"

Charles reached over and cut a slice of pizza for himself, his eyes concentrating on the pizza. "One or two. But they're cool. It's about respect. They know what I'm about as a police and as a person, and that's all that matters to them."

"Yeah, but do they respect who Charles *really* is?"

"Man, c'mon. It ain't nobody's business who I sleep with."

Otis chuckled, "Yeah, I bet you don't feel that way when they talk about their women. They can live their lives just as free as anything while you have to tip around on eggshells. You know that ain't right," he said as he gathered up the dishes and headed for the kitchen. "I'll clean up." He was enjoying the taunting.

"So you don't think being who I am is my business?" Charles called out from the living room.

Otis stood in the dining room holding a dish towel. "Nah man. All I'm saying is ain't no business good business if you're ashamed of it. Now if you wanna get real respect, then do like The Staple Singers said. Respect yourself."

"Man you need to take that bullshit back to New York," Charles laughed.

Later, when Otis had finished the dishes and returned to the living room he found Charles fast asleep on the sofa. He looked at him, the rise and fall of his chest against the tight tee shirt, his large arms, one across the slight mound that formed his belly and one thrown relentlessly across his eyes. His lips were parted slightly and Otis could hear the soft rush of air move from his throat.

The television screen rolled on in colors of blue, white and beige as the newscaster bid everyone a pleasant evening, and Otis picked up the remote and switched the channel. Then he slid back down onto the floor where he sat earlier. He wondered how it would feel to be in a relationship? He hadn't been in a meaningful one in almost twenty years, since he was with Terrell. He had tried. Several times he had tried, but it just never seemed to pan out. There was always something that crept in the way of the relationship. The relationships he had usually lasted no more than a few months; a year, if lucky. They, the men, were usually either too overbearing, or they were too weak. In any case none of them were ever able to meet his ideal. An acquaintance (he had no one he truly called a friend) once accused him of holding onto the memory of Terrell, but Otis knew that wasn't true. The memory he had of Terrell had shifted in the winds of time and now stood as an object to be purged, not embraced. At least that is what he had decided.

Just then, Charles turned on his side, half awake. "What'chou watchin'?" his voice was full of sleep.

"I don't know. Some show about- - shit, I don't even know."

The two of them chuckled at Otis' response before falling back into silence.

"I guess I'm not being a good host am I?" Charles had placed one of the throw pillows full under his jaw as he closed his eyes once again.

"No, you're okay."

"Well I'm off tomorrow, so we can hang all day. Unless you have something to do."

"Nah. I'm free."

"Cool," Charles muttered. "You can watch whatever you want. I'm just lyin' here for a bit."

Otis continued to jump through the channels of the TV. He wasn't much of a TV person. Actually, he didn't do much of anything except work, hang out with a few acquaintances and lie around home listening to music; with the exception of work, those were the things that gave him the least amount of challenge and so those were the things that gave him the most pleasure. Finally, he settled on a station.

"Found one, huh?" Charles muttered.

"Yeah, for the time being."

"Well now, you can always turn it off." Charles smiled and, with one hand, massaged Otis' shoulder.

~ ~ ~ ~

"What did your father say?"

"Nothin'. But he looked at me real strange. Like he wanted to say somethin'."

Otis leaned forward, resting his arms on his legs, and looked into the night. He and Terrell had made plans to meet that evening. It was two days before Christmas and school was out for the holidays. He knew he was putting their relationship at risk, but he couldn't wait the week or two to see him again.

The air was cold and clear, and moved like smooth crystal in his nostrils as he breathed. They sat on the bleachers of the football stadium behind the high school.

"So I guess we gotta be cool, huh?" Otis spoke as he continued to stare into

the darkness.

Terrell didn't respond for a second or so; then, "I guess so."

Otis cocked his head and looked at him, "Now you know that's bullshit, don't you?"

Terrell thought for a second before breaking into a laugh, "Yeah."

"Look, I got somethin' for you." Otis stood and put his hand into the pocket of his leather coat. "Merry Christmas." He grinned as he presented a small package to Terrell.

"Otis- -"

"Wait." He turned and went over to his car that sat just a few feet away. In a moment Donny Hathaway's 'This Christmas' rose from the eight track. "Now." He said as he stood once again in front of Terrell.

"Aw man..." Terrell moved the alligator skin wallet around in his hand. "But I didn't get you anything."

"It's cool."

"Nah man, I- -"

"Nah, really. It's cool. I had the money to do it. And besides, it's something you'll need when you start workin'." Then a smirk came to his mouth, "And it's somethin' you can hide from yo' ol' man."

"Wait." Terrell raised his hand to the back of his neck. "Here." He removed a chain from his neck. It's a St. Christopher's medal."

"You sure?"

"Yeah. Let me put it on you."

As Terrell started to stand, Otis gently pressed him back down; then he turned and sat between Terrell's legs.

"This is really nice, man."

"Thanks."

"Your father won't miss it, will he?"

"Uh, uh. As a matter of fact, he'll probably be glad I got rid of it. He thinks Catholics are evil."

Otis looked up at Terrell with an incredulous expression.

"Aw, he thinks everybody's evil," Terrell said as he dismissively waved his hand.

"Mm. Man you got a rough life," Otis said as he leaned back in Terrell's lap.

Terrell nodded his head as he wrapped his arms around Otis shoulders. "It'll get better."

"I hope so."

They sat in silence on the bleachers listening to the music for a while before Otis spoke. "I just wanna spend Christmas with you. That's all."

"Me too."

Otis raised his face to Terrell and they kissed each other lightly on the lips. The music continued. Barbara Lewis sang "Snowflakes" as Otis lay against Terrell.

~ ~ ~ ~

Chapter XI

The bishop had been talking to his mother. Terrell could tell.

"... and I'm sure Karen could use your help with the kids down there," the bishop offered.

"They're fine. I just spoke with her and she said everything's going fine." Terrell sat in his office and tried to keep his attention on the ledger on the computer. His neck was getting tired from holding the phone against his shoulder.

Bishop Abrams went on about the strength of the husband and how he was the pillar of the family. Terrell could tell by his voice that he was speaking out of coercion; and that actually he wished Terrell could stay a little longer to move the church project along. But apparently, Mother Abrams, from the coaxing of Terrell's mother, had twisted his arm. "It's just until next week," Terrell protested. Then he heard his own voice and figured the bishop had too. Now the bishop was probably wondering why he was offering such a protest about being with his own family. There was a slight pause on both ends of the phone before

Terrell spoke.

"I'll fly down tomorrow."

"That's the right thing to do Brother Mitchell."

* * * *

It was eight o'clock when Terrell placed the call to Atlanta. After he hung up from his conversation with Bishop Abrams that afternoon, he had called Karen's parents' home to let her know of his change of plans, but all he got was the answering service. He'd left a message telling them that he would call again around eight o'clock. Now the phone rang a few times before it was answered.

"Hello?"

"Babe?"

"Hi. We got your message this evening when we got in. We were gone all day."

"Oh. How are you doing?"

"Fine. Those kids of yours are a mess. They just keep us cracking up down here. My family is just crazy over them."

"Well of course. We've got some fine young'uns, you know."

"Of course I know that. So is everything alright?"

Terrell clicked his tongue. "Now why wouldn't it be? You just do not believe your husband can go a week or two without burning down the house."

Karen laughed.

He continued. "You know, I decided that instead of waiting until next weekend to come down, why don't I come on down this weekend instead?"

There was a brief silence before Karen spoke. "Why? I mean... Are you finished with the church project?"

"No."

"Oh."

"What's wrong?"

"There's nothing wrong. It's just that I thought you were coming down next weekend."

"Is there a problem with me coming down this weekend, instead? I mean, you sound like you don't want me to come down."

"Terrell... hold on. Let me go into another room."

He held the receiver to his ear as he heard his wife walk through her parents' house. He heard a door close. Then she came back on the line.

"Terrell, I thought part of this whole thing was also to give each other some time apart."

"That was your idea, not mine." He felt his anger rise then crash. He had not taken Karen's comment of down time seriously. She had offered it in such a non committed way that he had no idea of its gravity. "But, hey, if it's going to be a problem, then I'll just come on down next weekend." He attempted to control his anger, but it rose from his chest to his mouth. "Or maybe I won't come at all since you don't seem to want me there."

"I didn't say that."

"Believe me, you did. Look, I'll talk to you later. Tell the kids I love them. I guess that's the only reason I should come down there."

"Terrell--"

He hung up the phone.

* * * *

"Glad you could make it." Stanton walked over to Terrell's car. "The other day, it didn't sound like you were gonna show."

"Yeah, well, I thought I might be inconvenienced," Terrell said as he got out of his car.

"Well, you need a little escape," Stanton said as he put his hand on Terrell's shoulder. "Do you play poker?"

"No."

"You will."

Terrell looked along the sprawling one-floor home and noticed the expensive cars lined along the driveway. "What's this? The black millionaire's club?"

Stanton laughed. "Kind of."

The two of them walked up to the front door and were met by a tall man with a neatly trimmed gray afro.

"Stanton. How's it going?" the man greeted.

"You know. Same ol' same ol'. Look, I want you to meet a friend of mine, Terrell. Terrell, Jerry."

The two men shook hands.

"Come on in Terrell. Glad you could make it."

"He almost didn't," Stanton said as he and Terrell stepped into the house. "Said he was almost inconvenienced," Stanton said with a wink.

Jerry laughed, "Well you're not alone, Terrell. Some of the other brothers in here had to shuffle and bow to make their way here too. The wives don't like them going out too often."

"I can relate," Terrell chuckled.

"Well make yourself at home. There's beer and drinks in the kitchen. Got some finger food, and Rueben just ordered pizza. He said finger food just won't do. Niggers!" Jerry made his statement with a large grin.

The poker game was already in progress as Stanton and Terrell walked into the living room. Everyone greeted Stanton when he entered the room, then hurriedly turned their attention back to the game.

Stanton went around the table and introduced each person. "This is Harland, and Darnell, and this monkey ass man is Clyde, and Rueben." Each man raised his hand and greeted Terrell. "Fellas, this is a buddy of mine, Terrell." They all chimed their greetings. Then he turned to a large over stuffed sofa, "What's up Arthur?" he said to a lone man who sat on the sofa holding a drink. "And this is Arthur. Arthur, Terrell."

Arthur smiled and extended his hand. Terrell noticed that Arthur was dressed differently from the rest of the men. He had on a gray work uniform and black work boots unlike the other men who were dressed in slacks and polos. And his overall appearance was slightly rough around the edges, a five o'clock shadow and large calloused hands; hands that seemed too large for his slight frame.

Terrell shook his hand and noticed the strong grip.

"Let's go get something to drink," Stanton suggested as he walked towards the kitchen. Terrell followed close in tow like a school kid.

The kitchen seemed as expansive as the rest of the house. It gleamed in a dark sterile way from the polished black marble of the floors and counters, and the brushed chrome furniture that shone like dull stars. In the distance Terrell could hear the sound of music rising from below. "Jerry's not married is he?" Terrell asked.

Stanton was busy fixing himself a drink. "Yeah, he's married. Why did you ask that?"

"This doesn't seem like a woman's kitchen."

"They don't live together. It's a long story. Go on and fix yourself something."

When they returned to the living room the poker game was winding up. "Next!" one of the players called out.

"C'mon. Let me show you how to play." Stanton tapped Terrell's arm with his elbow.

"Nah man. I'll only cause you to lose."

"You can't do no worse than these two." Darnell laughed as he gestured towards Clyde and Harland.

"Nah. You go ahead," Terrell said to Stanton.

"There's a pool table in the basement," Stanton said.

"I'm cool. I'll just watch you guys for a while." Terrell felt too embarrassed to admit that he didn't know how to play pool either. He was embarrassed to admit that he knew very few games since, growing up, his father had always considered them too be tools of the devil. So he went over to the sofa and took a seat.

"The pizzas are here," Jerry called out as he walked from the foyer carrying three large boxes. "You know where to find them." Then he disappeared down the hall as he headed towards the kitchen.

In a bit Jerry came back into the living room carrying a plate with two slices of pizza. "Help yourself to some pizza Terrell."

"I think I will." Terrell got up and walked towards the kitchen.

"Where's Arthur?" Jerry asked, noticing that Terrell now sat alone on the sofa. Then he caught himself. "I know where he is. Watching some damn movie. I better tell him the pizza's are here," Jerry laughed.

"Yeah, you know him and his movies," Rueben replied.

Terrell was slicing the pizza when Arthur entered the kitchen.

"Alright," he mumbled.

" 'ey," Terrell returned.

"I see he got enough pizza this time," Arthur spoke as he walked over to the counter.

"Looks like he got more than enough," Terrell said.

"Nah, this is enough." He began fixing his plate, putting several types of pizza on the plate. "This should be enough to last me while I finish checkin' out this movie."

"What are you watching?"

"Some flick about a dealer."

"Oh."

"This one's good though. You oughta check it out."

"Guess I will."

Just then the sound of heavy footsteps came from below. The door to the lower level swung open and three young men came into the kitchen.

"'bout time," one of them exclaimed as he eyed the food. Two of the young men were tall and very lean. One had a close cropped fade, while the other one had his hair in braids that ran back to the nape of his neck. The third one had a very athletic build and a strong jaw that jutted from his face. The shape of his face reminded Terrell of his father's face. They appeared to be somewhere in their early twenties, definitely no older than twenty-two or twenty-three.

"What's up?' The one with the braids spoke to Arthur.

"What's up?" Arthur replied with a guarded tone. Then he turned to

Terrell. "Ready to check out that movie?"

"Okay."

They walked back towards the den carrying their food.

"How many rooms does this place have?" Terrell asked as he walked

alongside Arthur.

"I don't really know. I haven't been in all of 'em. But it seems like a lot,

don't it?"

"Yeah," Terrell answered as he glanced down a hallway before turning into

the den.

There was something alien about the house; the walls, the very space within

the house seemed to light just above Terrell's head out of his reach. Everything

seemed so elusive. Even the movement of the people within the house seemed just

beyond his comprehension. He wasn't sure whether to move out of the way of

something that threatened to drop or just let it all ride. Karen's voice from the

previous night came to him; distant, indiscernible, it faded even more as if a door

was being closed; then emptiness set in.

Terrell and Arthur had just gotten into the movie when one of the men who

had been at the poker table, Clyde, stuck his head in the doorway. He had one of

the young men with him, the one with the braids. "You and your movies," he said

to Arthur, shaking his head. Then he looked at Terrell, "Don't let him turn you

into a couch potato." He said this before making his way down the hall with the

young man.

Terrell looked at Arthur, but Arthur didn't seem to register much of an

expression as he continued to watch the movie.

From the living room the sound of laughter and the flick of cards signaled

the end of another hand of poker. "Damn!" (Laughter), "Why didn't you throw that down?"

Arthur looked at Terrell. "Looks like it's 'bout time for me to go on out there."

Terrell smiled.

"Arthur!" a voice called.

"Tol' you," Arthur shook his head.

"You want me to stop the movie?"

"Nah. I done seen it before. You go 'head. It's really good, I'm tellin' you." Arthur got up and left the den.

From down the hall the faint sound of voices and movement came through the walls of the den, muffled, sometimes rumbling, competing with the movie Terrell watched. He looked towards the wall in the direction of the voices as if he could see the source of the sounds. He wanted to see the room, and he wanted to see the voices and the movement. He wanted to, but at the same time he didn't.

"I see I'm going to have to move my play room." Jerry smiled as he stood in the doorway of the den holding two glasses. "Want some wine?"

Terrell looked at him for a quick second, adjusting his sight as if the man holding the two glasses was an apparition, "Yes. Thanks."

Jerry gave Terrell the glass. He then sat in a chair next to the sofa on which Terrell sat. "I feel like I'm being a bad host." He spoke in the tone and cadence of so many white people Terrell encountered in his office. "These knuckleheads keep me running. That's why sometimes I dread having our get together over here."

"Oh, it's not always here?"

"No way. Takes too much work to entertain."

"You must get some pleasure out of it, though." Terrell smiled.

Jerry sipped his wine. "What makes you think that?"

"Just the feel of this place. It's like it was designed for entertaining."

Jerry grinned, "Well when I designed it I did think a lot about entertaining."

"What does your wife think about it? I'm surprised she didn't have much say in the design."

"What makes you think I'm married?" Jerry joked as he twisted the gold band on his coral colored finger. "And what makes you think my wife didn't have a hand in the design?"

Terrell hunched his shoulders, "I don't know. I don't feel the touch of a woman. I know my wife would never let me design our home alone."

"Or at all," Jerry laughed.

"Or at all," Terrell agreed.

Jerry sat back in the chair. "Well my wife and I have our understanding. She has her life and I have mine. And we've been married for a long time. It's called respect."

Terrell nodded his head, "Mm. That's unique."

"Respect?"

"No. The space between the two of you."

"Oh. Well it is different, but not unheard of. So how long have you and Stanton known each other?"

"Not that long. Not long at all. He's working on a project that I've been appointed to oversee."

"Bishop Abrams' church."

"You know the bishop?"

"Who doesn't? He's a stalwart in the black community." Jerry spoke with the formality of someone commissioned to recite a sonnet. Leaning forward, he continued, "Are you a member of Bishop Abrams' congregation?"

"Yes. Yes I am."

"For how long?"

"For my entire life. I was christened there." Terrell bit at his words. He wasn't sure why this man wanted to know so much .

"Then that's why Stanton seems to know you so well."

"What do you mean?"

Jerry's hazel eyes twinkled a bit, "Let's just say Stanton's been on the periphery of your church for many years, so he probably watched you grow up."

"I don't know." Terrell hunched his shoulders and felt a slight breeze cross his chest.

"Well anyway, welcome to my humble abode." Jerry raised his glass. "Go ahead and drink your wine. You be my guest and I'll be your host."

And with that, Terrell took a drink from the glass.

"So are you a part of Stanton's campaign, Jerry?" Terrell asked as he swallowed the sweet white zinfindel.

"Oh we all are in some way or another."

"We?"

"Yes. All of us here tonight. And you will be too if you're not already."

"He keeps trying to recruit me."

Jerry laughed, "I can believe that."

"But circumstances keep me ... us from accepting," Terrell continued.

"Us meaning?"

"Me and my wife."

"Ah. Well between Stanton and the bishop, I'm surprised you and your wife have held out this long."

"My wife thinks we should join the campaign, but I'm not sure if I have what it takes."

"I'm sure you do. If you didn't Stanton wouldn't be so adamant about bringing you on board. Stanton is usually a good reader of character. That's what he and I have in common. You see, we can both look at a person and in a moment's notice assess his qualities." Jerry snapped his finger. He took a long sip of wine before leaning closer to Terrell and motioning him to also take another sip of his drink. "And from what I can see, Stanton has good reason to ask you to join his campaign. You see, you are a person who's concerned with details. You're able to see things that many times go unnoticed. Isn't that so?"

"I don't know. I guess so."

Jerry grinned, "And you're humble too."

A sudden sound came from the room down the hall. It was deep and singular. It caused Terrell to look towards the door.

"I didn't know you could hear all that down here." Jerry was laughing as he spoke.

"What is it?" Terrell asked.

"Oh. You don't know?"

Terrell looked at Jerry without speaking.

"C'mon." Jerry set down his glass and motioned for Terrell to follow him.

They walked a bit down the hall. The voices from the poker game in the living room fell into the background as Terrell traveled deeper into the house.

"I told you I have my little play room," Jerry said, and with those words he turned the knob of a door and opened it. It was a large room with shelves filled with videotapes and audio recordings. All about the room there were sofas and chairs. And reclining on one of the large chairs was the young man with the braids. He was naked, leaning back in the chair watching, almost simultaneously, a porn film on a giant TV screen and a half naked Clyde who was on his knees, his head moving rhythmically up and down the young man's long curved dick.

Terrell stood weak kneed, swayed slightly. "Oh."

"Stanton didn't tell you?" Jerry looked surprised. "He should've told you."

Terrell could only shake his head.

Jerry quickly closed the door. He nudged Terrell's arm. "Come on."

* * * *

Terrell stood outside and stared at the swimming pool. The clear water moved sullenly and lapped at the tiles of the pool. "How long have you been doing this?"

"A long time," Jerry said as he stood with his hands in his pocket.

Then he led Terrell to one of the poolside chairs. "You know, I really thought you knew what was up. I can't believe Stanton would invite you here without letting you know." He glanced through the large glass door where the poker game continued, the players unaware of what had taken place.

"No, he didn't."

"I guess this a dumb question to ask, but are you okay- - with all this?"

Terrell shook his head, "I don't know."

Jerry peered at Terrell, "You're still here so I guess you can relate, at least to some degree."

"What're you saying?"

"What I'm saying is that as an adult, a grown man, you can relate to the fact that being an adult means making decisions. And we chose to make ours long ago."

"What, engaging in pornography?"

"No, about living our lives. Now look, I don't want to make you any more uncomfortable than you already are, so if you'd like to leave, then I can understand. But I don't want you to leave feeling like we're a bunch of freaks here. Far from it." Then he paused before continuing, "And I really don't want you to share this with anyone. Okay? I mean a lot of people can get hurt. A lot of important people."

Terrell looked curiously at him. "No, I would never do that. It's your business." Then he sat for a while and looked at the water. "How long?" he suddenly repeated. "You never answered my question."

"Since our college days. Most of us went to school together. UC. In those days there weren't many of us on campus. So of course the black students would come together and party. That's how I met Darnell and a few of the other brothers. At first it was all the brothers and sisters, but then some of us picked up on- - variations, if you will, and, well, we started our own little community. And from there it just kind of grew." Jerry sat up and rested his arms on his knees. "And we've done some great things since we've been coming together."

"How?" Terrell gave Jerry a look that was mixed with incredulity and slight scorn.

"Terrell, what you saw in there is something that just happens every now and then. We're more than that. There've been brothers who have had their careers built on our support. How do you think Stanton was able to get where he is today? Me and some of the others who worked to network, set up opportunities. And they've done the same for me." He raised his hands. "So what if we have a little offside thing going on? Black men have benefited from our group." He stopped talking and measured Terrell's expression. Seeing the dark look on Terrell's face, he sighed, "I guess you should go. I'll get Stanton."

Terrell went into his pocket to retrieve his car keys but kept his hand there once he had grasped them. He walked to his car accompanied by Stanton who walked alongside him half diplomat, half emperor. A full moon pushed it rays through the cool night air and lighted their way past the other cars in the driveway. Stanton had tried to dissuade him from leaving but Terrell was anxious to go. As he walked along the driveway Terrell looked at the cars as he had done earlier that evening, but now they appeared more like coffins than expensive automobiles.

"I feel like you're making me the bad guy here," Stanton spoke as they arrived at Terrell's car.

"I don't intend to do that."

"Oh, so it's just my conscience, huh?"

"And I certainly don't have anything to do with that either. You know who you are. I'm just now finding out."

Stanton looked at Terrell and his eyes blazed in a quick second then receded. "Please man, don't play smug with me. I feel bad that you had to see what happened in there, and that's why I'm here with you. But don't play holier than thou with me."

"Man, what are you talking about, 'holier than thou'? Just because I can't get into where you and your friends are coming from? Look, I simply know where I want to be with my life, it has nothing to do with being smug or patronizing."

Stanton placed his large frame slightly against the door of Terrell's car as if he wanted to keep Terrell from leaving. "I just think you need to think about all this."

Terrell removed his keys from his pocket. "What's up with all this? You and Jerry seem so afraid that somebody might blow your covers. You know, if I were you I wouldn't do anything I would be ashamed of. I told you I don't have any intention of going any further with this. That's why I'm leaving. Now excuse me."

Stanton moved out the way.

Terrell pushed the automatic lock release and the soft sound of the car unlocking was heard. Then he looked at Stanton. "Why did you invite me here in the first place?"

"I was just doing a good deed. I guess it's the scout in me."

Terrell looked at Stanton but had no words. He was unsure of the statement he'd just heard. The words had come so easily from Stanton's lips, but they fell heavy on Terrell's ears, weighted with heavy meaning.

Stanton continued, his expression changing to a wry smile. "I thought I was doing you a favor because it was something you needed."

Terrell dropped his hand from the car handle. "And what do you know about what I need? You know, these past few weeks we've been working together I've noticed you always seem to think you know what's best for people."

Stanton grinned. It was obvious he was used to such a comment. "I guess it's my personality. I'm a scout and I'm a therapist. I'm cool with that."

Terrell shook his head and opened the car door.

"And I also know what you're going through," Stanton continued. That's why I took an interest in you."

Terrell stopped in his tracks. "You don't know anything about me. I guess that's how you move into other people's lives, by claiming to know more about them than they know about themselves. Man you need to leave that for some other sucker." He got in the car and started to close the door.

"I was there when you and Otis were together," Stanton blurted out.

Terrell looked at Stanton with a surprised expression on his face.

"And it's never gone away. I can see it Terrell. That's why I'm trying to help."

"Stanton, man, don't mess up what little relationship we have left." Terrell closed the door and drove off.

* * * *

The house was more silent than he ever remembered. He had tried to sleep but he couldn't, so now he sat in the large easy chair in the den and stared at the TV. The light and movement of the picture filled his eyes and the voices filled his head. But they only lasted for seconds at a time because they moved against the tide of his thoughts.

Too much had happened in the last twenty-four hours. It was something he thought only happened in fiction. But it was real. The sound of Karen's voice as she sought to keep him from coming to Atlanta. It was real. The sound of Stanton's accusation. It was also real. But the funny thing was that he wasn't surprised at the turn of events; he was just unprepared for it.

He knew that one day Karen would want to talk more about Otis. He had warded off her approach for many years, but it had become impossible to go any further. She loved him but despised the part of him that was able to love another man. For years he tried to convince her that his affair with Otis had been little more than an adolescent indiscretion, but he knew she didn't believe him. He could see it just behind her lips when she smiled, just shy of the next phrase she might utter.

And Stanton. He had never seen Stanton until a few years ago when the bishop introduced them at a meeting on the unveiling of the plans for the new church. Yet it was obvious that Stanton had been somewhere on the periphery of his life, somewhere where he stood unseen and unheard until now. Everything was happening now.

The evening he'd spent at the house with the other men would forever be a part of his memory. He'd never seen anything like it before. How could they live their lives with the kind of cool and confidence they had displayed that evening? It was as if they felt it was their right, their birthright to live that way. He recalled the casual air, the disengaged faces of the men as they sat at the poker table engrossed only in their game. And he recalled Jerry's demeanor as he recounted the years they had been gathering; his eyes, the way his mouth curled slightly at the corners showed more reminiscence than shame.

Then his thoughts drifted to the young man leaning back in the chair, naked, his long torso sloped like a valley; taut and sinewy, smooth, his hairless stomach rippling down to an extravagant bush of curly black hair. He could still see the large black dick, long and thick with a slight curve disappearing, wet and slick halfway in Clyde's mouth then out again. He felt his own dick begin to harden as he recalled this. His hand moved down to his crotch and grasped his dick through his pants and held it tight as he recalled the young man's face with it's eyes weakening from pleasure and the dark braids that ran the length of his head to the nape of his neck catching the light of the room as he moved his dark face up once, then back down to the man between his legs. Suddenly, as if a force of recognition had taken over, Terrell tore the image from his head. Immediately, he pulled his hand from his crotch; and there in the loneliness of the night it came roaring in through the darkness. Truth.

Chapter XII

"Brings back memories, doesn't it?"

Otis looked at the shoulder pads he held in his hands. "Yeah." He was helping Jun prepare equipment for football season. He shifted the pads causing them to clack slightly as he measured their weight. "Oh yeah," he repeated with a grin.

Jun continued to unload the equipment. "You know, there was a time I thought me n' you could've been out there in the pros. He smiled without looking at Otis. "We would've made history being the first set of brothers to play together for a pro team."

Otis set the equipment down along with the rest of the inventory. "Really?"

"Yeah."

"Hmh. I dunno, man," he said as he pulled more equipment out of the crate. "I don't think I woulda made it to the pros. Too many rules."

His brother looked at him. "Too many rules? It's about discipline."

Otis hunched his shoulders, "Too many rules for me."

"Well that's too bad, 'cause you were a damn good player. Both of us were."

"That's true." Otis smiled in agreement.

Jun looked at his brother. "But you know, I'm kinda glad I didn't go pro too. I mean I look at some of them brothers and they got so many of their priorities fucked up. I probably woulda been just as fucked up as some of them."

"Maybe not, man. You had some good values instilled in you."

Jun got up, his round belly pressing tight against his polo shirt. He lifted another box into his massive arms and set it in front of the bench onto which he was to sit. "I don't know man. I had some royal fuck ups in my younger years without being in the pros. So I can imagine what I might've done if I had had all that money- - and the women..." He shook his head, "Kenne forgave me before, but I don't think even she could've been that forgiving."

Otis didn't respond in order to give his brother a chance to change the subject. It worked.

"And about Dana," Jun suddenly said, "Don't let her attitude bring you down, y'know?"

Otis shook his head and was about to speak when two young men, both of them Jun's players, came into the equipment room.

"Where's Strayhorn and Woods?" Jun called to the young men.

"They on they way," the red one with the curly hair answered.

"Okay. Start checkin' those pads for any damage. "I'm gonna step outside for a bit."

The sky over the stadium was a deep azure; only wisps of white interrupted its serene notion. Along the highway behind the school, cars whizzed by like glinting flies in the afternoon sun. The two brothers climbed into the bleachers and relaxed their aging backs against the benches.

"Jun, you know, it's not Dana that's gettin' to me. I mean, like I don't expect nothin' from her anyway. But it's Daddy. It's like he still won't admit that he was wrong the way he treated me."

"Daddy? Why do you say that?"

"We talked the first day I went over there- - and it's still like he thinks I was wrong."

Jun spread his arms across the bench, extending one of them behind his brother. "Who do you think paid for your attorney? If he had been so against you, then he wouln'ta shelled out all that money."

"And I appreciate that. But it was almost like it was his duty to do that. I mean, shit, I was gonna go down and that was all there was to it. The system was gonna take me down no matter what. But when you see your world closin' in around you, you wanna see the faces of your loved ones smilin', tellin' you that no matter what happens they'll be there for you."

Jun looked across the field. Then, pulling his arms in, he slid one of his hands down his belly letting it come to rest just above his belt. "You know, you're expecting an awful lot when you ask people to understand you." He patted his brother's leg with the other hand, "But remember, what's most important to a person is that he understands himself."

Otis sat for a second before responding. "Yeah, but it would be good if at least your ol' man was on your side."

Jun broke into a loud laugh. "Man, look at you, poutin' and all. You know what? You and Daddy need to get a grip. It's like you got a whole world around you and all y'all doin' is buzzin' around one piece of shit on the basement floor.

Come on Otis, man."

Otis turned his head away for a moment. Looking out over the field, he saw a falcon. It soared like a black kite against the distant blue sky.

"Have you been to see Mama and Daddy this week?" Jun suddenly spoke, breaking the spell.

"Not yet. I was plannin' on stoppin' by there earlier today but Ma mentioned that Miss Susie was on her way over. I told her I would stop by later on."

Jun laughed. "Miss Susie. Yeah man, she's still a trip. Still chasin' down young boys." He continued to laugh as he slapped his knee. "Remember how she used to ask us to go to the store for her?"

Otis grinned and nodded his head.

Jun continued, still laughing. "Man, I used to take the money and run outta there."

"It was definitely a trip," Otis said. Then he looked up at the sky once again. The falcon had disappeared.

* * * *

"Boy, you better come in here and git you somethin' to eat." Otis' father was sitting in the living room on the couch, his dinner in front of him on a T.V. tray.

"Yessir," Otis said. "Where's Mama?"

"She and that ol' crazy Susie went somewhere. They'll be back soon." His father scooped rice and gravy into his mouth. "Grab one'a them trays and eat out here."

Sitting in the living room with his father brought back memories of the many nights his family would sit around watching T.V. The cool winds of a late autumn eve would dance just outside the door portending winter while inside the light of lamps and the faces of his family created a warm, orange glow. But like everything else, seasons change; and in time someone opened the door and the chill came in.

He remembered one particular night. It was Christmas Eve. He and his father had been assigned the task of picking greens. Jun was away at college. His mother and the two older girls had cordoned themselves off into the kitchen where they moved amid a flurry of activity as they made final preparations for Christmas dinner. He could hear their voices, hurried but cheerful as they talked to each other.

In the living room the warm smell of meat, breads and gravy swam through the air and made Otis' nose dance. Courtney couldn't have been more than one and a half at the time, and she crawled along he and his father's laps laughing and pulling at the leaves of kale and mustard greens as Otis and his father placed them into a large kettle. Everything about his father that evening seemed intentional. The way he pulled at the greens, separating the leafy flesh from their stems; the way he talked to Courtney; even the way he reacted to the evening news on the television, everything seemed intentional.

After a few comments about events on the news, his father asked him, "Everything goin' okay at school?"

Otis looked at him with a look of mild surprise. "Yessir," he answered. His father's demeanor that evening had made him feel uncomfortable. His mind whizzed through events trying to recall any infraction that would have warranted a call from school; but he couldn't think of any. He wanted to ask his father why he

posed such a question, but he was afraid of hearing the answer. Yet he knew he
would hear the answer soon. "Why?" he nervously asked.

"What do you mean, 'why'? Can't your ol' man ask you 'bout school?"

"Oh. Yessir."

"I was just wonderin' how things were goin' since you left the team."

Otis hunched his shoulders. "It's goin' okay."

Courtney pulled up on her father's shirt and tried to feed him a leaf. He
mimicked an eating motion causing her to giggle.

"Tangey been callin' for you," his father said as he lowered Courtney back
into his lap. "She said she ain't seen you much. Said she thought you was sick or
somethin'."

Otis felt his head lower slightly as if he suddenly needed shelter. "I'm
gonna see her."

"I know how that boy friend and girl friend thang can be. But we ain't been
seein' much of you neither." His father had stopped picking the greens and spoke
directly to him.

"I- - I been busy."

"With what? You ain't playin' football no more and I don't see you round
here studyin'."

"Daddy, I'm alright. When I get my report card you'll see. I just got some
things on my mind right now."

His father didn't say anything. He just looked at him, then went back to his
chore. A few months later he would learn of Terrell.

"That's some crazy stuff." His father now spoke as he pointed his fork at
the T.V. screen. "How they gonna do away with affirmative action? Talkin' 'bout

even playin' field. How can the playin' field be even when they own all the playin' fields? Give me a piece of the playin' field, then we can call it even." He spoke as if he was addressing an invisible listener.

"I guess they want us to trust them. You know, 'just trust us. We promise we'll be fair," Otis kidded.

"Shiiit. Fair based on what?"

Otis looked at his father and smiled. It had been a long time since he had experienced one of his father's diatribes. There was a time when he would grow tired of the sound of his father's voice; but now that same voice warmed him.

His father continued. "That's why I had to turn to haulin'. When I tried to do construction work they wouldn't let me in. White boys came and took all the jobs, all of 'em."

"Well, at least you had somethin' to call your own, huh?" Otis knew his father was proud to be an independent man.

"Yeah. And that's why I taught y'all to be self-sufficient too. Own your own." Then he began counting on his fingers. "Jun got his own home and some rental property; Dana got some, and Munny got this house when me 'n Momma are gone. And Momma said you got your own place up there too."

"Yessir."

"That's good." He took a bite of food. "It's expensive up there though, ain't it?"

"Yessir. I got my apartment through foreclosure."

"That was smart."

"Yep."

"... You live there by yourself?"

"Yessir."

"Oh." His father turned his attention back to his plate. "Out of all my kids, you had it the roughest. But you made it through. I'm proud of you." He spoke, nodding his head, as he looked at his plate.

"Thanks."

"Just keep goin' forward."

"Oh, I'm definitely gonna do that."

"Yeah, well everybody says that; but everybody don't know where forward is. Make sure you plan each step."

Otis smiled. "I will."

The back door opened and his mother and Miss Susie came in. He couldn't see them, but he could definitely hear them, especially Miss Susie. His mother spoke in a low controlled voice as if to counterpose Miss Susie's bellowing one.

Suddenly Miss Susie rushed to the living room. Standing in the entrance of where the dining and living rooms met, she put her hands on her hips. "Where's that boy?" she yelled.

"Shhh!" Otis' father hissed as he put his finger to his lips.

"Oh you shush!" she said as she spread her arms and waddled over to where Otis sat. "Stand up here!"

Otis glanced at his mother who stood with a smile of helplessness on her face just a few feet behind the bellowing lady. He stood and stepped from behind his food and was immediately pulled into Miss Susie's arms.

"Boy, look at you! You lookin' good! Time ain't had no effect on you either."

Otis saw his mother giggle.

Miss Susie smelled slightly of Noxema. Or was it split pea soup? He couldn't tell. Her dark skin was blotched with lighter patches of brown, compliments of years of skin lightener; and her face, a strange ashen color, felt like paste as she pressed his cheeks against hers.

"Don't we look good together? I always did say that."

Otis looked down at the little woman under the red dye job and then at his mother.

"Oh stop it Susie. You know he don't want no woman your age."

"Girl, what you talkin' 'bout? I still got it in me."

"Then you better take some penicillin." His father blurted out.

"Oh shut up." Miss Susie swatted at Otis' father.

"Come on by and see me before you leave." She spoke to Otis as she tapped his shoulder.

"...Yes ma'am."

"Woman he got better things to do than stoppin' by to see you." Otis' father enjoyed the sparring he and Miss Susie engaged in.

"It's better than sittin' 'round yo' ol' ass." She put her hands on her hips and leaned forward. Then she turned back to Otis. "Now make sure you stop by." Otis nodded his head as she walked back towards the dining room, her knit pants stretched across her wide hips.

"That woman gets crazier by the day," his father said.

Otis laughed.

Otis' mother was putting away some canned goods when he walked into the kitchen. "Is she gone?"

His mother laughed. "Yeah. Thank God."

"Oh you know you like it." Otis waved his hand as he walked over to the sink and began to clean his plate.

"Don't. I got that." His mother called to him.

"Ma, it's just one plate." He continued to clean his dish. "Miss Susie gives you some laughs, don't she?"

"Yeah. I guess so. But I feel kinda guilty sayin' that. It's like I'm just usin' her for a joke or somethin'."

"I'm sure she knows how she stands with you. To tell you the truth, I think she enjoys crackin' people up."

"Mmm." His mother nodded her head in agreement. "You get enough to eat?"

"Yes ma'am. Had a nice meal and some conversation with Daddy."

His mother nodded. "It's about time."

Otis smiled. She was right. He went back into the living room to sit with his father one more time before he left for the day.

Miss Susie's house was near the end of the street. And walking down that street felt just as it always had to him. Familiar. His entire childhood had been spent there. The homes that were there twenty years ago still stood; only now they were dressed with fresh coats of paint, and some even boasted new windows. They were small homes, made of the barest of material, so Otis was surprised that all of them were able to withstand time. But their permanence was their strong point because they had been built as a testament of a race and as a reply to the white folks who had said Lincoln Heights would never make it.

Jackson Street, like most of the streets in Lincoln Heights, had attitude. Its pavement bumped when it wanted to bump, slumped when it wanted to slump and sometimes it even knotted when it damn well pleased. But none of that attitude bothered Otis as he walked along the way. It was as if his feet and ankles had memory of each indentation along the road.

"Come in, come in." Miss Susie greeted him as he stepped through the doorway. Her ash colored face seemed to float, unattached to her body, against the shadows of the house. "I thought you wasn't gonna come. 'Oh he don't wanna see no ol' crazy Susie.' That's what I said to myself." She spoke as she closed the door behind her, shutting out all hope of sunlight.

He stood in a darkened living room. All the shades were drawn, as they had always been. But now they were stained yellow from years of exposure. He recalled that she never raised those shades. The curtains were always open, but the shades were always drawn. The house had a warm, dusty smell that collected like powder around his nostrils as he breathed. And the stillness. Nothing moved except the hands of a clock that sat upon an old Muntz T.V. marking its time in a catatonic rhythm.

"Here, have a seat. You want somethin' to drink? Some lemonade?"

"No ma'am."

"I don't have the beauty shop no more." She started as if she was already in mid conversation. "Got too old. I tried to hold onto it as long as I could. Even hired some young girls, you know to pull in a younger crowd."

"Yes ma'am."

"They did bring in a younger clientele; but I couldn't keep up with all them hairdos these girls be wearin' now. Hair up to here with straws in 'em an' things. Shoot." She flicked her wrists.

Otis laughed. "Yes ma'am, I know what you mean."

"Yes chil' times do change."

"So you sold the shop, huh?" He searched for further conversation.

"Yeah. And it's the best thing I ever did. Antonio was growin' up and I wanted to spend more time with him."

He'd forgotten about the child. He knew when he left that she was
pregnant. It had caused a sensation that the middle-aged beautician had had a
child at her age; but what had caused most of the talk was the fact that she had it
out of wedlock. That was excusable for a younger woman. After all, there's
always a place for ignorance, but not for a woman well into her forties. And to
top that off, she proudly refused to name the father. It was as if it was all a badge
of honor.

"How old is your son now?"

"He'll be nineteen in December."

Otis took in the dimly lit house with its old stuffed furniture covered with
brightly flowered upholstery. The still, the silence. He wondered how a child
could have kept its sanity in such a place.

"But enough about me. Tell me about New York. I been there lots of
times, but that was like forty-six, forty-seven years ago since the last time I was
there."

Otis chuckled, "Yeah, well a lot has changed since then I'm sure."

"So go on, tell me." Her rheumy eyes danced in the dim light of the living
room. She was like a chubby faced kid in an old woman's body. "What part do
you live in?"

"I live in Brooklyn."

"Brooklyn," she repeated.

"Yes ma'am."

"Now I know where the village is. But I never used to go to Brooklyn
much. Mostly I know the upper part of Manhattan. You know, Harlem, then over
to The Bronx. You ever go to Harlem?"

"Oh yeah. All the time."

"The Apollo?"

Otis smiled. "Yep." He enjoyed bringing some happiness into the old woman's life. He always did. "Some of the best concerts I ever been to was at the Apollo. ConFunkShun, Labelle, New Birth, The O'Jays- -"

"Oh I like Patti Labelle. She's good. Now let's see, the last concert I saw there was Dinah Washington."

"Really?"

"We was surprised she came 'cause by then she was The Queen. Before Aretha Franklin. So we didn't expect her to come back to The Apollo, but she did."

"I bet she was hot."

"Who's The Queen, now?"

"Ma'am?"

"Who's The Queen, now? Aretha?"

"Probably so. Either her or Whitney Houston. But I think 'retha still holdin' it. Too much history."

"That Whitney Houston can sing too. I used to tell Antonio about New York." She spoke as she rose from the couch. She walked across the room to a curio cabinet. "I tol' him you live there. I tol' him maybe he can go and see you sometime. Here he is." She handed Otis a gold picture frame.

Otis squinted his eyes to get a good look at the picture.

"Let me turn on a lamp," she said as she leaned to an end table and clicked a switch. "You can't see black in black." She laughed and clapped her hands at her own brilliance.

The young man in the picture was indeed dark. Like night dark. He was in a full white linen suit that made his complexion appear even blacker. His sharp, high cheekbones, well defined lips and oval shaped eyes gave him the strong features of a Wolof prince, especially the deep stare.

"And he's tall too. Not quite as tall as you, but almost." She looked down at the picture in Otis' palms and slowly shook her head. "Sometimes I worry about him. He keeps so many secrets. Won't let me in. Maybe you can talk to him when he comes to visit you."

Otis looked over at her sad face.

"I just wanted you to see him," she said softly as she gently removed the picture from Otis' hands. She got up and placed the picture back in the cabinet. "He's a good boy." She spoke more to herself than to Otis.

He watched the older woman as she walked back to the couch. "He can come and see me anytime he wants, Miss Susie."

She smiled. "Thank you."

Chapter XIII

She said she didn't like the photo because it made him look like a criminal. Maybe she was right.

Otis looked at the photo as it lay on the passenger seat of his car. Antonio stared back with vacant eyes. It was the eyes that made him look threatening; they gave no glint of happiness and foretold of no hint of remorse if there was ever to be any. They just stared. And the cigarette that hung from his lips only heightened the anticipation of danger one felt when looking at the photo.

The next day Otis had gone back to see Miss Susie. Actually, he had not gone back to visit her so much as to learn more of the young man in the photo. Since he had seen the picture a few days earlier he could not keep his mind off it; and when he had returned she had opened the door, smiled and said, "I knew you would come back."

That evening he learned more about the boy. He learned that he and the boy were about the same height; and he discovered the boy had no middle name and that his first name was given to him because his mother had always wanted to go to Italy.

But when Otis asked if the boy might be his son, Miss Susie had smiled and said, "Now you know I don't like tellin' all my business."

He had paused and looked at her. He didn't press the question any further, or grab the foolish old woman in her collar and demand a reply. Instead, he watched her face as it turned into a cracked smile.

He knew she had always been good at keeping secrets. She was the only woman he'd known to whom men would share their deepest thoughts and their most fragile emotions. They had always done so because she always understood them and she would always keep their confidences locked behind her smiling face.

Sitting across from her, he wondered how many secrets her aging mind held. He knew some of them, and watching her, he was well aware of one; the one that grew out of one night twenty years ago.

The rush of a late autumn wind had chased everyone from the street that night. He remembered that there was no sound around him save the cackle of fallen leaves being blown across the ground. The silence of the streets and the sound of dead things in the wind seemed like an elegy for the weight he carried in his heart that evening.

It had been only a few weeks since he was forbidden to ever see Terrell again. Terrell's family had contacted his family and made aware their outrage at what had been going on between the two young men; so his family had assured them that he would never go near their son again.

In the weeks that followed, the school, having been made aware of the possible contact between the two lovers, had removed Otis from his regular school and had placed him in a special one for juvenile offenders, having accused him of menacing.

At home matters were no better. While he stood his ground and defended the love he and Terrell shared, his mother could only look at him in search of resolution and his father, well, he simply would not look at him at all. So he spent many of his evenings away from home, drinking and wandering lonely places. He would go home only when he thought his family had gone to bed; he could not bear to see the casts of their faces.

He made his way along the dark streets that night, stumbling not from the breaks in the asphalt, but from the scotch he had been drinking for much of the evening.

The houses that lined Jackson Street sat sleeping in the shadows. It was what he wanted as he lumbered past the homes of people he had known all his life. These same people now acted as if he was invisible, but he wasn't bothered because he now rendered them invisible as well.

As he neared home he noticed another house. It was Miss Susie's house. There was a single light on in her house and it shone like a lantern against the night. He stopped walking and looked at the window from which the light came. Its ocher hue seemed to splay from the window and dissipate into the night. There was something so lonely about the light, so wanting the way it reached into the night that Otis felt a kinship to it; he understood its desperation and witnessed its frailty against the consuming night.

Drawn by the lighted window, he crossed the street and stumbled into her yard. The sound of music from a phonograph drifted out her window. Dinah Washington sang "This Bitter Earth", her blue voice drifting through the night and settling around his head as he sat on Miss Susie's porch and began to cry. He was

too drunk to remember why he was crying, but he knew he had earned the right to
the tears that flowed from his eyes and rolled down the back of his hands as he
rested his face on his fists.

He sat there on the porch and sobbed all while the music played. It wasn't
until the last song ended that the front door opened and Miss Susie stood there in
her robe. She looked down at the sobbing young man on her porch. "Otis? Otis,
baby what's the matter?"

His throat was too knotted to answer.

"Why're you sittin' on my porch this time of night?" she continued. Not
receiving a reply, she looked over at the darkened house in which he lived, and
suddenly her understanding of his predicament became clear. She understood the
foolishness of her words so she squatted and, with her hands cupped under his
arms, half lifted him. He lumbered to his feet. "Come on," she said. And they
went inside.

So much had happened to him since that night that he hadn't given much
thought to it. But now upon his return, the evening he spent with Miss Susie had
become more important than he ever imagined.

* * * *

Miss Susie had given him the address where Antonio lived. She said he
lived 'with some gal' in Walnut Hills. She said she had been to his place once or
twice but said she hadn't been back because she didn't like his girlfriend.

Now, turning down the street, he slowed as he searched for the address. He
found it about midway down the block. It was a two-family house that was in
need of repair.

He pulled up to the curb and turned off the engine. Looking up at the second floor where Miss Susie had said Antonio lived, he watched the windows hoping someone might come to one of them; he felt that could serve as his first step towards the meeting. But no one did so he got out and walked to the building.

There was someone in the apartment because he could hear music coming from the windows. At first he was calm, but now as he stepped onto the porch, his stomach fluttered and his breathing quickened. He inhaled and let out a slow breath, then he rang the doorbell.

He heard someone come down the stairs, and then saw through the lace curtains a figure that was slight in build.

A young woman pulled back the curtain to the window of the door. She studied Otis' face, her own face curling into a quizzical expression.

Otis pushed a smile across his lips in an attempt to win her confidence.

She opened the door, peering around its edge. "Yes?"

"Is Antonio home?" He heard himself and wished he had made a different approach.

"No…" This time the young lady's hand tightened around the edge of the door as if she was prepared to shove it closed if any danger became apparent.

"I'm a friend of his mother, Miss Susie." *That's better.*

"Oh," she replied as she opened the door wider. "Is something wrong?"

"No, no. Everything's fine. I just happen to be in town and decided to drop by for a visit." He hoped his face still held a pleasant expression because the young lady continued to study him.

"Well he's not here right now. But what's your name and I'll tell 'em you stopped by."

"Otis. From New York," he said, hoping 'New York' might spur Antonio's memory of the stories his mother used to tell him.

The young lady grinned and put her hands on her small hips. "New York, huh?" Suddenly she seemed enchanted.

Otis nodded. "Yeah."

Her grin suddenly lowered into a slight smile and her eyes moved over Otis' body, then back to his face. "You wanna come on in?" Her voice softened. "I ain't never met a man from New York." She continued roaming his body with her eyes.

Otis grinned a 'thanks, but no thanks' kind of grin. "No. I just wanted to holler at Antonio before I left."

Suddenly the young lady's expression dropped, defeated, then her face closed, becoming almost like a period. "Well, I ain't seen him. Ain't seen him in a coupla days," she huffed. Then, quickly, she shut the door.

Otis stood stunned for a second before turning and walking back to his car. He would try later after stopping once again by Miss Susie's house; maybe she would know more of Antonio's whereabouts, but for now he headed for Mt. Auburn where he had made plans to hook up with Charles.

Chapter XIV

"Here I am thinking you're in the shower, and yo' ass still in bed." Otis walked into the bedroom careful not to spill the coffee he was carrying and to keep the towel around his waist from falling. He set the two cups on the nightstand.

"I don't usually get up this early on my days off," Charles growled.

"Well it was your idea that we run to the mall then meet Shirley for lunch."

"I know."

"Speaking of that, is it alright if my sister joins us? She works downtown too. Sugar, right?" Otis asked as he took the lid off the sugar bowl.

"Just a little. Yeah, it's cool. So I guess I get to meet the family now, huh?"

Otis laughed. "Let's not rush it. Here."

Charles sat up and took the coffee. Then he handed Otis the phone.

"Hello? Courtney?" Otis spoke as he poured cream into his coffee. "Yeah I'm all right. I don't need you takin' care of me. I been out here longer than you, remember? Look, I was callin' to see if you wanted to meet me and some friends for lunch today. Hold on." He looked over at Charles, "Where are we meeting?" Then back into the phone, "Aroma. It's - - yeah on seventh street. He called there? When? Oh. Okay, I'll listen. Okay. See you at twelve."

He hung up the phone and turned to Charles. "I gotta listen to my messages," he said before picking up the receiver once again. "Courtney said I had an important phone call."

After going through a number of messages he finally got to the one he sought. It was from a co-worker, the only one to whom he felt some degree of closeness, and to whom he had given Courtney's number just in case there was some news about the status of his employment.

"Hey Otis. This is Emory. Got some good news. Patrick, up in personnel, said you can come back. They'll see it as medical leave. But there's one catch. You have to seek therapy. Now I know you're probably saying 'fuck that', but think about it. You need to call 'em as soon as possible to let 'em know if you'll accept. Do it, man. Do it."

"By your expression I can't tell if the news was good or bad," Charles said, leaning back against the headboard.

"Huh? Oh. Yeah, it was good news. I got my job back. Well kinda."

"So what's the terms?"

"Mmh," Otis hunched his shoulders.

"I can understand if you don't want to discuss it. I wasn't askin' just to be nosey. But if the terms are cool then you should take it. You ain't gettin' any younger, man."

Otis turned to face him, "You don't think I know that?" he grinned.

"Well, you need to think about it more."

Otis leaned back against the headboard and stared ahead.

Charles looked at him. "You'll make the right decision. Now I better start gettin' ready."

Otis nodded his head as Charles got out of bed. Then, "Charles."

"Huh?"

Otis grinned and undid the towel around his waist. "Let's be a little late."

* * * *

Otis tapped his fingers to the music as he and Charles drove along Columbia Parkway. He looked out the window at the bright sunshine that played off the Ohio River like small diamonds dancing on water. "I really like this song," he said as he looked over at Charles.

"Me too. Who is that?"

"Somebody. I don't know. Some hip-hopper."

"It's nice."

Otis nodded his head. Then he turned to Charles with a slight smile. "You ever notice how a lot of those hip-hop videos are?"

Charles continued to look ahead. "What do you mean?"

"How some of the brothas in those videos seem so gay?"

This time Charles glanced at him. "What?"

"You heard me." Otis now grinned. "They may not act feminine and shit, but they still act like they doin' somethin', you know..."

"See now, you're just trying to fuck with me."

Otis laughed. "Well check some of 'em out next time. You'll see what I mean. The ones who be with their boyz and they all have their shirts off and hugging on each other and shit."

"Yeah, but I doubt if they are," Charles defended.

"Why not? Now I know you ain't stupid."

"I don't know. I guess I just gotta get used to this gay thing."

"Or at least get over your insecurities." Otis smiled and patted Charles' thigh.

"So Otis. Who is the friend who left you that message? Is he a friend friend? Or is he just a friend?"

"He's more of a friend, I guess."

"More of a friend."

"Yeah."

"More of a friend," Charles repeated. "You don't sound too sure."

"Well, I'm not too sure about a lot of things these days."

They arrived downtown just before noon. As they walked into the courthouse, Otis heard the din of voices echoing through the imposing lobby; the sound was one of hushed conversation. His mind drifted back. He could remember the cuffs on his wrists and the shackles on his ankles. *Why did they have to do that?* He remembered the fear and the sense of hopelessness as he was led from the waiting room into the courtroom. He remembered feeling like he was marked and had nowhere to run, no one to turn to. He remembered how, on that day, he simply submitted to the hand that was dealt him.

"There's Shirley." Charles' voice brought him back to the present. Looking across the lobby Otis saw Shirley talking to a tall silver-haired white man. Both of them had on business suits and moved with the studied mannerisms of people who were groomed to take care of business. She turned her head slightly to acknowledge that she saw them before continuing her conversation. A few passersby waved at Charles and more than a few, mostly black officers, stopped by to chat. The whole scene there in the courthouse seemed, at times, as if a fraternal order were convening.

Then he looked at the many black and white faces around the lobby, faces stripped bare by their indigence. They stood in deference to the business suits and uniforms looking slightly confused. Every now and then a white man in business attire would motion one of them aside; he would put his hand on the back of the person and lead him to a quiet place and after talking to him would place his hand on his shoulder, shake his head and lead him into a room. All of this transpired within the bizarre elegance of the courthouse with its grand foyer and massive chandeliers. It was, indeed, a beautiful place at once morbid and inviting, ostensibly impersonal.

The tall man and Shirley ended their conversation and she walked across the lobby to meet Otis and Charles. "Hey boyfriends," she grinned. "I was hoping you would make it," she said to Otis and gave him a hug. He noticed how uncommonly strong her arms were as they encircled his neck. "I kept asking Charles when you were going back. I wanted to see you again before you left."

"I'm not quite sure when I'll be going back. Soon, though," Otis answered as the three of them left the courthouse, Shirley in the middle, and walked down the stairs to the street.

Main Street was crowded with government employees in their various guises. Vendors lined the curbside with a sundry of sandwiches and drinks, while suspicious looking brothers darted among the crowd seeking to escape the light of their deeds.

"Who was Milton trying to set up this time?" Charles inquired of the tall white man with whom Shirley had been talking.

"Nobody, surprisingly," Shirley replied.

"What is he, the D.A.?" Otis asked.

"He's one of the assistants. Always out to get somebody," Shirley said.

"Well, now you gotta admit, that's his job." Charles came to his defense.

"Yeah, but he likes burning people. And you know that, too." Shirley spoke as she slapped Charles' arm.

Charles smiled and hunched his shoulders.

Otis had been checking Shirley out as they walked down the street.

"You know Shirley, you look kinda different from when I first met you."

"Is that good or bad?"

"Well, both of you are fine," he grinned.

"Oh. Well thanks. Heeey..." She suddenly called out, waving her hand, "But it's probably because I was drunk that night."

"You weren't drunk."

"You never know with her. I've seen her drink to infinity and still make it home before crashing out," Charles commented.

"That was only once."

"Twice. No, four. No- -"

"Boy shut up." The three of them laughed as they strolled up East Seventh Street. "I'm the same ol' me under this suit. Same ol' rah rah girl," she continued. "I don't believe in changing for nobody."

"I know what you mean. That's the way I am on my job," Otis agreed.

"Oh yeah." Charles spoke as he crooked his neck towards Shirley. "He's been offered his job back and he's not gonna take it."

Shirley looked over at Otis, "Why not?"

"I didn't say that," Otis protested.

"You said, 'Well- - kinda'. And you know what that means."

"Look, you better make that move, boy." Shirley took Otis' hand and gave it a gentle shake.

They arrived at Aroma and found a seat at a table not too far from the window.

"You hold the table. What're you having?" Charles asked of Shirley.

"I'll have a reuben," she said without looking at the menu.

"You come here a lot, don't you?" Otis laughed.

"I try to. I like giving my business to the community. Besides they make some damn good sandwiches and some good ass coffee."

Otis followed Charles to the counter. He looked around the snappy eatery done up in wild cantaloupe and tangerine colors and saw that it was becoming crowded as people streamed through the door, "I better make up my mind."

He and Charles returned and placed the meals on the table. "Looks like this place is going to make it. It's got a nice crowd. And a lot of white people too. That's usually what makes you or breaks you."

"But look at all the Nubian brothers '*in heah*'," Shirley smiled as her eyes moved across the restaurant. "And especially that one, standing at the counter in the navy blue Armani."

Otis turned to look at him. The man was definitely hot, but he wasn't sure how to respond, not because of Shirley, but because of Charles. He still wasn't sure how comfortable Charles was with himself. He glanced at Charles who looked towards the man in the most casual way and slightly bobbed his head as if he was listening to music. Then he turned back around without saying a word.

Shirley tapped Charles' arm, "You know who he looks like?"

"Who?"

"That statue we saw when we were in Central America. You know, the one in the museum."

"Oh."

"Yeah." She turned to Otis. "Have you ever been to Central America?"

"No."

"It's nice. You need to go, get a little taste of black history."

Charles rolled his eyes, "Here we go."

"What?" Otis asked as he unfolded his napkin.

"Man, don't ask that," Charles warned as he shook his head.

Shirley turned to Otis. "We went down to Costa Rica a few years ago. They have these busts of black men in the National Museum; they're of an ancient people who lived in Central America over a thousand years ago. And that man looks like one of the busts."

"Oh, okay," Otis said as he glanced back at the handsome dark skinned man.

"And now on to something else." Charles sighed.

Otis looked at him, "Man you should feel proud."

"I do. But I don't want to sit around and hear a history lesson right now."

"He doesn't wanna hear much of anything that's outside of the mainstream," Shirley laughed. "It's too much for him. Mister conservative," she quipped as she picked up her sandwich.

Shirley turned once again to Otis. "But about your job; you really should go back to it. If you feel it's time to make a change you can always look for another one while you're still with that one. You got that apartment to pay for I'm sure and you don't want to lose that. What are your mortgage payments for that anyway?"

"A lot. And I probably will go back there."

"See? There he goes again," Charles said.

"Well, I know I will. It's just that right now I got other things to think about. But I know I have a time restriction placed on me. I'll jump on it. Don't worry."

At that moment Otis looked out the window and saw Courtney waving at him as she walked to the entrance of the café. "Oh, there's my sister."

"She's so pretty," Shirley said as Courtney walked towards their table.

"She's tough," Charles added.

Courtney's deep cinnamon complexion complemented the aroma of the coffee and spices that filled the air of the café; and her tall stature, long almond shaped eyes and the braids that hung down her back made her appear as exotic as the foods the café served.

Otis and Charles stood as she walked up to the table. "I was beginning to think you weren't going make it," Otis said and gave her a kiss on the cheek.

"We had a little celebration at the office and I lost track of time."

"Oh. Well Court, this is Shirley. Shirley, Courtney."

"It's nice to finally meet you," Shirley said as she shook Courtney's hand.

"Same."

"And this is Charles."

"Good to meet you Charles."

"Likewise."

"I'm glad to know my brother made some friends since he's been back."

"Well it's been our pleasure to know him." Shirley smiled as she looked over at Otis.

Charles nodded his head in agreement, his eyes still wide and focused on Courtney.

"What're you having?" Otis asked.

"We had a mass lay out at work and I ate like a pig, so I'm not that hungry. I'll just have a latte and a fruit bowl."

"I'll get it." Charles was quick to respond, and in a second was gone to place the order.

Shirley looked at him with raised eyebrows; then she smiled and looked over at Otis who shook his head.

"So, Otis said you work for P&G."

"Yep."

"That's a pretty conservative place, isn't it?" Shirley asked.

"Not anymore. I mean, how else are they going to recruit world-class employees? You know?" she said waving a finger, "They even provide benefits to life partners now."

"What?" Shirley exclaimed.

"You sure about that? Here in Cincinnati?" Otis asked.

"Yep."

Shirley nodded her head. "That's good. But it's still hard to believe."

"What?" Charles asked as he returned to the table with Courtney's order.

"Courtney was just telling us that P&G offers benefits to life partners now," Otis said.

"Oh." Charles spoke in a noncommittal tone.

Courtney turned to Shirley. "And I hear you work for the county. Which department?"

"Records."

"She's records manager," Otis added.

Courtney raised her eyebrows, "Wow. Keeper of secrets, huh?"

"I guess you can say that; but it's mostly managerial stuff, you know."

Courtney picked at a piece of melon, "I know if I was in that position, I probably wouldn't want to see information like that all day long."

"You just don't look at it. You see it but you don't look at it," Charles said.

"You work there too?" Courtney asked.

"No. But I know what it's like." He spoke as he lifted his drink to his mouth. "Believe me."

"You'll never guess what he does," Otis interrupted with a grin.

Courtney eyed Charles for a second. "Well the first thing I would think of is a bodyguard. I mean, the way he's built and all."

"Close enough," Otis said. "He's a cop."

Charles winced. He wondered if he could get Otis away from calling him 'cop'?

Courtney cocked her head slightly, "Oh. Now that's a job."

"Oh yeah," Charles responded with pride.

"Look at him, actin' like Barney Phyfe," Otis laughed.

"Well I think he's justified," Courtney said. "That's dangerous work."

"Thank you." Charles answered.

Otis looked over at Shirley who could only roll her eyes.

"So how long have you been on the force?" Courtney continued.

"A long time. Eighteen years."

"That is a long time."

"But enough about him... there's too many other things we can talk about in an hour," Otis said.

The rest of the lunch went on, but as it did Otis fell into a noticeable silence.

"You okay?" Courtney asked her brother. "You've been kind of quiet."

Otis looked up from his meal. "Huh? Oh. Yeah. I'm okay. I was just sittin' here chillin'."

Courtney looked at her brother as if she didn't quite believe him. It was as if something had come along and caused his mood to suddenly darken. "Oh." She didn't pursue the matter any further.

In a while the four of them left the café. Shirley and Charles shook Courtney's hand and wished her well. Otis gave her a hug. "I'll see you this evening."

"I hope so. I haven't seen you in a couple of days," she smiled. Then she kissed him on the cheek and waved to Shirley and Charles.

After having seen Shirley back to the courthouse, Otis and Charles walked back to the parking lot.

"Man, are you sure you okay?" Charles asked.

"Yeah, I'm okay. I just got somethin' on my mind. Look, can we call it a day? I need to do somethin'."

"Yeah, that's cool," Charles said as he unlocked the doors of the truck. He looked across at Otis with a puzzled look on his face.

They headed back to Charles' house in silence.

Suddenly Otis spoke, "Fuck it. Let's go on with our plans."

Charles glanced over at him. "Nah it's cool."

"Nah man. We planned this day and we should carry it through."

* * * *

Before, they had only sucked each other's dicks. But now, as the afternoon promised evening, they fucked. And they fucked hard, and with passion. Before they had placed kisses on each other's lips as they watched each other cum. And Charles had been astounded at the size and power of Otis' dick as it had pulsed before spurting. But now he was beneath Otis, locked in a silent struggle, his legs and arms around Otis' back taking the large dick, each stroke becoming more acceptable. He could feel something in Otis, the way he held him down on the bed and buried his head into his neck. He could've sworn he heard him sob.

* * * *

"So, the prodigal son returns." Courtney lounged on the sofa as she watched TV.

"Okay mother. I said I was coming back."

"And speaking of mother, Momma said to call her."

"I was gonna go over there tomorrow anyway. But I'll give her a call."

"Still go over there. It has been twenty years, y'know."

"I am. And don't start that shit with me. What'cha watching?"

"Jeopardy."

"Figures. I got us some beer."

Courtney watched her brother go into the kitchen. "A forty. Figures," she countered as he pulled the two large bottles out of the bag. "Oh, and I hope you weren't expecting dinner. I didn't feel like cooking."

"Nah, I ain't hungry."

"Good."

Otis walked back to his bedroom to drop his valise.

"Shirley and Charles seem like cool people," Courtney called out.

"They are." Otis spoke as he went into the bathroom to piss.

"So is Charles your new friend?"

"Nah." His voice came around the bathroom door as it opened. "We're just friends," he spoke as he went back into the kitchen to retrieve one of the bottles of beer and two glasses.

"Ooh, just a 'ho," Courtney exclaimed with a click of her tongue.

"Ain't nobody no damn ho'." He returned to the living room and moved his sister's legs that had been strewn across the sofa.

"You are. What about your friend, Emory, up in New York?"

"He's a co-worker, not a friend."

"I bet he doesn't think so. Come on, why would he waste his calling card on you if he didn't think something different?"

"I told him to let me know if something happened on the job."

"Otis..."

"I don't know. I guess he just knows how to be a good friend slash co-worker."

"Now y'know y'wrong."

"No I'm not. Me an' him go way back. I mean, we tried to start somethin' once but it just didn't work out."

"On whose part? Yours or his?"

"He just wasn't the one, that's all."

"Boy you are in so much denial. And you're a liar, too." She poured herself a glass of beer before curling back up on the couch, her legs under her. "Have you even been in a relationship since Terrell?"

"Yeah."

"How many?"

"A few."

"And what happened?"

"None of 'em worked out."

"None of 'em? Now just listen to you." She leaned her head forward as if to plant a thought in his head. "You haven't had even one stable relationship in twenty years."

"Yeah, well maybe I would have if everybody would've left me 'n Terrell alone."

Courtney clicked her tongue, "Boy, you need to get over that."

* * * *

Later that night after Courtney had gone to bed, he sat alone on the couch; the image in his head was as sharp as what he had witnessed that afternoon. He hadn't wanted to say anything to anybody; he only wanted to run to the door of the café and stop the man who had passed the window. He wanted to call Terrell by name, to stop him. But again, as before, he hadn't been able to respond. And again, as before, he watched as Terrell passed by.

Chapter XV

The waitress led Otis to his table; she moved quick for her age, as if years of waiting tables had engendered an eternal youthfulness to her stride.

He had requested that particular table because it lent a view of the kitchen area.

"What can I start you off with?" The waitress asked as she pulled a pen from her brown wig.

"I'll start off with a cup of coffee."

"Okay." She began to scribble. The fragrance of floral perfume, and spearmint with a hint of stale liquor stirred about her as she moved. "I'll be back with your coffee." And she left.

He looked around the restaurant at the few patrons before settling his eyes on the area that led to the kitchen.

The waitress returned with his coffee and he placed the rest of his order.

Before she left he asked, "Is there an Antonio Burton who works here?"

"Yeah. In the kitchen," she said, pointing with her pen. Then she caught herself. "He's not in trouble is he?"

Otis smiled and shook his head. "Nah. I'm just a friend of the family."

"That's good. He's a good boy. I'll let him know you're here," she said before scooping up the menu and heading back towards the kitchen.

In a few minutes he saw a young man look around a corner from the kitchen. He checked Otis out before disappearing back into the kitchen. The young spy wasn't Antonio so Otis guessed he had been sent by him to scope out the scene.

It was about five minutes after the reconnaissance that Antonio came out. He was tall and slim with the same dark features as Otis. As he approached the table, moving in a slow loping walk, his eyes flashed with a quick reckoning, with the light of knowing without having known.

Otis stood and stuck out his hand. "Antonio?"

"What's up?" He shook Otis' hand.

"I'm a friend of your mother."

Antonio looked at him for a moment. "You the one from New York, ain't you?"

"... Yeah... I was in town and, your mother wanted us to meet."

Antonio pushed his hands into his pockets.

Otis continued. "I thought maybe we could get together after you get off from work."

"I got things to do."

"Tomorrow maybe?"

"Still got things to do." Antonio turned to leave then he stopped; something like guilt held him. "Shit. Okay. I get off at three."

"Today?"

"Yeah." He headed back to the kitchen.

* * * *

The sign read 'The Majestic Apartments'. The lettering on the sign had once shone in a brilliant gold color befitting the building's name, but now the gold had become more of a pallid yellow blotched with black stains. The two men walked through one of the arches of the wall that enclosed the courtyard.

Coming into the courtyard had an uplifting effect as one would walk from the hard gray and black of the squalid streets into the lushness of the green enclosure. But then that enlightened feeling, the feeling that one had stumbled upon paradise would come crashing to an end when one eyed the building. The Majestic was a large five-story structure of blond bricks that half encapsuled the courtyard. The doors and the windows were barred almost as if to contain the last vestiges of hope more than to keep burglars out.

Otis looked up at the canyon of windows that all appeared as dark eyes, sullen, looking down on him. "Whose place is this?"

Antonio walked a little ahead of him. "Mine."

"I thought you lived in Walnut Hills?"

"Oh," Antonio laughed, "I do, sometime. But when I wanna get away, I come here."

It was one of the few times they had spoken to each other since leaving the restaurant.

The weight of concern landed in Otis' chest. How could this kid afford two apartments? He felt all the answers and none of them were good.

Antonio unlocked the large steel doors that stood oddly in a palatial doorway and they ascended the stairs. The building was surprisingly clean except for the carpet that held years of renegade soil, having found a home settled deep, black, in the ugly green material of the hallway. "I ain't got much. I'm just gettin' started," he said, speaking into the door as he turned the lock. The sound of a radio came from inside the apartment. "It's gonna be tight when I finish though," he continued. And he opened the door to a bright, airy room that was sparsely furnished. The smell of Lysol rushed to Otis' nostrils as he stepped inside.

"Make yourself at home," Antonio invited as he motioned to the sofa, which was the only piece of furniture; the other items were a television and a boom box. "Want somethin' to drink? I got a coupla forties on ice." He spoke as he walked into the kitchen.

Otis followed him. "That sounds nice. I could use one." He felt strange talking that way to the young man who might be his son, but it was all there was to say at the moment.

"I don't do much eatin' when I get home 'cause I eat all daylong on the job."

"Yeah, I can tell by the empty fridge," Otis said as they walked back into the living room.

Antonio turned off the radio and turned on the TV; then he sat down beside Otis.

"So what made you come back after all these years?" He spoke as he went in his pocket and retrieved a bag of weed and papers. Reaching for a newspaper on the floor, he began rolling a joint using the newspaper as a lap tray.

Otis took a breath to shake his sudden feeling of paternalism. "I needed to come back to take care of some loose ends." He wasn't sure if Antonio knew why he had left.

Antonio chuckled, his eyes focused on the weed being rolled, "And see, I thought maybe you realized you forgot somethin'."

"No, I didn't forget anything. Not a damn thing." Otis was looking at the bottle on the floor. "But looks like there was some things I didn't know about." He picked up the bottle and took a drink.

"So I see we on the same page." Antonio spoke as he completed the paper construction. He lit the joint and took a drag. "Why did you leave me alone with her?" He extended the joint to Otis who declined. He had to be a father.

"Like I said, I didn't even know you existed." He turned to his son, "So I guess she admitted the truth to you, huh? 'cause she wouldn't tell me."

"Me neither. I kinda figure it out the way she was always talkin' to me about you, where you was, when you comin' back to take me on a trip an' shit. She even used to keep your picture by her bed."

"A picture? Of me?"

Antonio nodded. "I think she stole it."

Otis shook his head.

"I love her, but I think she's a witch," Antonio suddenly declared.

"What?" Otis turned to him with raised brows.

"Why else would she sit up in that house with all the blinds closed? And some of the weird shit I saw..." Antonio looked out across the room before continuing. "You know she used to make me eat my nails?" He looked at Otis with a smile; he knew his father would find his words incredulous. "When she used to clip my toenails or fingernails she used to save 'em. Then she would chop 'em up and boil 'em 'til they was real soft and mix 'em in with my food. Said she didn't want them to get wind of me. She always said they was people out to take me from her." He took another a drag.

"Who?"

Antonio hunched his shoulders. "I dunno. She didn't never say." He spoke with his lungs full of smoke, letting small wisps of air escape as he continued. "She used to lock me in my room sometimes for a entire day. Shit was crazy, man. But even then I still loved her, and still do.

Otis looked at him as the smoked encircled his head. "You should love her, she's your mother."

"But I still think she a witch or somethin'," Antonio insisted.

"Man, she ain't no witch. Just a little eccentric, that's all," Otis defended.

"Yeah, well she got you didn't she? I mean, how can some old broad get somebody young to go to bed without performin' some black magic or some shit like that."

Otis looked sideways at him. "She wasn't so old then."

"Yeah, well, she still got you."

"Look," Otis continued as he folded his hands, "I'm sorry I haven't been there for you."

"It's cool. It's kinda fucked up, but it's cool. Shit you didn't even know about me. Besides, I'm makin' it, as you can see." Antonio waved the bottle through the air, having lifted it for another swig.

"But I just want you to know that I'll be there for you for the rest of our life."

Antonio broke into loud laughter. "Man, you sound like we in a movie or somethin'."

"So what? I don't care what it sounds like, it's true."

Antonio nodded his head as he set the bottle back on the floor, the braids on his head moving against the afternoon sun like tamed serpents. "When you goin' back?" he asked.

"In a week or two, I don't know. I want to spend as much time with you as I can."

"And then y'gone, huh?" Antonio looked at the joint he held, unable to look at his father for the reply.

"I'll be away," Otis corrected, "But not so far this time."

"Hmh," Antonio grunted as he lifted the bottle to his mouth once again.

Otis wanted badly to convey the commitment he knew his son wanted and that he knew he should give; it was what good fathers do. Should do. But, in reality he just didn't feel that way. Commitment. No. Seeing his son was more like a visit to a trophy he had earned. His son was not to be loved, but to be cherished as a mark of Otis' success as a man, not as one in need of the love of a father. Yet he did want to be that way, a good loving father just like... his father...

"So is it okay for me to see you again?" he continued.

"Yeah. I guess so." Another toke.

Otis went into his wallet and pulled out a slip of paper. "Here's how you can get in touch with me, here and in New York."

Antonio took the information and studied it trying to give it relevance.

"How can I get in touch with you next time?" Otis asked. "I don't want to be running around town looking for yo' ass."

"I'ma have a cell phone soon. You know where I work, though. Other than that I'll just have to call you."

Otis stood to leave. "Two apartments and a cell phone. How are you pulling all that off?"

Antonio grinned wide as he followed Otis to the door. "I got benefactors."

Chapter XVI

"Wha'chou doin'?"

"Watchin' T.V."

"How come you ain't studyin'?"

"I already did. How come you ain't studyin'? Where are you?"

"Down here on the corner. I wanna see you."

"What? I can't."

"Is yo' moms and pops up?"

"No. It's just me and my sister."

"Then come on outside."

"It's rainin'."

"Don't you think I know that? I wanna see you. Tell yo' sister you takin' out the garbage or somethin' and meet me out back."

"Is that all the garbage you could find?" Otis' voice cut through the clatter *of the rain. He appeared like some tall dark spectre, his deep complexion and dark clothing barely visible under the black umbrella that shielded him from the rainy night.*

"I took the garbage out earlier this evening." Terrell squinted under his umbrella as the rain splattered from the garbage can onto his face.

"Come on." Otis raised his large umbrella higher and extended his free arm.

"Man, you gon' git us killed."

"It won't take long. Like I said, I just wanna see you. Is your sister nearby?"

"Nah. She's upstairs in her room."

"Then..." Otis gave Terrell a light kiss.

"Otis..." Terrell looked around the courtyard at the other apartments. "Somebody might see us."

"No they won't. It's nighttime and it's rainin'. Ain't nobody gonna be lookin' out they window." He put his arm around Terrell's back and held him closer. They engaged in a long kiss.

After the kiss Terrell laid his head on Otis' chest. He felt the solid muscle and heard the deep thumping of Otis' heart. He could have stayed that way all night. Out the corner of his eye he saw the figure of a man jump out of a car and rush into one of the apartments. He didn't know whether or not the man saw them, but there was something about getting caught that relieved him.

"Like I said, I just wanted to see you." Otis' deep voice rumbled through his chest.

Terrell held him tighter.

* * * *

He didn't always think of Otis. Karen seemed to think he did; and she would tell him so if he looked too long in the direction of another man, or if he appeared to get too comfortable with one of the men at church, especially if the man was handsome. It bothered him that she felt that way, but he accepted it. It was something to which he deferred.

But memories are like crickets. Anxious ones. They leap at the slightest provocation. And now he wondered what was provoking the memories he was having. The night before he had thought of Otis. Even that afternoon, while out to lunch with some of his co-workers, he thought about him. It was almost as if he had expected to walk upon him on the street. And what would he have said to him? What would he have done? And more than anything, how would Otis have received him? It was strange.

His mother was sitting at her puzzle table as he came through the door.

"Hey Ma," he said as he kissed her on her cheek.

"Boy, I was wonderin' when you were gonna show up."

"It's just a little past five."

"There's some chicken, rice and greens in the kitchen." She anticipated his visit; she knew that was one of his favorite dishes.

"Yes Ma'am. You still workin' on that puzzle? Too tough for you, huh?"

"No. You have to do better than this to beat me with a puzzle."

"Then why haven't you finished it? I got that one for you two weeks ago."

"I'm tryin' to make it last. I figure I'll give you and Charmaine time to buy me another one before I finish this one."

"Oh. You know they have three dimensional ones."

"What's that?"

"Instead of being flat, they have all four sides."

"Oh. That should be a challenge."

"Then I'll get one of those for you next time. Have you eaten?" he asked as he walked through the dining room.

"I don't want anything right now. I'll eat later. Me and Mozelle ate a big lunch."

"Where did you two fly girls go today?" Terrell came back into the dining room and sat across from his mother's workstation.

"The usual: the rec center and shoppin'. Oh. And we went to Vine Street Elementary."

"Why?" Terrell sopped up gravy from his plate with a piece of bread.

"We did some story telling."

"Oh. Did the kids listen?"

His mother looked up, "Of course they did. All kids like stories."

"Yeah, I guess so."

"And they're no different down there, you know."

"I know." Terrell answered with embarrassment.

"Charmaine and the kids were here earlier."

"D'Andre too?"

"Yeah. He's lookin' good, too. I'm glad he's eatin' right at school."

"Trust me Ma, that's all you do in your dorms besides studyin'. I have to see him before he goes back."

"He said he likes it there," his mother continued.

"That's good since his first year was so hard. But I told him that was normal."

"I'm so proud of him. I'm proud of all my grand kids."

"Yes ma'am."

"And your father would be proud of him too."

Terrell's father had taken D'Andre as his own after Charmaine had him. At first they were concerned that their father had taken him under his wings. They knew of his sternness and the heavy hand with which he ruled over his family; they didn't wish that on D'Andre. But surprisingly, he was more accommodating to his grandson. They had a friendship; something he'd never had with Terrell or Charmaine. Maybe it was because D'Andre wasn't of his seed that Terrell's father felt he had no direct control over his life. Or maybe it was because he felt sorry for the little fellow whose mother had only been eighteen years old when he was born and whose father had only given him his name before he left town. Maybe that was why. And maybe that was why Terrell's father and D'Andre remained close. Even after Leon came on the scene and took him as his own; he remained close to his grandfather until the day his grandfather died.

"I'm so proud of him," Terrell's mother repeated as she held a piece of the puzzle in her hand and searched for the empty space.

"Me too."

"You'll be with Kenya and Abassi soon too." She didn't look at him, but continued to look for the empty space.

"Yes ma'am."

"Is it this weekend?"

"No ma'am. Next weekend."

She looked at him. "Next weekend? I thought Sister Abrams said- -"

"Well, me and Karen talked and we decided next weekend would be fine."

His mother looked at him for a minute. "Well, I guess you two know what's best." She looked back down at the puzzle. "Good. Ah. There it is," she said as she snapped the piece in place.

           After he left his mother's house he started for home. He wondered if his mother's concern that he rush to Karen and the kids was out of her love of family or was it due to a lack of trust of his character? He wanted to believe it was the former, but he couldn't help but wonder otherwise.

           Everyone seemed to watch him as if he was deserving of being monitored. "The narrow path is the best path," they would say whenever he would hint of straying; or, "You're blessed to have a good wife like Karen and such beautiful kids." They would make these comments with a smile and searching eyes.

           But he was becoming tired of the narrow path. It was confining and monotonous.

           Sometimes he would sit at home in his den and dream of escaping his life. Karen would think he would be working in his den, but imagining is what he would really be doing.

           Of course he usually left his imaginings there in the den. He could never abandon his family. But he could make just one run at life before he went to join them. Just one. Besides what does Karen care, he thought. She didn't even seem to want him around.

           The evening he'd spent at Café Cin-Cin with Stanton was different from his usual evening. The conversation had been daring and full of challenge, unlike the ones he had with his wife and members of the church. And then the incident with the hustler...

           He turned the car around and drove back towards downtown. On Montgomery Road he came to a stop at a traffic light in The Five Point district. On all sides of the large intersection were drug dealers. He watched them as they strode along the sidewalk taking care of their business, their baggy jeans slung low beneath their hips and gold teeth that flashed like quick bites of light as they called out to each other.

He got caught up in the fast pace and the craftiness with which these young brothers conducted their business. It was a sight he'd seen mostly on television, but not in his circle of acquaintances and surely not in Mason. He could hear Stanton laughing and chiding him about his small life.

A car horn blew.

He looked in his rearview mirror at an exasperated driver who waved him on.

Once he got downtown he parked and sat for a minute. He wasn't sure which way to go. He knew he didn't want to go home. There were no messages waiting for him and he decided not to make any phone calls that evening. Karen and the kids seemed so busy these days.

He noticed his attire and slowly removed the tie from around his neck and spread the collar of his shirt; then he got out of the car and started walking. He decided not to head north because that would take him across Central Parkway and into Over The Rhine. He knew he would stand out like a sore thumb there; he could even get robbed there, he considered, as he walked westward up Seventh Street.

He thought about Stanton. He wasn't sure why, but he did. Maybe it was the walk through Piatt Park. He and Stanton had strolled there the time they'd gone to the Y together. And it was there, in the same park, that Stanton had played the man who had called out to him. Terrell now guessed the man must have been one of Stanton's little secrets.

He was still in shock over Stanton being gay. It was almost absurd to him that a man of Stanton's stature in the community could live such a life under cover. People like him just didn't live that way. Besides, he stood to lose so much. But there it was. He wondered how Bishop Abrams would react to knowing that one of his 'pillars of the black community' was gay. He knew he never would divulge the secret, though. Too messy.

He had walked a while before he came upon a couple of men standing outside a bar. By their gestures Terrell figured there was some type of transaction taking place. It appeared as if one of the men was asking the other for a loan. They appeared to know each other so Terrell didn't think the man in need was a street beggar. Anyway, it wasn't his business so he navigated to the opposite side of the walk to avoid them. The bar they stood in front of was called The Phoenix; the sign above their heads declared the name in weak red letters. Terrell had seen the place many times, but only in passing. Every time he had walked by the bar he could hear voices and music roll through the doorway and onto the street. It had always been a place of slight curiosity to him; but this evening the curiosity gave way to intrigue. This evening he wouldn't pass it by. Yes, he assured himself, he knew of the possibilities that temptation could present once he crossed the doorway; hadn't he been warned enough against them? But that day it was just those possibilities that drew him forward.

The door of the bar was open which made it easier for him to step inside. A breeze stirred by ceiling fans rushed across him cooling the thin veil of perspiration that covered his skin. He walked over to the bar without slowing to take a look around.

"What can I git 'chou?" The bartender was quick to notice his presence and had left his conversation with some of the patrons to serve him.

"... Rum and coke ..."

"Light or dark?"

"Light(?)"

The bartender pulled up a glass and a bottle, "Double?"

"Yeah."

The bartender didn't seem to smirk, so Terrell felt accomplished.

"Three twenty-five."

Terrell gave him a five. "Keep the change."

The bartender smiled. "Thanks."

He didn't want to sit at the bar so he turned to look at the tables that lined the wall. There was a nice crowd, but not too full. He spotted an empty table and took a seat.

The bar was long and kind of narrow. There was nothing fancy about it; no shiny brass railings, or classy renderings touting imported ales. It was a hole in the wall. The red glow of the sign outside seemed to carry over into the interior; a red hue that came from an indiscernible place mixed with the low light and created a charge in the air. All around were signs that seemed to have been placed wherever there was space. Some of them were electric blue and blazed against the red hue, while others were posters of white and light skinned black women sexily posing next to bottles of beers. The clientele was mostly black, middle aged, working class; and by their appearance were probably unskilled laborers, Terrell assumed. But there were some white people there as well, and everyone seemed to know each other, calling to each other and hugging on each other.

He stirred his drink and started to take a sip. Then he paused and looked at the glass. Since he was unsure of the establishment, he used the stirrer as a straw instead. There was music pumping out of a jukebox that sat halfway along the distance of the wall, briefly interrupting the flow of tables. Barry White was playing:

"Your sweetnes is my weakness, yeah, yeah"

Terrell remembered that song and smiled as he lightly moved his head to the beat.

From where he sat he could see much of the bar. The two men who had been out front of the bar now stood by the cigarette machine at the entrance. They were holding glasses of beer and continuing their conversation. The one man seemed to be getting nowhere with his sell. Terrell took another sip from his drink as he considered that this was only the third time in his life that he had ever been to a bar. The first time had been when Otis and he had snuck into Central Café. He wondered if Central was still around.

'Almost forty years old', he thought. He wondered how he could have let so much of his life go by without experiencing its fullness.

Barry was reaching a climax:

"Your swee-eetnes, is my wee-eeaknes, uh huh, uh huh"

A woman jumped from her seat and began to wiggle at her table while the men pumped their fists and laughed.

Terrell couldn't help but laugh himself.

A man at the bar laughed and looked at Terrell while pointing towards the woman. "She crazy, man," he exclaimed.

Terrell nodded as he continued to laugh.

There was a lot of movement in the bar. Men, some of them in their early years, some of them around Terrell's age, came and went in an incessant flow. Sometimes they stayed long enough to have a drink, and at other times they would leave their drinks for a minute and would step outside or to the back of the bar.

The bartender smiled and pointed to Terrell, questioning if he wanted another drink.

Terrell hesitated, then smiled and nodded his head as he got up from the table.

"This time git two straws." The man who had spoken to him earlier joked. "Maybe you can get more of a rush that way."

The bartender grinned and plopped two stirrers into the glass.

"Thanks. I'll give that a try." Terrell laughed. He sat back at his table and continued to check out the scene. A few of the guys eyed him suspiciously as they went about their business; while some merely seemed curious about the brother in the white shirt.

He grinned to himself. He was just as curious about them. These were the people he was to avoid. They were the ones who spoke in ravaged voices and whose lives, he believed, were lived with abandon. Surely they couldn't be on the narrow path. But tonight, he wanted to stray into the larger world with them.

The bartender served him a few more drinks as Terrell now sat at the bar and talked with the bartender and another man. The conversation was lively as the three of them talked about everything from politics, to the police, to women. It felt good to let loose without having to watch your tongue, he thought.

Soon he rose to leave. He shook the men's hands, wishing he had known them longer than for just a couple of hours, and he left. He knew he would be back before he headed for Atlanta.

As he stepped outside the bar, he looked up at the sky. It was deep and full of stars. He smiled and walked to his car.

* * * *

The next evening Terrell attended a meeting at the church with the bishop and Stanton. He sat quietly and watched as Stanton laid out the request for proposals. He hadn't spoken to him since that evening at Jerry's house. That had been over a week ago. He hadn't been sure how he and Stanton would act towards each other the next time they met, but everything went fine. Stanton had greeted him as if there was nothing more than business between them.

The meeting was brief. It had mainly been to present the RFP's and to assess a possible cost overrun. Stanton promised to minimize the overrun as much as possible, but assured them there would be one.

As the meeting wound down Stanton once again gave a pitch for the project. Then, leaving copies of the proposals, he requested a reply as soon as possible. "I hope we can get this done before you head down to Atlanta next week," he said to Terrell. They looked briefly at each other; then, with a brief nod, Stanton left.

After he left Terrell turned and noticed the bishop had a curious look on his face. He knew the bishop had picked up on the silent exchange between he and Stanton, yet the bishop seemed to hold his tongue. He gathered the papers on his desk where he stood. Then he tapped their edges against the cherry wood top before setting them down.

"Well? What do you think?" he finally asked before raising his hand. "Ah. I know what you think."

"You know we're going to have to go before the board with these numbers, Bishop."

Bishop Abrams gave a light smile. "Yes, I know. Come on. Walk with me to the store. I have to get some tobacco." He picked up his pipe and walked around the desk.

"I love hearing the sound of little black kids playing." The bishop spoke as
he and Terrell stepped outside into the warm evening air. Down the street the
calls and laughter of children could be heard from the nearby projects. "All that is
gonna stop soon. You know that, don't you?" He continued, "They're tearing all
this down. They've already leveled half of it."

"Yessir. I know."

"And what won't be torn down will be remodeled."

The bishop and Terrell walked down the front steps of the church and made
their way up the street past turn of the century brownstones that lined the avenues.

"The voices will change, the laughter, the music. All of that will change
when this neighborhood is re-done. They say this'll become a mixed income
neighborhood. But you know that the people who'll control most of the resources
won't be you or me." Now he walked slowly, with his hands clasped behind his
back. "And that's the reason I chose to keep the church down here. That's why I
wanted the new church built right here in The West End."

"But I agreed with you, Bishop." Terrell defended.

"I know. And thanks." The bishop smiled and patted Terrell on the
shoulder. "But you know some of the congregation wasn't too thrilled with the
idea. They wanted to move out to Forest Park." The bishop laughed. "Notice. It
was Forest Park. Not Blue Ash. Or Kenwood. They won't let too many of us out
in those parts."

"Well, you know how that is Bishop. We think moving out to Forest Park
is like we're movin' on up." Terrell heard his words and blushed slightly because
he lived not too far from Forest Park.

"The new ghettos," the bishop continued. "But they don't seem to realize that." He shook his head. "We have to sop letting them shuffle us around from place to place, Terrell. We're not on their plantations anymore." Then he paused as they arrived at the store, "Or are we?"

Terrell held the door for the elder gentleman. The Bishop and the shop owner had a friendly relationship. They chatted a bit while the proprietor rang up the tobacco. He was a short, stout man, the proprietor, with a thick moustache that spread across his face in a perpetual run as he laughed and joked with the bishop. Terrell stood by and responded with quick smiles as the two men talked.

"Well, take care Hassad," the bishop waved as he and Terrell left the store.

They walked back down the street, neither of them saying a word. Finally, Bishop Abrams spoke, "See what I mean?" he said as he stopped to tap his upturned pipe against a tree. Years ago that store was owned by a Jewish man. Mr. Feldstein. Now it's owned by an Arab." He chuckled. "They're both nice men," he continued, "But that's not the point. The point is that that store has never been owned by a black man. Even though it's sitting smack in the middle of a black neighborhood. Terrell, that's why we have to hold on to something down here. Property value is about to go up and this neighborhood is going to become hot. That's why they want us out of here; and that's just why we need to keep the church here." He shook his pipe in the air. "And that's why we need to make the new church the grandest testament to our people. And that's why I'm going to need you by my side when we go before the board."

Terrell looked at the bishop as they stood under the tree. The bishop's light complexion had taken on a sudden warmth, like the sun at dusk, and his eyes looked deep into Terrell's. Terrell answered in a slow, deliberate tone, "Bishop, you know I'll always be there for you."

Bishop Abrams laid his hand on Terrell's shoulder. "You don't know what you're getting yourself into." Then he smiled and the two of them walked back to the church.

Terrell couldn't believe what he had heard. Bishop had told him of the plans to force him into retirement. He said he had heard it through 'an unidentifiable source'. He said the letter warned that Pastor Calloway, the assistant pastor, was engineering a coup against his leadership. "The letter said there was a number of the congregation that felt 'I was too old'." He had said this with a hurt look in his eyes. "Hey, I like Mahalia, and they like Kirk. What can I say?" he had tried to joke, but the pain was there.

Terrell walked up the street to his car. His mind went over the faces of the congregation and over his years at the church. He'd been there since birth. Most of the congregation had since left and many of the older ones were departed. He couldn't believe that the church, his family, would do that to the man they dearly called Papa. Yet he had grown to never doubt the word of the man called Papa.

He got to his car and unlocked the door. He looked around at the neighborhood, the ghetto. Bishop was right. It was home.

Now, as he got into his car, he wondered what he could do to continue the bishop's vision? He wasn't sure, but he knew there must be a way. He just had to figure it out. But not at that moment. At that moment he was still slightly shaken by the revelation, and suddenly felt exhausted. Somehow God and coups didn't mix. But it wasn't about God, was it? It was about power, earthly power, the power that men seek.

He started his car and pulled away from the curb. He could use the type of easy conversation he'd gotten the other night at The Phoenix.

As he walked into the Phoenix he noticed that it was a bit more crowded

than the day before. This caused a bit of uneasiness in him. He walked to the bar
and stood behind another man who was ordering a drink. There were now two
bartenders. The one who had waited on him the day before noticed him and
smiled.

"Rum and coke?"

"Yeah." Terrell was pleased the bartender remembered him.

"Two straws." The bartender grinned as he put the drink in front of him.

Terrell paid for the drink then stepped aside to look for an empty table. As
he stood in the aisle a young man passed by him, bumping his arm and causing
him to spill a bit of his drink.

"My bad." The young man spoke as he made his way to the back.

Terrell steadied the rest of the cocktail and nodded his head.

There was a table near to where he stood that wasn't full. He glanced at it,
but wasn't sure if he should intrude in the circle of three men who sat there. But
one of them noticed him and spoke up.

"Ain't nobody sittin' here." He spoke as he pulled a chair from the table.

"Thanks," Terrell said as he sat down.

"My name's Ernest," the man said as he extended his hand. He was a stout
man in his late fifties. He wore a Kangol and glasses that sat slightly low on the
bridge of his nose.

"Terrell."

The other man extended his hand. "Derrick."

The third man also reached his hand forward. "Will."

"We were just sitting here reminiscing about in the day. You from here?"
Ernest asked. He had a matronly air.

"Yeah."

"What part?" Will asked. He, as well as Derrick, appeared to be about Terrell's age.

"Lincoln Heights."

"You from The Heights?" Ernest asked in mild disbelief. "You don't seem like you should be from there."

Terrell smiled. "Well I am... originally."

"Those niggas crazy out there," Will testified.

The other man, Derrick nodded his head in agreement as he lifted a glass of beer to his mouth. The amber liquid stood out like gold against his dark complexion.

Ernest continued. "But I guess like anyplace else you have good families and then you have... not so good families. You seem like you came from one of the good ones."

"I don't know about all that." Terrell laughed.

"Yes you do. And I can tell because you carry yourself with the kind of self esteem people from good backgrounds do." Ernest spoke with an air of expertise as he stirred his drink. "I come from a good family, so I can tell."

"Welll..."

"Shit I know I ain't from no good family," Will interrupted as he sat back in his chair. "And I ain't ashamed of it." He leaned back in his chair while reaching his hands forward to play with the sides of his glass.

Terrell noticed how red his hands were and the very light complexion; he thought of the definite white blood the man must have in his family tree.

"Me neither," Derrick boasted.

Ernest defended their shortcoming. "It's okay. We're all struggling."

"Shit, if you black, you strugglin'," Derrick said.

"Yep," Terrell agreed.

" 'ey. You know Melvin Symington?" Derrick asked as if his memory had suddenly been jarred.

Terrell squinted as he tried to recall the name. "Melvin Symington..."

"Yeah. Lil' short nigga with good hair."

"Oh yeah. I know who you're talking about. I didn't know him personally."

"I used to date his sister, Debbie. Fine ass red bone. Long, pretty hair."

"I remember her, with her fine ass self." Derrick grinned and rotated his glass on the table.

Ernest rolled his eyes. "Good hair, red bone," he mocked. "All hair is good, and everybody's complexion is beautiful."

Derrick waved his hand. "Aw man, you just jealous. 'ey, I know I'm black and got bad hair. But I admit it."

Terrell self consciously stirred his drink.

Ernest sat very erect. "Well I know I'm beautiful, and I am not like these two." He used his stirrer to point to Derrick and Will.

Terrell felt slightly embarrassed. He glanced at Will who didn't seem phased by the conversation one way or the other; instead, he was beginning to get a little high. His complexion had begun to turn ruddy and his eyes were becoming rheumy. "We're all beautiful," was all Terrell could say.

"So, Lincoln Heights, huh? I remember a little about it," Ernest continued. "The Magic Moment, Mann's Lounge," now he stirred his drink in an exaggerated fashion, "Club Ebony; Country Preacher," he leaned a bit forward and looked closely at Terrell. "And I remember people, too."

"Yeah, an' if walls could talk I bet we would hear some shit," Will said.

Ernest grinned down at his drink as if it was a pool of memories, "Mm hm."

"I didn't get around much, so I didn't know too many people," Terrell said.

"Now if I was a gossiper, I would call names. But I'm not." Ernest put his stirrer in his mouth and beamed superior. Then he plopped the stirrer back into his drink.

"Oh yeah. Lincoln Heights has changed so much from the old days," he lamented. "But I guess that's everywhere. Even downtown, here. We used to jump down here."

"I remember that," Derrick said.

"Me too," Will agreed, his words slurring.

"I know y'all do. I remember you two urchins," Ernest quipped.

Derrick grinned.

At that moment Will looked towards the bar. " 'ey. What's up?" he spoke to someone.

A man at the bar turned towards the table with a drink in his hand. "What's up?" He laughed and reached across to grasp Will's hand.

Terrell recognized the face from the party at Jerry's home.

"What's up Arthur?" Ernest greeted.

" 'sup, man." Derrick waved.

"This, uh, I'm sorry man, what's yo' name agin?" Will asked Terrell.

Arthur looked down at Terrell and smiled. "We met before. What's up?"

"Nothing much."

"I bet he remember the ol' days. Don't you man?" Will asked Arthur. "Central, The Post, Badlands..."

"Oh yeah," Arthur grinned.

Terrell knew of those bars also. Otis had taken him down on the block once when they were dating. They had gone to Central Café, and then around the corner to The Post Café. They had tried to enter Badlands, but they were carded. He recalled how, in Central Café, Otis had been able to get a drink by having an older acquaintance buy it then slip it to him. Terrell could've gotten one that night too, but he didn't drink back then. Besides, it had been hard enough to convince his father to let him go out; God knows what would've happened if he'd come home smelling like alcohol. But that was the only time he'd gone down there. He was young then, hopeful and in love. It had been a wonderful night. He'd never seen so many people, people just like himself, enjoying themselves as he had that night. They were people who laughed and spoke in strident voices instead of running in search of shadows. It was a night he would always remember.

But that had been the last time he was there, because not long after that night his world began to collapse.

"...Yeah but he wasn't no urchin," Ernest continued, speaking of Arthur.

Derrick pulled his beer from his mouth. "Man, you keep callin' us urchins. What's a urchin anyway?"

Ernest smiled and looked at Terrell. "You tell 'em."

Terrell grinned. "An urchin is a kid of the streets. Usually they're orphans; but hey, he said it, I didn't."

Derrick's eyes widened from disbelief. "I got a momma."

"Well y'all didn't act like it."

"Ma-a-an..."

"You didn't. Young boys hangin' round bars tryin' to run games and take advantage of people."

"We wasn't no boys. Shit we was teenagers, wasn't we Art?"

"Like I said, 'boys'. And don't try to pull Arthur into this, because he wasn't like the rest of you."

Terrell and Arthur laughed.

"Well shit, y'all didn't have to deal wit' us," Derrick challenged.

Ernest pointed his stirrer "*Y'all* didn't deal with you. Maybe some of those other girls did, but I wasn't tempted by you bucks."

"Well you used to give me money."

"That's because I thought you were cute. But I didn't want to have you." Then he looked at Derrick and gave a wry grin, "And you still are," he said through puckered lips.

Everyone at the table broke out laughing.

"You silly, man..." Derrick blushed.

It was hours later and several rounds passed when Terrell prepared to leave.

"So soon?" Ernest asked.

"Yeah. I have to head on in. I have a phone call to make and get ready for work tomorrow."

"Yeah, I gotta get to work too," Arthur said as he put his empty glass on the table.

"Aw, that's too bad. And just when the fun was starting," Ernest said.

Derrick agreed, "Yeah."

"Well it was nice meeting you Terrell. And I hope to see you again." Ernest shook Terrell's hand.

"You will."

"Same here," Derrick said with a wave.

Will was nodding out.

"And you take care too Art," Ernest said.

THIS PLACE OF MEN

Derrick nodded in agreement.

"A'ight," Arthur said. "Y'all take it slow. Oh, and tell Will, too."

Terrell and Arthur stepped outside of the bar and stood under the glowing
sign.

"Good to see you again, man." Arthur said as he shook Terrell's hand.

"You too. You need a lift?"

"Well, yeah, if you headin' towards Evanston."

"I can drop you off. C'mon."

"I didn't expect to see you again after the way you left outta Jerry's," Arthur
spoke as they got in the car.

"Yeah. Well I wasn't expecting anything like that."

"Stanton shoulda told you."

"Does that kind of stuff go on all the time?"

"Nah, not all the time. And they pretty cool people. Jerry, Stanton and all
a'dem."

Terrell turned onto Gilbert Avenue and headed north. "How long have you
been going over there?"

"A long time."

"... How long?"

"... Since I was young."

They drove on a bit.

"It ain't like they doin' something wrong," Arthur defended. "I mean, it
ain't like they messin' around with little kids or nothin'. I wouldn't be hangin'
around 'em if that was happenin'."

"I don't know. There's still something wrong with it."

"Like what?"

"Well for one, most of 'em are probably married."

"How you know? I'm not. And Stanton ain't."

"But Jerry is. And I bet some of the other ones are too."

"You ain't stopped to think that maybe some of their wives might know."

"What?"

"Jerry's wife knows. She gay too."

For a moment Terrell was speechless. Then, "Does she live there?"

"Sometime."

Terrell slowly shook his head. "That's wrong, man. They got any kids?"

"Yeah. But they grown."

"I wonder where their heads are," Terrell tsked.

"I dunno, but Jerry seems fine and so do his wife. I'm sure if the children was fucked up, then him and his wife wouldn't be so at ease, y'know."

"Their kids probably don't know."

"I don't know." Then he looked over at Terrell. "But that's a lotta supposin' you doin'."

Terrell reached down and pushed a button on the stereo, changing from a CD, to the radio.

"Who was that you was playin' before?"

"Some guy named Ismael Lo. He's from Senegal."

"Where's that?"

"West Africa. I collect African music."

Arthur nodded his head, "He sounded pretty smooth. Mellow."

"You wanna hear it?"

"Yeah."

Terrell pushed the controls again and brought the CD back on. The mellow

strains of Ismael Lo's acoustic guitar and his soft tenor voice rose in the car.

"That is so smooth," Arthur smiled.

After a while, Terrell spoke. "So what keeps you going back there?"

Arthur paused a bit before speaking. " 'cause they my friends. I been

knowin' 'em for a long time and they always been there for me." He looked at

Terrell. "I don't know if you ever needed somebody to talk to, but I did. And

they was there." He paused again before continuing, "I had it rough, man. All my

life I had it rough. My momma died when I was little and my daddy had to raise

all of us by hisself. And that's hard to do when you got five kids, all boys. We all

worked a lot to get through but you know how it is. Eventually, some of my

brothers got caught up in the streets so it was mostly me'n my father tryin' to hold

things together for the younger ones. That shit's tough on a young boy, y'know.

As I got older I knew that I was - - you know, I was different, and I needed some

people to connect to. And that's where they came in. And it's been like that ever

since."

"Does your father know you're gay?"

"I'm sure he do by now. He ain't in his right mind though. Got

alzheimer's. But I'm sure he did before he got sick. All my brothers do too, but

we just don't talk about it. They see me come 'n go an' that's just the way it is."

He turned quietly and looked out the windshield.

Terrell pulled up to Arthur's house.

"Thanks for the ride, man," Arthur said. "I gotta git in here an' make sure

my father ate right today." He got out of the car and leaned forward into the

cabin. "Let me give you my number so we can keep in touch."

Terrell gave him a pen paper on which he scratched down his number.

"Call me anytime."

"Alright."

Arthur stood to walk away but again leaned back down to the window.

"They good people, man. They the one's got me my job down at Cinergy."

"I'm sure they are." Terrell said.

"And Terrell, man. It's deeper than you think."

Chapter XVII

It was dark by the time Otis made it back to Courtney's apartment. He had been to visit his parents. He had also stopped by to see Miss Susie once again. He had hoped maybe she would inform him of how to get close to the distant young man who was his son, but she was just as elusive as before. After he left her house he had walked backed to his parents' house and spent more time with them and Munny.

Munny had been her usual self, quiet and accommodating to everyone's needs. Once he even had to put his hand on her shoulder to detain her just so he could get his mother her reading glasses. She was the image of a spinster living at home with her parents. She was approaching middle age and was still romantically alone. But she didn't appear to be lonely. Never once to Otis' memory had his sister dated, nor did it seem to be that important of a matter; so everyone learned long ago to understand this nice silent china doll as simply their sister and their daughter.

The evening had been just like old times. His father had moved to his favorite easy chair and his mother to her favorite spot on the couch with her legs curled and her feet tucked underneath her. She had always sat like that so her body experienced little strain in her older age to still curl in that comfortable position.

Otis had sat in one of the high back chairs while Munny silently sat at her mother's feet at the opposite end of the couch. It had been a beautiful evening of family discussion, some gossip and most of all, lots of laughter.

Now, as he came through the door of Courtney's apartment he saw her rushing down the hall towards her bedroom. The air was filled with vibrant fragrances that rose from the bathroom.

"Where you goin'?" He asked.

Courtney came back from her bedroom. She was in a robe; and on one arm was draped a pair of dress slacks while in her hand she held a blouse. "Out."

"You ain't asked me."

"Shooo'! I'm grown." She flicked her hand palm forward and snaked her neck. Then she tossed her blouse to her brother. "Iron this for me." She then turned and hurried back to the bathroom.

"So who is he?" Otis asked as he set up the ironing board.

"His name is Kelly." She was calling from the bathroom where she had left the door open.

He could tell by her voice that she was peering into the mirror applying her make-up.

"Kelly. I haven't heard you talk about him."

"That's because I haven't. We've known each other for about three years now. We used to work together."

"Oh." He began to iron the soft silk blouse, making sure the temperature was right. "Is he your boyfriend?"

"No." She stuck her head around the corner. "Now do you think you would have been here all this time without having met my boyfriend if I had one?"

"He must be takin' you out to a nice place."

"To a movie and then to dinner. We're going with some friends."

"What 'chall goin' to see?"

"I dunno. It really doesn't matter." She called back, again from in front of the mirror.

"As long as you see him, huh?"

"Yeah. I guess so." She mumbled her reply.

"So he is your boyfriend then."

"No." She was now rushing back to her bedroom.

"How come?"

"Because he just isn't." They were now calling back and forth to each other.

Otis finished ironing the blouse. "I'm comin' back. You decent?"

"Come on." She stuck her hand around the half closed door and took the blouse from his hand. "Thanks."

Otis stood outside the door and continued his conversation. "So you were bein' nosey about me, what about you and... Kelly?"

"What about us?"

"How close is he?"

"If you mean, do we spend the nights together, no." She opened the door and adjusted her blouse. "Because that's a special thing. And we decided that we would take our time before we committed that much. And besides, I don't sleep around."

"Well, that's not where I was goin' with that. But still, watch your heart."

"I do. I guess that's why I'm not in a committed relationship." Then she stopped for a second. "Do you hear us? Do we sound paranoid?"

"Nah, I don't think so. You can really get hurt if you open yourself up too much."

"Yeah, I guess so. But I also know you have to take chances."

"Just know when to slack up."

Courtney chuckled, "Okay."

As Courtney left, Otis stood on the balcony and watched she and Kelly drive off. Her friend seemed like a nice enough guy; but still, Otis felt uneasy. There were so many ways for a person to get hurt.

He walked back to the living room and turned on the T.V. He watched it for a while until his mind began to lose contact with the story on the screen, the carved faces, the mundane plot. He really wasn't there that night. He was somewhere else. He needed to be somewhere else. He turned off the television and walked back onto the balcony. He stood with his hands in his pockets and looked out over the street. The night had lowered itself like a blanket over Bond Hill. The light from the houses below lined the avenue like a necklace and the street lamps glowed like breaks in the night.

He was aware that he wasn't home. The journey back to Cincinnati had been necessary. It was a journey twenty years in the making, but now it was time to go home. He had walked the streets that once knew his name, had spoken to faces that remembered him; but those streets and those faces were no longer a part of his life. Cincinnati used to be his home, but now home was New York, and he had to return there. The next morning he would call his job. But tonight he would have to make some decisions.

Chapter XVIII

"Antonio?" His mother's eyes were wide with shock.

"Who?" His father asked.

"Antonio," she said, "Antonio."

"Who's that?"

"Susie's boy."

"That nigga? He ain't none 'a my grandson!" His father reared back in his chair.

Otis took it all in; his mother sat, her head moving, making tiny circles as she tried to absorb the message. Across the table from her, Courtney reached and held her hand (that was why she wanted to accompany Otis when he broke the news), while Munny stood in the corner huddled safely against the refrigerator unsure of the role she should assume and unsure of what her thoughts should be.

His father continued his tirade, waving a large finger through the air. "That boy ain't no grandson 'a mine."

"How can you say that?" Otis demanded.

" 'Cause he ain't, that's how."

His mother turned to his father. "Stop it Clarence. Now just stop it."

"I'll be damned if I'm 'a claim him. I'll be damned!" His father yelled and slapped the table so hard that the salt and pepper shakers leapt and landed on their sides. Then he jumped to his feet and stormed out of the room.

Otis' mother called after him, but he didn't answer.

A silence fell over the kitchen after his father left. It wasn't the kind of silence in which shame is held, suspended, rather it was the kind of silence in which thoughts conjugate and resolution is borne.

"Antonio," his mother softly repeated, this time her voice seeded with resolve.

Courtney nodded assurance, her hand still atop her mother's.

Then his mother smiled, and the smile turned into a giggle. "Me an' Susie sharin' a family. Almost related."

But in a fading moment her smile began to dissipate and her eyes dimmed. "And she never told me." Looking over at Otis, "How can I ever trust her again?"

A voice came from the corner of the kitchen. "Maybe she didn't want to hurt you." Munny stood in the shadow of the corner her eyes querying her own reply.

"I think Munny's right, Ma," Courtney said. "I don't think she was being malicious, just safe."

Their mother sat for a while before letting out a heavy sigh. "Yeah, I guess so. She has been a good friend. And you're both right, she wouldn't do anything to intentionally hurt me."

Otis added his sentiment. "She just did somethin' stupid, that's all."

Courtney shot him a disapproving glance before turning back to her mother. "Besides, it took two to make it happen," she added.

"Let me go and talk to your father," their mother said as she started to get up. But Otis stopped her.

"Ma, let me talk to him."

"No, no. You two'll just end up arguin'."

"Maybe that's what they need to do," Courtney assisted.

Otis got up and left the kitchen.

"Don't y'all start arguin'," his mother called after him.

Otis walked out onto the porch where his father sat looking at his folded hands as if he was trying to divine an answer from them.

"We gotta talk." Otis spoke as he stepped out onto the small porch that sat just two steps above the yard.

"We ain't gotta do nothin'," his father pouted. He continued to look down at his hands. "I'm tired of it all," he said.

"Tired?" Otis sat on the railing. "You ain't gotta do nothin'. I'm the one who gotta deal with this, not you." He paused and shook his head, "But I'll tell you what I am tired of; you pushin' me away whenever somethin' comes up you don't like."

His father looked over at him. His eyes seared with anger. "I ain't never pushed you away."

"What is it about Antonio you don't like?" Otis spoke calmly.

"He ain't my grandson. That's all."

"Yes he is."

A moment passed before his father spoke. "He- - he's just part of that crazy ass Susie. Sitting up there in the dark all the time, actin' all weird."

"That's Miss Susie. You shouldn't take it out on him."

"You ever see the way he look at you? Just somethin' mean and sneaky about him."

"Daddy..."

"And he used to look... dusty all the time."

Otis turned his head; he was tired of the same old episodes with his father. He saw two boys walking down the street. They kicked at tiny rocks creating a clacking sound. The image reminded him of better times. Then he turned back to his father. "How come you gotta respond like a child to things that bother you?"

His father raised his hand and pointed at him. "I raised a family. Can't no goddamn child raise a family. You would know that if you didn't do so much runnin' yo'self. So don't try that shit with me boy!" He turned his head from Otis. He spoke in a low voice, "How come you can't be responsible? Just for once."

Leaning towards his father, Otis spoke through clenched teeth. "That was almost twenty years ago. All of it. And I been responsible for everything that happened since. And what do you think I'm doin'? Walkin' away from the situation?"

"If you had 'a stayed around you woulda known what had happened, but you way up there in New York hidin' from everybody."

"And what difference would it have made on your part, Daddy? If you don't like the boy now, would you have felt any different then? Nah, you wouldn't."

His father continued, looking Otis dead in the eyes. "You left with trouble and now, here you come years later still with trouble."

At his father's words, Otis jumped up. "Hey, you don't have to worry about it. I'll be gone in a few. I'll make damn sure I'm gone." He stepped down into the yard, then turned back to his father.

"You know, all you need to do is show Antonio some love. That's all. I ain't askin' you to take care of him. I can do that. Hell, he's almost a man. He can take care of hisself. But all I'm askin' is that you show him some love, and if you can't do that then you need to search yo'self because Antonio ain't the problem. You are."

He didn't wait for a reply from his father. He got in his car and drove away.

* * * *

An evening rain had come and wet the streets. Otis left the bar to which he had gone after leaving his parents' house. He wanted to wash his thoughts away with the liquid he rolled down his throat, but he knew what could happen if he drank too much. Actually, it was the fact that he didn't know what could happen that kept him sober; and he needed to be sober, to be without the visions, so he could take care of his affairs.

He drove to Antonio's apartment. There was a light on in the apartment so he got out of his car and went up to the front door of the building.

The rain had created a mist that gathered in the dark courtyard and played against his face as he approached the door.

When he got to Antonio's apartment he heard the radio playing but heard no sign of movement. He assumed Antonio wasn't there and that he kept the radio on to keep burglars away, or maybe to dispel Miss Susie's spirit.

He knocked but no one answered. He looked at his watch; it was almost nine thirty. He didn't want to wait around for long because he wanted to go back to Courtney's apartment. She had called him twice since he left his parents' home, but he didn't answer her calls.

He walked down the long hallway from the apartment and down the stairs.

As he walked through the courtyard he heard Antonio's voice. Then he saw him standing outside a car, the door open, talking to the driver. It was a big car, long and white and sleek. Otis couldn't see the driver's face because Antonio stood in the way.

Antonio said his goodbyes and shut the car door, then the car moved on into the lights of the city.

" 'ey, what's up?" Antonio said as he spotted Otis. "I thought I saw yo' car."

"Just stopped by to see you, since you ain't called me."

"Antonio let out a small laugh. The smell of alcohol rose on his breath. "Yeah..." was his only reply.

"I thought you was supposed to call me?"

"Why? You know where I live."

Otis stiffened. "What's this sudden change, man?"

"What sudden change? I'm the same me. I ain't changed none."

Otis sucked his teeth. "Look, I thought we could see a lot of each other before I went back."

Antonio shook his head. "Man, you got me fucked up. 'Before you go back'. Listen to you. I ain't goin' back with you, am I?"

Otis didn't respond.

"Like I said, you got me fucked up," Antonio repeated as he started past his father.

"I want to get to know you," Otis said.

"What, you wanna certify me or some shit?" Antonio stood facing Otis, his eyes wide. "How you sound?" Then he turned and walked to the courtyard. Then, turning back to his father, "Have you told 'em about me?"

"Yeah."

"I bet they was happy to hear that bit of news." Then he continued on into the courtyard.

Chapter XIX

"What's up?"

"I was sleepin'. What time is it?"

"I don't know... 'bout three."

"You okay?"

"Yeah."

"You sound kinda down. You sure you okay?"

"Mm hnh. 'ey, I just wanted t'say I'm sorry 'bout the way I talked to you the other night. I don't know, I was trippin'."

"That's okay. I figured that's all it was."

"Love and pain. It's crazy, y'know?"

"I know. Look, maybe we can hook up later on tomorrow."

"...I don't know... I think I wanna move slow on all this."

"... Okay."

"But I'll be callin' though."

"A'ight. Now you need to get you some sleep."

"I will. 'ey."

"Huh?"

"Would you stay a little longer if I asked you to?"

"Yeah."

"Oh."

"Goodnight."

"Goodnight, Daddy."

'Daddy.' It was more than a word. Given the tongue that speaks it, it becomes an invocation, a moment of definition; and for Otis, the morning Antonio spoke the word had been a defining moment.

To go from being unaware of his son's existence to being called Daddy was amazing even for one such as Otis, who had lived so many cold, cold years alone, locked in the gray silence that had settled in his heart.

But now he sat on the balcony in his robe and watched the orange sky of a new day. There was dawning within him a reason to do more than merely exist on the salt of bitterness; there had come to him thoughts that were light and open, consideration of things new and of possibilities borne of hope instead of maneuvers borne of desperation. There was now purpose.

He understood Antonio's confusion about wanting to get close to him. It wasn't about hatred, but of fear. Distrust and fear. He understood because he knew those feelings firsthand.

But all the feelings of fear and distrust had to be conquered because the both of them had to find new ways of seeing things and new ways of being. It was the only way they would be able to come together.

* * * *

A few days passed before Antonio called again. He had asked Otis to meet him downtown at Lytle Park. He had also suggested that Otis 'dress up a bit'.

"Dress up? Why?"

"It's a surprise. But don't dress up too much 'cause I ain't got no *real* dressy stuff."

It was warm the evening he went to meet his son. The hard shadows of the day had begun to soften under the retiring sun as Otis rolled up to the park. He saw Antonio sitting on a bench. His neck was bent and he rested his elbows on his knees. There in the waning light he appeared as if he was in prayer.

Otis slowed the car and let it drift to a stop, to do otherwise: to brake hard or to blow the horn would seem obscene for such a tranquil moment.

Antonio looked up and noticed the car; a slice of a smile crossed his face.

" 'ey," he greeted as he rose from the bench. He had on a pair of oversized jeans and an equally oversized shirt and his hair had been freshly braided. Otis nodded slightly as he appreciated his son's handsomeness.

"Lookin' good kid," Otis complimented as his son slid into the passenger seat.

"Thanks. You too."

"Thanks." Otis had on slacks and a white cotton dress shirt.

"But you almost got too dressy. A tie and you woulda overdid it." Antonio warned.

"Well, you know... I'm from the ol' school."

Antonio laughed and nodded in agreement.

"Now. Where to?" Otis asked.

"I was thinkin' a movie then we can get somethin' to eat."

"Okay."

After they left the movie, they headed along the riverfront to a restaurant.

" 'tonio you sure you can afford this? Otis looked up at the restaurant that sat atop a hotel.

"Don't worry man. I got it," Antonio assured.

"At least let me help out a little."

"A little is too much. I wanna treat you."

Otis sighed. "Okay."

"Besides, I always wanted to go up to that restaurant. It revolves, y'know."

"Yeah, I remember when they built it."

"That long ago, huh?" Antonio looked sideways at him.

"Yeah. And we both still standin'."

They lauged and got out of the car.

There were a few other people on the elevator as they went up to the restaurant. They were all well dressed in suits and ties, the ladies in nice after five outfits. Antonio stood to one side of the car; he kept his eyes on the lighting numbers as they announced each floor, and at his sides his arms hung loosely, but his hands were working feverishly as he rubbed his fingertips nervously together. He was new in the world. He had never been beyond the world of black blue collar except as servant, but never as peer. Or at least in an attempt to be.

Otis picked up on his discomfort and shifted his body, letting his hand bump against his son's; but he made it appear accidental. It worked. The contact of his hand eased Antonio's tension. They looked at each other and smiled. Otis was glad to be there for him.

Chapter XX

"It's deeper than you think." That was the warning Arthur had given him; and now those very words moved in his head as he sat in church and watched Stanton work the congregation.

The bishop had invited Stanton to speak that Sunday to get his campaign off the ground, and he did it in inimitable style. The sanctuary was filled to the rafters and heads nodded to the words of the large man in the pulpit.

Behind him, the figures of the bishop and Pastor Calloway seemed to shrink almost to the point of invisibility as the towering presence of Stanton took center stage.

Leaning on the podium he reminisced of days gone by, of the days when black folks were self-reliant; and from there he explained the dynamics of deprivation, lingering at times on the pain that black folks experienced, and then, with a thrust of his hands, admonished the power mongers who wished to keep the status quo. All the while he extolled the virtues of his plan to liberate his brothers and sisters- - God's children- - from the throes of the enemy.

Terrell sat through as much of the speech as he could endure, but soon the scene became too much for him, so he stepped outside to get some air, leaving behind him the sea of plumed hats and hands waving like hydra.

On the steps of the church, Terrell gripped his bible as he wondered how someone as sleazy as Stanton could have maneuvered his way to the pulpit of Savior's Temple.

Maybe the talk around church was right, he thought, maybe Bishop Abrams *was* becoming too feeble to lead his flock. To have Stanton up in the pulpit, up there with the righteous, instead of down front of the congregation did indeed wax of feeblemindness.

But there was nothing he could do about it, nor had he a desire to because he was beginning to let go of some of his responsibilities to the church.

This change of attitude bothered his wife as well as some members of the church, but his feelings were honest and he was at a time in his life when honesty and truth seemed to seep into his every thought and were beginning to affect much of his reasoning. He had not voiced his decision to relinquish any of his responsibilities; in fact, he had barely made a decision at all. It was something that was just happening, a series of subtle changes in his character that had come as silent as the changing light of a day; and it was something that caused his interest in his church to fall like petals upon the ground.

So now, under the governance of truth he stood on the steps of Savior's Temple, his beloved home, with his back to the calls of the congregation, and faced the silent street where nothing moved in the afternoon sun.

That night the stillness remained; it had held since that afternoon, on through the evening, and on through dinner at the bishop's home where he had watched the talking heads of the distinguished guests. He had watched them as they mouthed words that were unintelligible to him, made so by a deepening disinterest in their conversation.

Whereas before the stillness had presented a sense of wonder, then as a respite from the talking heads, it now brought about a sense of anxiety; instead of calm it now seemed like the frozen moment that occurs between events, like the moment before the insane steps off the ledge, or the moment before a victim's breath is snatched away. It was a moment that seemed to preclude a horrible act, but just how horrible the act, he could not say; nor could he even imagine just what the act might be. But it was there, this act; and it was assembling itself, taking joints and extensions to form arms and hands with which to manipulate moments in order to create an event, a singular decisive event.

For Terrell though, his awareness was only of the space created by the act and in that space was the stillness, and the anxiety.

And it was the anxiety, that unconscious anticipation of an unprepared moment that caused him to search for some type of comfort as a relief from the tension; even if only to return the stillness to its sense of wonder.

It was what he had tried to do earlier when he had called down to Atlanta, and later, when he had read his bible. But he had come to realize that what he needed most was the voice of someone who might understand him, so he picked up the phone and placed a call then he waited for Arthur to answer.

Chapter XXI

Otis awoke with a jolt. Again, it was the dream. Always, it was the dream. Sometimes it came in full, like an ocean; while other times it presented itself in portions. Small, filling portions. But always, it was there. That night he recalled the holding cell where he had sat with two other men while they awaited their trials.

He had been given what was to him an odd request that he dress up in order to go before the judge. It had been agreed that there would be no need for a trial, only sentencing, so he had found it stupid to dress up for his own funeral. But his parents had followed the advice of his attorney; so he sat in the cell in a pair of tan dress khakis and a crisp white shirt that had been starched as if the laundering had been the last act of love his mother had been able to give him. The shirt had been his, but he wasn't sure where the khakis had come from. He had sat on a hard chair and looked at his wrists. They appeared strong and elegant next to the starched white cotton and beneath the chrome handcuffs. At times he would flex them and imagine the cuffs breaking, the nightmare ending. But it didn't.

The bailiff, a middle-aged man with salt and pepper hair, looked over at him. His steely blue eyes and angular jaw seemed to tweak from the satisfaction he got from his job. He walked over to Otis and lifted his elbow. C'mon. You're up."

Otis got to his feet and walked alongside the bailiff who led him to the courtroom.

The room felt like a circus and he was the animal to be tamed. He felt ashamed as he walked across the floor under the lights and the eyes of onlookers. He looked over the observers until he spotted his parents. His mother sat limp, her eyes were red while his father sat stiff, his arm around his mother's shoulders, and glared at him.

A bit away from his parents two men caught his eye. One man, a tall very light skinned man sat motionless. He wore a clerical collar and his face had an expression of pity. But the other man, the one with the caramel complexion and the features similar to Terrell's glared at him with an anger that surpassed his father's.

Otis' attorney pressed down on his shoulder and seated him, and it was then, facing the bench that he noticed the judge had no face. Where there should have been a nose, a mouth and eyes was only pink flesh. He felt a great fear come over him as the judge cocked his head to one side and from the face without eyes or mouth, seemed to grin lasciviously at him.

That was when he awoke from the dream. He lay in bed and felt his heart pounding. From Courtney's room he heard her move in bed. It had been the dream, but now he was safe.

Someone had suggested once that he record his dreams so he could look at them in the light of day, and that that might help him overcome them. As usual, he hadn't taken the advice, but now, maybe he would. So there, in the dark he went over the dream image by image until he had recalled the whole thing.

But something else came to him during his reflection. The two men. He was sure one of them had been Terrell's father; but the other one, had that been Terrell's pastor? And if so, he was sure he had seen his face somewhere else.

He got up early the next morning. He wanted to see Courtney before she left for work.

He walked into the kitchen where she was eating a bowl of cereal.

"Mornin'."

"Morning. You're up early."

"Yeah. I wanted to see you before you left for work." He pulled out a chair and sat. "I'll be heading back next week."

Courtney set her spoon down in the bowl. "I kind of figured that. There's only so much you can do." Then she looked closely at him. "You sure you've done what needs to be done?"

"For the most part, yeah."

"That doesn't sound too promising."

"I got more ahead of me than what I left behind. And like you said, I can only do so much."

"Yeah. You can't get too caught up in the past. Have you let Momma know?"

Otis shook his head. "Nah. I just decided last night." He clasped his hands. "It's gonna be hard leaving her again."

"Putting it that way gives it all some hope. At least it sounds like you won't be gone for good."

"Nah."

Courtney smiled, "I bet Dana's gonna clock when she hears this."

Otis waved his hand, "Fuck Dana."

"Well that's what I say too."

She picked up her spoon and held it, empty before her. "I'm going to miss you." She put the spoon back in the bowl. "It seems like just when I start to get to know you, you up and leave."

Otis slowly nodded his head. "Yeah. But don't think of it like that this time, because I won't be out of reach. And of course you can visit any time you want."

"I better have that kind of invitation." She got up and took the bowl over to the sink. "You know it's just that for once I had somebody to talk to." She put the dishes in the sink. "You can't talk to Momma and Daddy about some things," she turned back to Otis, "And Jun, well he's so much older and he's gone on with his family; Dana's too judgmental, and Munny, well you know how she is- - as long as everybody's happy she's fine with it."

She came back and sat across from her brother. "All the time you were away? I always felt I knew you. I couldn't remember you; but from hearing all the stories about you when you were growing up I came to feel like you were somebody I could relate to. That's why I always kept in touch with you."

Otis smiled. He put his hand on hers. "I didn't know that."

She nodded.

"Well that means even more that you should come on up to visit me. But I'm gonna tell you, in the meantime you should find yourself a good friend to talk to. We can always use that, maybe even two of 'em."

"I guess... I just don't feel comfortable talking with too many people."

"It wouldn't be too many, just that one close friend, like a brother." He looked at her for a moment then squeezed her hand. "And I'll be that brother, okay?"

Courtney smiled, "Okay. But get ready, because I got a lot to share."

"Hey, call me; come on up."

"Yeah," she said.

"By the way, that Kelly seems like a nice guy; and a cutie too."

"I know. We have nice times, but I think he wants to get serious now."

"And you're not ready, right?"

"Right. See I told you we have a lot in common."

She looked at her watch, "Oh shoot. I better get out of here. Talk to you later." She grabbed her clutch and rushed out the door.

* * * *

His mother was in her garden when he arrived later that morning. He saw her through the back door as he walked into the kitchen. She was bent over a row of kale with a sprayer.

He called her before coming to the door so he wouldn't startle her.

"What's up?" He greeted cheerfully.

"Hi baby." She raised a cheek for him to kiss. "Tendin' this garden. Lord, if these damn bugs don't leave my garden alone..."

"You still at it with bugs?"

"When they messin' with my garden I am."

He watched as she sprayed the plants. She never liked bugs.

It would be hard telling her he was leaving. "Let me do it." He took the can from her and began to wet the leaves with the fine mist.

His mother picked up the hoe and continued the turning she'd begun earlier.

"You up mighty early," she said as the steel blade tore through the soil.

"Yes ma'am. I got tired of just lyin' around."

"I guess so when you use to doin' somethin'."

Otis stepped over a few heads of greens in search of more bugs.

His mother spoke as she continued to hoe. "You visit any of your old friends?"

"No ma'am."

"You should."

"I don't know... it's been so long."

"Sounds like a good reason to visit 'em, don't it?"

Otis didn't answer.

"Miss Susie said y'all had a nice time the other day," his mother said.

"We did. Surprisingly. I guess I'm older now so I can see her more than just a crazy ol' woman."

"She's a good person. Got a lotta wisdom."

"And experience. You know she used to live in New York?"

"No."

"You shoulda seen her face when me and her was tradin' stories."

His mother chuckled, "I bet she had some good ones. Is that why you asked for her number last night?"

He hesitated before answering, "Mm hm."

Leaning a bit forward, his mother narrowed her eyes. "It's dry," she said as she inspected the soil. "See how light and powdery it is?"

Otis looked over at the spot to which she pointed. "Yeah, it is. I'll get the water hose." Otis took the hose and walked past his mother where he began wetting the soil she had already tended.

"Ma?"

"Hm?"

"I'll probably be goin' back next week."

"I know." She spoke without looking his way. "I figured that's why you came here so early. I'm gonna miss you."

"I won't be gone long this time."

His mother continued chopping at the soil.

"I'll be visitin' all the time," he continued.

"I hope so." She stopped her chore and looked at him. "I don't wanna have to think it's gonna take another twenty years to see you."

Otis smiled. "Nah. Everything's different now."

"I'm glad to hear that. Now finish with that waterin' so we can sit and talk."

Otis and his mother sat at the kitchen table of the sun filled kitchen. "What about Antonio?" she asked. "You just now startin' to get to know your own son. Don't that bother you to be leavin' him so soon?" Otis' mother sipped a cup of coffee.

"Yes ma'am, it does. It's something we'll have to work out."

His mother nodded her head in a non-committal manner.

"Hey ma. How do you feel about Antonio?"

"Oh I never had much of a problem with him. He was kinda bad when he was growin' up, but most boys are. More than anything though, I always felt a bit sorry for him. He had no business growin' up in a house like that. Alone. No brothers or sisters to talk to. And that Susie," she shook her head, "She had him all wrapped up in that weird world of hers. Wonder if the boy didn't go crazy."

Otis looked down at the cup in front of him. "Yeah."

"But she took good care of him. Dressed him real nice and made sure he never went hungry or anything like that, but..."

"I know."

"The boy was angry," his mother continued. She looked over at her son. "Is he still angry?"

"He deals with it."

"I hope so."

"One thing he does need though is to know he has a family here in this house who will love him. It's important to him. He's never felt like he ever belonged anywhere but in that messed up world of his mother's."

His mother sighed. "I'm workin' on all that. Been talkin' to your father 'bout his attitude. Everybody else seems fine."

"See if you can get Daddy to change his mind. Antonio don't need to be walking into a house with a lotta bad vibes."

"Your father'll come around. He always does." She paused. "Now how about you? Where will you be?"

"I'm gonna be there for him and everybody else."

Purpose.

"That's good to hear. Now I'm gonna hold you to that."

"Yes ma'am."

"Now what about that other boy?"

"Other boy?"

"The one from long time ago."

"Terrell?" Otis stood at the kitchen sink and washed his hands.

"The one who was part of all that mess. Have you seen him?"

"Terrell. No ma'am."

"Good. 'Cause it might bring back bad feelings." She took another sip of coffee. "But if you feel you have to see him, to talk to him, then you should."

"I haven't quite decided," Otis said as he dried his hands.

His mother sat her cup down. "Now I find that hard to believe. You done had almost twenty years to decide."

"I know. But I don't know how I might feel if we come face to face."

"I'm sure you two will be fine. Both of you are older now. You gonna act like two grown men and talk it out."

"It ain't that easy."

"It should be."

"Why do you say that?" he asked as he poured himself a cup of coffee.

"Because the situation is pretty much over."

Otis walked to the kitchen table and sat across from his mother. "Over, huh?"

"Mm, hmh. What's done is done."

All is as it should be. He had read that somewhere once. It was in a book he'd gotten from the library while in prison. He never thought he would remember anything from the book, but he did now.

"So now y'all, you and Terrell, are closin' chapters. Ain't no need to get riled up when you closin' chapters because then you can go on to the next chapter."

With the closing of one door comes the opening of another. Otis nodded his head. "Yes ma'am."

"But you gotta make sure you really closin' the chapter. So if it takes seein' Terrell to close it, then go and see him."

Otis grinned and leaned across the table and kissed his mother. "Ooo. My momma so smart."

"I thought you knew that."

"I always did," he nodded.

* * * *

After Otis left his mother he headed up to Mt. Auburn.

Charles was already home when he arrived. He was washing his truck in front of his house.

Looking at Charles, Otis noticed his husky form as it strained to reach down to wash a lower panel of the truck. He realized how alone Charles seemed. He never spoke about knowing many people, or hardly of anyone; he never spoke of friends or family, only of Shirley.

"What's up, Big Poppa?" Otis greeted as he got out of the car.

" 'ey, what's up?" Charles answered through huffing breaths. Beads of sweat crowded his forehead.

"Look like you havin' problems reachin' that lower panel."

"Yeah man," he blew. "This shit is gettin' rough."

"Gotta lose some of that stomach, man. You ain't gonna be catchin' no criminals like that." Otis picked up a cloth and began assisting his friend. "Damn, I stopped by to see my mother and ended up helpin' her in her garden, and now I'm helpin' you wash your car."

"So you makin' the rounds today, huh?"

"Yeah."

"Well thanks for helpin' me out."

"No problem. The reason I'm makin' my rounds today is because I decided to head on back, next week," Otis said as he slung a soap filled rag against the hood of the SUV.

"Yeah?"

"Yeah."

"So you made that call, huh?"

"Yeah. Like y'all was sayin', I can't risk blowin' everything."

"Nah man, that wouldn't make no sense."

They washed the truck for a while, neither of them saying a word.

After a while, Charles continued. "Nah, 'cause none of us are gettin' any younger."

When they finished, they drove across the river to Devou Park where they found a nice spot on a bench. The Cincinnati skyline loomed just beyond the park like a giant peering over the horizon.

"You finished with your business?" Charles asked as he looked across the river at the gleaming buildings.

Otis nodded his head. "Yeah." Then he turned and looked at Charles. "No."

Charles gave him a questioning look.

"Man, I think I have a son."

Charles looked at him with raised brow. "What, you just finding out about him?"

Otis nodded. "Yeah."

"Damn." Charles scratched his head. "How do you know?"

"I don't know for certain, but I'm pretty sure."

"I think you'd better make damn sho', bruh."

"I know. But man, you gotta see him. He looks just like me."

Charles chuckled, "Man we *all* look alike. Don't you know that?" Then he became more settled. "So what makes you think he's yours?"

"I saw his mother and it's like she just kept pushin' him on me. Been keeping him up on me all the years I been away, and promising him I was gonna come back for him."

Charles shook his head. "That don't mean shit." He looked back at the skyline. "So you slept with her, huh?"

"Yeah."

"Mmh."

"Charles, man, I know he's mine."

"How many more do you have?" Charles spoke while still looking out across the park. His words were tinged with bitterness.

"None."

Now he turned to Otis. "None that you know of."

Otis looked at him. He was unprepared for Charles' reaction.

Charles turned to him again. "I don't know why I'm bothered by your little disclosure. I guess I just thought I knew you."

"What are you talking about? You do know me."

"And I guess now you're thinking 'and what difference does it make?'"

Otis didn't respond.

"It doesn't," Charles sniffed. "It really doesn't." But it did; something deep inside him had allowed him to feel that Otis belonged to him. His thinking had warned him that such a thought was foolish, but his emotions had told him otherwise. For so many years he had felt alone, unable to trust anyone to love him and then Otis came along, but now he found himself being jettisoned back to the same place he had been for so long. Alone.

Otis looked at him. He wanted to say, 'y'damn right it don't make no difference', like he had told so many others. But tonight it would be a lie. He wasn't in love with Charles, but he realized that he did like him enough to want to remain a part of his life as long as he, Charles, would allow it. And for the first time in years Otis experienced these feelings without fear.

"'ey Charles. I want me and you to be tight, I really do."

Charles didn't say anything.

"And I want you to know me. That's why I'm telling you." He reached over and put his hand on Charles' shoulder. "You the only person I told this to outside of my family, so you know, well, you know you cool with me."

Shaking his head with a smile, Charles looked over at the bumbling man beside him.

"There's more," Otis continued.

"More? I don't know if I can stand any more."

"I never told you why I came back here."

"No."

"Somethin' happened to me a long time ago," Otis said. He looked at his hands that were clasped in front of him. "I was charged with rape."

"What?"

"Rape." He looked over at Charles who still had a look of disbelief on his face. "But it wasn't like it seemed. I mean, we were goin' together."

"How old was she?"

"It was a he. His name was Terrell. He was seventeen and I was eighteen. I was a few months older than him, 'bout five months. But we was both seventeen when we started goin' together."

"Hold up, don't tell me. His parents waited 'til you turned eighteen and came after you."

Otis nodded his head.

"That's fucked up." Charles slowly shook his head as he spoke.

"They said I got him drunk and took advantage of him."

"Did you?"

"Hell nah!" Otis spat. "We *had* been drinkin' when we went to bed for the first time. But it was gonna happen anyway, even if we wasn't drinkin' because we were in love. His parents found out and started trippin'. They kept tryin' to stop us from seein' each other."

"And they couldn't, so they got you with rape."

Otis nodded his head.

"Why didn't your boy speak up?"

Otis shook his head.

Charles put his hand on Otis' arm. "Man, I'm sorry about all that."

"It's cool. I just wish I could get past all that. But it's like I can't."

Charles looked at Otis for a while before he spoke. "What do you *need* to do?"

The two men left Covington and headed back into downtown. They drove under an immense, full moon. The warm night air rolled through the windows of the truck and escaped back into the night through the sunroof.

"I had a dream last night." Otis spoke as he hung his arm outside the SUV.

He looked around at the lights of the buildings and the people walking to restaurants and theatres. "I was before the judge for my sentencing, and it was a lot of people around. But I didn't recognize any of 'em but my mother and father. And then there was two other men there. I know one of 'em had to be Terrell's ol' man 'cause he looked just like Terrell. And he was with another man who had on one of them priest collars. And the way they was lookin' at me..."

"Was that just a dream, or did that really happen?" Charles asked as he navigated the truck through the streets.

"Yeah, it really happened. But I just keep havin' dreams about it."

"Who was the priest?"

"I think he was Terrell's pastor. He wasn't no priest, though. He just wore one of them collars. I know it had to be him because him and Terrell's father was the ones behind most of the shit. Bishop Abrams. I remember Terrell always talkin' 'bout him."

"Oh." Charles became silent then spoke suddenly. "Come on, let's go back to my house."

Chapter XXII

Terrell got off the elevator and walked through the large glass doors of the office. He was accompanied by one of his firm's attorneys. The receptionist smiled and waved at them as they came in.

"Hey Linda and Terrell."

"Hi Mia," Linda returned.

"Hey Mia," Terrell answered.

"Linda, you got a package here," Mia said as she handed a parcel to her.

"Oh, thank you." Linda took the package and read the label. "Oh, okay," she said to herself.

Mia was all smiles. Actually, all grins was more like it. In fact, she had the widest grin anyone at the office could remember. They had all conferred about it and had concurred; and under the track lighting above the desk, her grin seemed almost harlequinesque. She always dressed in matching colors, so if she wore a red dress she would also have on red stockings and red pumps. Today she was

done up in lime. Yet even the brilliance of all lime succumbed to the radiance of
her grin.

"Some man came here for you Terrell." She patted the red arbor of curls
atop her head.

"Who was he?"

"Here. He left you this message."

Terrell took the pink slip from her golden brown, taloned hands. It was
from Stanton. Terrell was surprised that he had stopped by. The note merely
asked Terrell to call him.

"Thanks."

"You welcome," she grinned.

Linda had walked on down the hall, her blond page boy lightly swaying
across the sides of her face.

"What do you think about my outfit?" Mia asked as she stood and ran her
hands over the material at her thighs.

"It's nice. Kinda bright, but nice."

"Well, you know a sistuh gotta be seen."

"Well, you can definitely be seen."

She giggled. "Thanks."

On his way to his office, he stuck his head in on Harlan. "Hey hey. What's
up?" he greeted.

Harlan looked up from his desk. " 'sup dawg?" He called all the brothers
at the firm dawg. Some of the white guys jokingly complained that they wanted to
be 'dawgs' too. But he said they didn't make the grade. He was just that way,
young and full of himself. And for that reason Terrell watched over him. "You
get that GenChem account?"

"Looks like it. Me and Linda are going to meet later on to put together our presentation. We think it'll be a good account."

"Well I want in on it."

"Man, you ain't even caught up on the Morris-Donaldson account yet."

Harlan waved his hand. "Man, just put me in."

Terrell laughed. "I'll see what I can do."

When he got to his office he listened to his messages. None were pressing so he decided to call Stanton back.

He waited while Stanton's secretary transferred the call.

"Hey Stanton. Just returning your call."

"Oh. Good." Stanton sounded as if he had been interrupted from something important. "Yeah. I just stopped by there while I was downtown to see if you and the bishop was still going to meet with the board. Time is of the essence, you know."

"I know. But really, I don't see why he needs me to help him make his case. I'm not on the board. I just report to it."

" 'cause you have influence, man. You got clout. That's why. Come on, now. You know they listen to you."

"To be honest Stanton. I don't think it's such a good idea to spend that much on a broadcast facility. I mean, there's licensing fees and all kinds of responsibilities that can come about. And the chances of recouping our investment is risky."

"All business is risk."

"Yeah, but we're not supposed to be about business. And anyway, I'll be in Atlanta by then."

"Well look, just think about the bishop. Maybe you can submit a letter of recommendation before you leave."

"Like I said, I'm still kind of up in the air about it."

"Write the letter. I'll talk with you later. Maybe before you leave. Oh yeah, Arthur said he saw you the other night. At the Phoenix. Man, what're you doin' at The Phoenix?"

"Having a drink."

Stanton chuckled. "A'ight man. I'll holler atcha."

"Later."

Terrell sorted through some notes then picked up the phone and called Linda. "Ready for that meeting? Ok, I'll be on down."

The clock on the dashboard was agreeable with Terrell. Six o'clock would allow him enough time to fix himself dinner, place a call to Karen and the kids and kick back for a quiet night in front of the TV.

He pulled the car into the garage and parked it alongside Karen's car. It seemed as if her car had been there for a long time. Once he walked into the house he immediately began removing his tie and unfastening his shirt. He took a meal from the freezer and put it in the microwave to cook while he took a quick shower and changed into comfortable clothes: a pair of loose fitting shorts, tee shirt and flip flops.

The meal was ready so he sat down and ate it in the kitchen in front of the TV set that sat on the counter. The food was good and the daily news interesting. He exhaled a soft rush of air to compliment his relaxed mind and took in the tranquility.

Around seven thirty he went into the den and called down to Atlanta. After a few rings, Karen's father answered the phone and chatted a bit with Terrell before calling Karen to the phone. But before she made it to the phone Terrell heard the sound of running feet and Abassi's voice.

"Is that my daddy?" he yelled.

Terrell laughed as he listened to the sound of his renegade child.

Karen's father scolded him for running and yelling in the house, but it didn't dampen his enthusiasm. Finally, Karen's father gave the phone to him.

"Daddy!"

"What's up Sport?"

"Nothin'. What 'chou doin'?" He was almost yelling over the phone.

"Okay, okay. Calm down. You don't have to be so loud."

Abassi caught himself. "Okay," he said in a more controlled volume. Then he repeated himself. "What 'chou doin'?"

"Talkin' to my sport."

"Me too," Abassi laughed. "Five more days," he called out suddenly.

"Yep. Five more days."

"And you'll be down here."

"Yep, I sure will. And I can't wait."

"Me neither."

Terrell was pleased to hear his enthusiasm. For a while it seemed he and Kenya were so busy enjoying themselves that they had forgotten about him.

"You been good?"

Abassi laughed. "Yeah. You ain't gonna haveta spank me when you git here. But Kenya been actin' up."

"What'd she do?"

"She got smart with Grandma. And guess what? Grandma spanked her."

"Well she should have."

"Yup. Momma tol' her she could."

Terrell wasn't too surprised with Kenya's smart ways. It seemed the older she got the more lines she tried to cross.

"Where's Kenya now?"

"She's out with our cousin."

"How come you're not out?"

"I'm playin' a game our other cousin'."

"I bet you got a lot of cousins down there, huh?"

"Yup. A whole buncha cousins. And Mommy said some more gonna be comin' next week when you come."

"That's right. They'll be coming from all over. Chicago, Alabama, Florida, Detroit- -"

"New York?"

"Yep."

"And California?"

"Yep. Even Alaska."

"Alaska? Where's that?"

"Far away."

"At the end of the world?"

Terrell laughed. "Some people think so."

He and Abassi talked for a while before Karen took the phone.

"Oo that boy can talk," she said.

"He got it honest," Terrell joked.

"Well I guess I can't argue that point."

"That's right. So how's everything going with the reunion?"

"Hectic. But you know I'm enjoying it."

"Jimmie make it down from Milwaukee yet?"

"Not yet. I think he's due in like next Wednesday or something."

Terrell liked Jimmie. They understood each other. "I can't wait to see him again."

"Yeah, I guess so," Karen replied. "How is everything going up there?"

"Fine. About to close on a new account and tying up the Richmond Brothers account."

"Oh. Well that's good... You put a lot of work into that account..."

He could tell she wasn't interested in his work. "Oh. Did you know they're trying to get rid of Bishop?"

"What? So they're really trying to do that?"

"Yeah. They are."

" So they're really trying to do it." She spoke mostly to herself.

"Yep," he repeated.

"And after all he's done for those ungrateful people. But the church has a right to call it to referendum. So there's still a chance."

"I hope so."

"Me too."

"So, like, you haven't been running up a lot of bills down there have you?"

Karen responded with mock dismay. "Of course not!"

Terrell laughed. "Yeah, well I know you."

"I just got a few things for the kids."

"And yourself."

"Just a few."

"Mm hm."

They came to a lull in the conversation. Then Terrell spoke.

"Kenya's out with her cousin?"

Karen answered, "Yeah. Tamika and Jocelyn."

"Tamika and Jocelyn. The two musketeers. I bet they're all grown up now."

"Yeah. They are. So... have you been spending a lot of time at the church?"

"Yeah, a little. Most of the work's been going pretty smooth."

"That's good. What have you been doing other than that?"

"Mostly working and relaxing."

"I know when I called earlier this week, you hadn't gotten in yet. It was pretty late."

"Yeah, it was, so I called that next day and y'all were out."

"Where did you go that night?"

"I just stopped off for a drink."

"You went to a bar?" Silence.

"By yourself?"

"Yeah."

"Oh..."

Another lull.

Finally, with a yawn, "Well, I guess I'd better get off this phone so we don't get any more bills," Terrell joked.

Karen didn't laugh. "Okay. So we'll see you Monday?"

"Monday evening. I'll be on the seven-thirty Delta. Flight one eighteen."

"Okay."

"Love you. And kiss the kids for me."

"I will."

He hung up the phone and sat for a moment in the quiet den. He had
promised Abassi he would be there in Atlanta next week; and he would be there.
But now he wondered how many more family reunions they would attend
together? Such a thought unsettled him, yet, at the same time it was a thought that
seemed to gain prominence in his mind because of its substantiveness.

He understood why Karen had always struggled to hold onto him. Though
she had always felt diminished by the knowledge that there was a part of him that
rued the day he chose to marry; and that deep inside he wanted to be somewhere
else and to live the life both he and, regrettably, she knew he was meant to live,
she held on to the marriage because she loved him, and, besides, it was the only
life *she* had been prepared to live. And even though he had always denied Karen's
claims of his desires, deep inside he knew she was right. But he had always felt it
was his duty as husband and father to disavow her assertions; and besides, he did
love her as well. However the love he had for her couldn't alter his true sexual
feelings.

His identity beckoned for change; it had been that way for a while but he
denied it satisfaction. But now he was at a point in his life in which he was
finding it more and more difficult to walk in the skin he'd been given. His
imaginings were beginning to turn into longings, longings that he live the life he
knew he was meant to live, and to travel a road that was much fuller than the
narrow one to which he had been assigned as a young man with no mind of his
own.

Because he did have a mind of his own, had always had one. However, any
effort at free thought had always been held at bay by fear of reprisal by society,
family and God. But that was no longer the case. He had had many years to live
by the rules of others, but over the years he had gained the confidence that comes

with age and now he was beginning to look at alternatives.

Karen had been right to concern herself with worrying what would happen if she ever left him to his own devices. Childish as he now felt, yes, she was right. The past days had come at him in ways unexpected. Yet he had been prepared to receive these days for all his life and he, hungry for a new life, had unconsciously sought what the past few days had offered. Now he wondered if he could ever go back.

After a while, shrugging it off, he picked up the remote and turned the T.V. back on. In a while one of his favorite shows would be coming on but that evening he didn't have much anticipation of it. That evening his favorite show was just another show, just as his day had merely been another day.

He recounted the events of the day. Nothing out of the ordinary. A tinge of frustration ran through him and left in its wake a distant light that flickered somewhere deep within him. He wanted to look at the light, but caution won over and he turned his attention to the still room in which he sat.

Later that night the phone rang, but he ignored it. He felt he had solved enough problems for the day. A bowl of ice cream and the T.V. had become his balm for the evening.

It was only nine-thirty when he began to doze off. He did it once. Twice. And the third time made him realize that he should go to bed. Suddenly the phone rang again, jarring him fully awake. This time he answered. It was a deacon from the church calling to bid him a safe trip and to give his regards to Karen and the kids. After some small talk Terrell thanked the deacon and promised to pass the regards on to the family. Then he hung up the phone. As he did so, he noticed a message alert on the phone base. He'd forgotten about the earlier call. He picked the receiver back up and went into the message service. The call had come in at eight forty-one. Then there was the message:

"Yeah, uh, this is Otis Carter. I'm tryin' to reach

Terrell Mitchell. I can be reached at (pause) 731-2278. Thanks."

Terrell caught his breath as he listened to the message. The voice. So distant, so familiar. He stood there for a second before hanging up the phone and, walking numbly across the room, he sat heavily in a chair and stared at the phone. Then, slowly, he walked back over to where the phone sat and pulled up the message once again; and almost without thought, wrote it down. Afterwards, he erased the message, folded the piece of paper in his hand and went upstairs to bed.

Chapter XXIII

1974

"I hope I didn't fuck up yo' shirt."

"Me too."

"A little soap and water'll git that out."

"...yeah..."

"What's the matter? I mean, like, I'll pay for it, if it don't."

"No, I think it'll come clean. It's just the smell."

"Oh. That should come out too."

"Why did it have to be alcohol? You ain't even supposed to be drinking anyway."

"It was a basketball game."

"But still..."

"Look, me an' my fellas like a little rum in our Coke. Why you trippin'? I said I would pay for it."

Dew hung in the crisp night air of autumn causing swirls of frost to curl from their mouths and dance like angels in the light of a full moon.

"It's not so much the shirt, man. It's what my father's gonna say."

"He gonna kick yo' ass? Over a goddamn stain on yo' shirt?"

"It's the alcohol. The smell of the alcohol."

"Aw that shit'll dry up. And the smell'll be gone by the time you get home. Just take yo' coat off and let the air get to it."

"You crazy? It's cold out here."

"Look, I'm tryin' t' help you. Yo' ol' man that strict?"

"Uh huh."

"So I guess y'all don't drink."

"Nah."

"Y'all must be religious."

"Kinda."

"What do you mean?"

"I mean, we're religious but we ain't that strict."

"Sounds like it."

"Only with some things."

"Like drinkin'."

"Yeah. It's cold."

"C'mon. Get in my car."

~~~

"I'm holding you up, ain't I?"

"Yeah. But it's cool. After all, it was my fault you got splashed, so I can deal with it for a bit."

"It is warmer in here."

"Yep."

(The click of an eight-track)

"If I gave you my love
I'll tell you what I'd dooo
I expect a whole lotta out of you, huh, huh..."

"So where are y'all headed to?"

"A party in Avondale. Wanna come?"

"Nah. I can't."

"Strict on that too, huh?"

"Not really. Only with strangers."

(Loud laughter) "Man you make me sound like a murderer or somethin'."

"No, I- -"

"It's cool."

"...You got to be good to me
I'm gonna be good to you
There's a whole lotta things you and I could do
Hey, hey..."

"You always so quiet in school. You an' yo' sister."

"Yeah."

"I bet you smart too."

"I just do a lot of studyin'."

"Is that why you an' yo' sister never come to any of the games? I'm on the football team, and I don't even remember y'all at any of them."

"You mean because we study a lot?"

"Nah. Strictness."

(Nodding).

"That's too bad 'cause you 'n yo' sister seem pretty nice."

"When you need me

I'll be right there beside you...

Sometime when you're feeling low

All you got to do is call me

Simply Beautiful..."

"Want a little help?"

"Huh? With what?"

"Gittin' out. I can show you around. Let yo' ol' man git to know me, and then you can hang out with me."

Smiling. "It ain't that easy. Thanks for the offer though." Touching his shirt, "Hey, my shirt is dry now."

"See? And the odor is gone too. Told you."

"Yeah. Well, I better go. Thanks."

" 'ey. What's your name?"

"Terrell."

Smiling. "Otis."

"I know who you are."

* * * *

Memories. Like anxious crickets ready to leap at the slightest provocation. Or butterflies ready to warm themselves in the sun.

Terrell stood at his office window and watched the sun move to the edge of the city. All day his mind had been on Otis. Thoughts left behind long ago had now returned. His eyes traced the outline of buildings against the changing sky. From where he stood, high above the city, the view was without boundaries. There, where the horizon sat, his longing took him even farther.

He looked at his watch and saw it was time to leave work. But more immediate, it was time to go and meet Otis; earlier, they had spoken on the phone and had made plans to meet that evening in Eden Park.

As Terrell arrived he saw Otis sitting on a bench overlooking the Ohio River; his back looked much broader than he remembered.

He walked towards where Otis sat and felt his emotions churn. There were so many feelings that he couldn't accommodate any one emotion in particular. All he knew was his chest was full and his stomach knotted.

Otis sat so still that Terrell didn't know if he'd seen him arrive.

"I didn't think you would show." Otis suddenly spoke without turning to look at him.

"I wanted to see you," Terrell said as he came upon the bench.

Otis didn't reply. He continued to look out over the river.

A thought came to Terrell: What if Otis was there to settle a grudge? This would be the perfect place to take it out. The thought crossed his mind as he looked down the steep embankment; yet, more than his own death was the need to see Otis' face once again.

He stood a little away from Otis and all he could see of him was his profile; but that was enough to incite renderings of days past. "We needed to see each other," he continued.

Otis sat a little longer before turning to him. "Yeah. We do."

And it was then for the first time in twenty years Terrell was able to see his face. Little about it had changed; it held the same dark beauty it had years ago, only seasoned. But there was something about his face that was disturbing. It seemed to know things. Things so personal and so intense that it humbled Terrell.

"Otis, I…" Terrell tried to speak but suddenly found his words inadequate. Otis nodded his head, "That's 'bout the size of it."

"Don't do this to me. I came here to see you. I didn't have to do this, y'know."

"Yes you did. You did have to come here. We both did. I guess we both did," he repeated as he turned his face back towards the river.

Terrell stepped closer, then sat down beside him. "You're right. I did have to see you."

Suddenly, out of nowhere, Otis spoke out. "You were wrong, man." He shook his head slowly. He seemed tired. His elbows rested on his thighs and his hands were clasped loosely between his legs. "What you did was wrong, Terrell, man."

Terrell paused for a second before speaking. "Otis, what could I have done? There wasn't anything I could've said that would've changed anything."

"You could've spoke up in my defense." He turned to Terrell, his eyes like flame. "They charged me with rape, man. And you didn't say a goddamn thing."

"Otis, man, they were gunnin' for you. They wanted to break us up and they wanted somebody to pay."

"Aw man you could've said somethin'. You could've told 'em I had just turned eighteen; how I was only a few months older than you; how we was really the same age. You could've told 'em how much you loved me. You could've done somethin'." His deep voice rose through the air.

"I was scared. I just… I just…" Terrell shook his head.

"You just wanted the whole thing to be over. That's all the fuck you wanted." Otis glared at Terrell.

Terrell felt himself shrink under the accusation; but he could only acknowledge it. "I just wanted the whole thing to be over," he confessed. "But I didn't want to hurt you. Otis, I would've done anything to keep you from being hurt. But there was nothing. Can't you see that?"

"Fuck it, man." Otis got up from the bench. "I don't know why I called yo' ass."

Terrell sat in silence for a moment.

Otis had walked a bit away and stood, looking down at the river's bend.

Terrell looked over at him. "I was seventeen. I was scared. I was always scared back then, remember?" He spoke in a soft steady voice. "Think back Otis. You knew that about me. Hell, you used to say how you were going to help me get over my fears. Become a man. Remember? That's the way I was back then; and you accepted it." He stood and walked over to Otis. "I'm sorry you were hurt. And you know that. In your heart you know that. But don't try to punish me for my weakness. You have to remember what I was going through back then."

"You didn't write or nothin'."

"I wanted to, but I knew you would write back. And that my father might see your letters."

"Your father!" Otis snorted.

Terrell looked around and saw some more people had arrived in the park. A young man pushed a swing in which his girlfriend sat. The sound of squeaking metal filled the air.

"C'mon man. Sit down." He motioned towards the bench and the two of them returned to their seats.

"After you left, I almost died. I couldn't sleep, couldn't eat; I couldn't think about anything but you," Terrell continued.

"I thought about you too." Otis had calmed himself and now spoke in a softer tone. "I was confused, man. I was hurt and I was angry; but at the same time you were here in my heart. And that's what hurted, man. You were still here," he patted his chest, "and you had turned yo' back on me."

"No I didn't."

"Then what the hell was it?"

Terrell didn't answer.

"When you did that it just added to the misery."

"I'm sorry..."

Otis blew a heavy breath. "Sorry can't change nothin'. I guess I wasn't even lookin' for an apology."

"Otis, man I wish there was something I could do to make things right."

Otis hunched his shoulders, "Maybe things are right. Maybe I just gotta learn to look at all this differently. But it's hard."

"I know." Without thinking, Terrell reached over and laid his hand on Otis' arm. He stiffened when he realized what he had done. He started to pull his hand away, but he noticed how Otis made no attempt to remove his hand. So he left it there.

"Otis, I'm glad you decided to come back."

"I had to. I started to call you sooner, when I first got here, but I couldn't. But I knew I had to before I left."

Terrell removed his hand. "You're not here to stay?"

Otis shook his head. "I live in New York. Been there for about sixteen years."

"Oh. I thought you had moved back."

"Nah. I can't come back here."

"Memories?"

"No, not really. It's just that I'm not a part of this anymore. I don't belong here. Twenty years ago they told me I didn't. And you know what? They were right."

"So when're you leaving?"

"Monday. That's why I had to see you today."

Terrell smiled, "I'm glad you did."

The sky had turned deep orange when Terrell and Otis walked back to their cars. Much had been said, with some things having been understood. When they arrived at their cars they hugged each other and made plans to meet the following evening.

The streets moved like water beneath Otis' car as he left the park. The evening had become a portrait; golden, still and silent. Though he drove away from the park, his thoughts were still there. He wondered if all he could say had been said; he wasn't sure, but he knew there had to be a point when all was said and done, or at least when he would have to accept the words that had been spoken. He was coming to believe that time had arrived.

He moved up Gilbert Avenue past The Baldwin Building. He remembered how he had worked there one summer when he was younger, helping move shipping crates. He recalled how he would eye the rows of baby grands, highly polished until their bodies shone like dark suns as they awaited a concert hall or some grand mansion in Indian Hill, or, maybe even Beverly Hills. He'd always wanted to play an instrument, or even to sing but the natural ability eluded him. Now Terrell, he could play the piano and sing. He could sing his ass off.

He wondered if Terrell still sang in his church choir. When they were younger he used to tell him 'Boy, if you get away from that church, you could make some big bucks singin'. But Terrell always replied that it was God who had given him his voice and it was God he would sing for.

It had been good to see Terrell no matter how much he had told himself it wouldn't be; deep inside he had always known it would be. The anger inside just never turned into hatred.

He arrived at Charles' house around seven o'clock. He pulled up behind his truck in the driveway; then he gathered his bags and went up to the house. He was about to ring the doorbell when the door opened and Charles stood there looking at him. Then without a word he pulled Otis close and they embraced as the door closed.

* * * *

The reason to live is to be. The reason to be is to live. Terrell's mother had told him that once when she had seen doubt cross his face. It was a lesson he remembered well, but was never quite able to abide by.

But for Otis it had been different. He had always lived his life with a keen since of awareness and adventure; and through it all he arrived looking good. Terrell thought this as he sat before his drink.

The Phoenix was busy but not crowded. Thursday evenings were more primers for Thursday nights and the weekends. From the jukebox R. Kelly's voice carried sensuous lyrics like Sam Cook before punctuating them with sharp staccato like Lenny Williams. Memories, like butterflies...

"You better drink that. You paid for it." A voice pulled Terrell's attention back to the moment.

He looked up to see Arthur in a gray uniform grinning over him holding a glass of beer.

"You better drink it before one a' them winos drink it through osmosis or somethin'."

"What's up Arthur? Sit on down."

Arthur pulled up a seat. "You must be inspectin' yo' drink 'cause I know you ain't meditatin' in here."

"Actually, this place isn't too bad to come to for a little meditation."

"On what, crazy niggas?"

Terrell nodded his head. "There's something to be said about that too." He looked at Arthur's uniform. "You just getting off?"

"Hell yeah. Had to do a little overtime. But it's all good. I was about to ask you the same thing."

"Nah, I got off regular time, five. I just went and met up with an old friend of mine. I hadn't seen him in almost twenty years."

Arthur held his beer half in the air. "That's a long time, bruh." He took a sip.

Terrell took a sip of his drink also.

"Y'all musta grew up together."

"Kinda. We knew each other growing up."

"He change much since you last saw him?"

Terrell was impressed with how much concern Arthur took in his conversation. Not too many people would go on in a conversation that didn't concern their own affairs. Terrell could see why it was Arthur, of all his siblings, who was his father's care giver.

"Surprisingly, no. I mean, of course there were some changes, but not like I would have expected."

"What, you probably expected him the be fat and bald?"

"No. I just didn't expect him to have held up so well."

Terrell looked at the glass as he rotated it slightly in his hand. "He was the only friend I ever really had."

"Really."

Terrell nodded his head, lifted the drink and took a swallow. "I'm gonna tell you something I don't usually tell people. Me and Otis used to go together."

"That's the one you saw today?"

"Yeah." He looked at Arthur. "You don't seem too surprised."

"Nah, I mean, you know, I kinda figured..."

"That I'm gay? Because I know Stanton? I didn't know he was gay."

"It's not that. I mean, like a lotta people are gay- - or whatever. But there is somethin' to you knowin' Stanton, hangin' here- -"

"This isn't a gay bar."

"But a lot of us hang out here; and look which ones you done got to know. You know, chickens always come home to roost."

Terrell hunched his shoulders.

"How long y'all go together?" Arthur continued.

"A year. It probably would've been longer if my father hadn't found out. How does your father feel about you?"

Arthur raised his eyebrows. "Man, I'm thirty-seven years old."

"I know, I know." Terrell took another drink.

"Look, before my ol' man got sick, me an' him had a understanding. We may live together but we both grown. That's the way my whole family feel."

Arthur tapped his fingers on the table to the music. "So you 'n yo' friend ain't seen each other in all that time?"

Terrell shook his head. "No. He left after that..."

"Y'all shoulda at least kept in touch."

"It was messy, man. Brutal. I felt like running away myself."

Terrell had another drink then decided to leave. The bar was becoming crowded and the din of voices and music rose the roof.

"Well, look, I'm outta here."

"A'ight. But look, call me if you need to talk. A'ight?"

"Okay." Terrell nodded his head as he turned and went towards the door.

Chapter XXIV

It wasn't supposed to have been that way. Looking into his father's eyes that morning. Eyes so full of contempt that all ties had been severed.

His father had little more to go on but the expression on Terrell's face after spending time with Otis, and suspicion.

"Git up an' git ready for church!" His father had spat.

Terrell was still groggy from sleep. "Yessir."

"Now!" His father tore the covers from the hide-a-away and flung them across the living room.

Terrell sat up in bed, the cool morning air racing into his skin. "Daddy- -"

"If you can stay out late with that boy you can go to church. Now git up!"

Terrell jumped up and began gathering his clothes. For the first time in his life he felt what it was like to be unloved. He felt small and dirty, unworthy of love from anyone... even God. His bare feet padded across the cold linoleum as he hurried to the bathroom. Even then he could hear his father mumbling something about 'two men'.

It wasn't supposed to have been that way; but it had.

~~~~

The memories circled through his head as he watched Charmaine tend to her plants. A late morning sun poured into the solarium and warmed his face. The air was stuffy in the enclosed room. "It's hot in here. Why don't you open up the door?"

"It's not that warm in here. The morning's kinda chilly." Charmaine spoke as she bent over and watered a fern. She was still in her robe and not ready for the day.

"Girl, it's sixty-seven degrees."

"If you're gonna sit there and whine, go on and open the door," she replied.

Terrell immediately got up and opened the door that led out onto a stone patio.

"You took off from work today?" Charmaine asked as she rubbed a leaf between her thumb and finger.

"Yeah. I called in for a rest day."

"And the real reason is? The reason you got me up when you know I worked late last night?"

"Otis is back."

Charmaine paused slightly before picking up the watering can. "So? It is his home." She turned and looked at him. "How do you know he's back?"

"We met up."

Charmaine rolled her eyes and shook her head. "You met up."

"Yesterday."

"That's a fine thing to do while your wife is away."

"He called me. I didn't call him. And what was I supposed to say, 'No'?"

"Yes." She sat the can down and seated herself on a wicker chair. Saying 'no' would have been fine Terrell. All that mess that happened to you two was years ago. I'm sure he's built his own life over the years and God knows you have."

"There was no closure to what happened."

"And why does there have to be? C'mon, you're old enough to know that we don't always have closure to things that happen in our lives. You know that. That's why we have faith and forgiveness, Terrell."

"But what if you have a chance to close a chapter in your life? You're gonna jump on it. You know you would."

Charmaine sat back in the chair.

"You know you would Charmaine. And that's all I'm trying to do."

"And what if he doesn't accept your offering?"

"Then I'll be able to walk away knowing I did the best I could do."

Charmaine sat silently and studied her brother's face. "I wonder if that's true, Terrell," she finally spoke. "I wonder if you'll ever walk away."

"What do you mean?"

"Nothing."

Terrell leaned forward. "Nah, c'mon. What do you mean?"

"What about your family?"

"What? What does that have to do with anything?"

Charmaine got up and picked the watering can back up. "How far do you plan to go with this… apology?"

"I'm not sure. That's why I came by. To run it all past you."

"Me? I told you what I think. The only person who can apologize to Otis is Daddy. And Lord knows he can't."

"- - and Bishop."

"Well you can forget that right now." Charmaine waved her hand and walked across the room. "Bishop believes with all his heart he did the right thing."

"But he didn't."

"So now you're gonna try to go after Bishop. See what I mean? Where does it stop?"

Terrell looked down at his hands as he contemplated his sister's words.

Charmaine continued to tend to her plants as she mumbled. "And you wonder why Karen's so insecure."

Chapter XXV

Otis got out of his car when he saw Terrell drive through the gate of The Vernon Manor.

Terrell parked his car alongside Otis' and walked over to him.

Otis nodded his head. "What's up?"

"Sorry I'm late," Terrell apologized.

"It's cool. I ain't in no rush."

The two of them walked up the driveway towards the restaurant.

Otis gave a sly sideways look at Terrell. "If I remember right, you were always late."

Terrell smiled and they entered the building.

"I used to always wanna come in here when I was growin' up," Otis said as he looked around the restaurant.

"Me too. The first time I came here was for a meeting."

"What kind of work you do?" Otis asked as he cut into a salad.

"Accounting."

"By the looks of that car you do more than just accounting. You must be a CPA."

"Yeah."

"You own yo' own firm?"

"I'm a partner."

"I always knew you would go far."

"It's just accounting."

"Yeah, but that's something you should be proud of."

Terrell hunched his shoulders slightly and took a sip of tea. "...What line of work are you in?"

"Warehousing."

"Oh good," Terrell gushed.

"Yeah, I made it through all right."

"You know, I always hoped you would. I always wondered if, well, if you were okay. Always hoped you were."

"Yeah?"

"Yeah. Otis, man you never left my mind. See, I always thought you would come back to Cincinnati; and I figured we would see each other again. I never thought you would up and disappear like that."

"At least not for twenty years, huh?"

"Especially twenty years. That's a long ass time to worry over someone."

"All you had to do was ask my family how I was."

"I wasn't sure how they would react to me."

"I think they understand that it wasn't you." He looked at the wedding band on Terrell's finger. "So you married, huh?"

"Yeah."

"How long?"

"Fourteen years."

Otis nodded, his eyes on his food. "How many kids y'all got?"

"Two."

"What about you?"

"One."

"You married?"

Otis smiled at him, then shook his head. "I'm true to myself, man."

"But you just said you had a child."

"That's another story. But like I said, I been true to myself."

Terrell bit into his dinner without responding.

"How's your mother doin'?" Otis continued.

"She's fine."

"I always liked her. She was always so cool. How 'bout Charmaine? She and Boy ever get married?"

"Nah man. He decided he wasn't ready. He up and joined the service."

"Oh."

"After he got her pregnant."

"What?"

"Mm hm."

"She have it?"

"Yeah. A boy. D'Andre. He's about eighteen now. She has two more kids through her marriage. She's been married now 'bout thirteen years."

"That's good."

"He's an engineer and she's a nurse."

"Mm."

"How's your mother doing?" Terrell asked.

"Oh she's doin' good. Retired. Finally."

"What about your father? He still in the hauling business?"

"Yeah. He's about to retire too, though. Can't get any contracts. White man's got 'em all sewed up."

"Like the stadium mess going on," Terrell commented as he separated a piece of bread.

"And he done lost most of his men 'cause ain't no work for a black man in construction. So yeah, it's time he retire."

"You know, I always thought you would've gotten into the construction business since it was in your blood."

"Shit, and walk around carrying dirt or directing traffic while the white boys pull in the skilled jobs? Hell nah."

"How long have you been with your job?"

"Thirteen years."

"So what's exactly involved in warehousing?"

"Not much. Takin' care of stock, trackin' inventory. Shit like that."

Terrell laughed. "You always know how to downplay things."

"Well that's all it is."

"I guess you like New York, huh?"

"Love it man."

"Never been there. Always wanted to, though."

"You should." Otis took a drink. "Yep, it's home. The first years were rough. But it's home now. I see you got a nice home."

Terrell raised his eyebrows, "How do you know?"

"I saw it. I looked you up in the phone book."

Terrell put down his fork. "So you've just been sitting outside my house?" His slightly round copper colored face flickered above the candle at their table.

"Nah. I was on my way to visit you but I saw you leaving with a friend."

"Friend?"

"Dark skinned brother; 'bout my complexion. Y'all left in a black Bimmer."

"Oh yeah. We're working on a business project."

"Mmh," Otis responded as he lifted a fork of food to his mouth. "Besides, I wasn't sure if you were living by yourself. I didn't wanna come bustin' in on you."

"My wife and my kids are out of town."

The server brought the rest of the meal to the table and re-filled their glasses before politely leaving.

"How's married life?" Otis asked.

"Good." Terrell answered as he pushed at a few grains of rice.

"Well I wish you all the luck, man."

"Thanks. I wish you the same."

After dinner Terrell suggested they take a walk. He said it was a nice evening and they both agreed they had lost so much time; so they left the Vernon Manor and walked down the street to The Civic Gardens where they strolled down winding lanes of plants and flowers with complicated names. Overhead, the gathering of trees formed a cool moist canopy and held back the sounds of the city.

"The air is so clean here," Otis said after taking in a deep breath.

"I guess you don't get much of that in New York."

"Clean air?"

"Well that, too. But I mean parks."

"Yeah," he spoke incredulously. "Central Park and lots of others."

"But not like here in Cincinnati. We have one of the largest park systems in the country."

"Oh really?" Otis replied with mock interest.

"Never mind." Terrell playfully elbowed him. It all felt like twenty years ago.

"You still full of information, I see," Otis laughed.

" 'ey, you know me..."

They walked a bit in silence as they enjoyed the lush greenery.

"You ever think about me?" Otis suddenly asked.

Terrell hesitated before he answered. "Yeah. I do. I used to wonder how you might look now. What your life was like."

"Like if you ruined it?"

Terrell looked at him.

"Well, I never hated you, man." Otis said. "I was angry. Pissed that you wouldn't stand up and defend me. But I never hated you. Pitied, yeah. Angry, yeah. But I could never hate you."

They made their way to the end of the gardens.

"Which way now?" Otis asked.

"Let's walk around a little bit," Terrell replied.

They moved out of the quiet of the garden and back into the din of the streets. It was a warm Friday evening and everyone moved like electric moths.

Cars rolled down the streets on dazzling rims, the music from the stereos competing for attention. Otis' eyes twinkled as he watched the display.

"That used to be us. Remember?"

"Yep."

"Nimrod used to be tearin' some ass."

Terrell nodded his head. "What happened to Nimrod?" He spoke through slight gasps as he and Otis walked up the incline of Reading Road.

"My father sold her. I needed the money when I got to New York."

"It would've been nice if you could've held onto her. A '68 Four Forty-two is a classic."

Otis kept his eyes forward. "Well, y'all saw to that." He spoke in a calm but indicting voice.

Terrell looked over at him. "Otis, look, we need to have a serious talk because... man, you ain't right," he said as he shook his head.

"How come I'm not right? You did what you did and that's all there is to it." He continued to speak without looking Terrell's way.

"Because you weren't the only victim. I was victimized too, you know." Terrell's breathing was becoming more labored. "Let's go back to the bar."

As they entered the restaurant they encountered a bemused maitre'd. "Back for seconds, gentlemen?" he asked.

"Yes. Can you seat us at a booth? We just want drinks and appetizers this time around," Terrell said.

"Certainly," the matire'd said as he led them through the restaurant.

The two of them placed their orders; Terrell paused to give the young lady a chance to walk out of earshot. Then he began.

"You know, I have spent years feeling guilty and wondering if you were okay. And now I see that you really are. You really are, Otis. But still, you want to come back here and throw your pain around. And you know what? Never once have you asked me how I was doing; to see if I survived without any scars. And that's selfish, man. Just plain selfish."

Otis looked at Terrell with continued calm. "Oh. So now you gonna tell me you suffered as much as I did."

"No I'm not. But I suffered too. I suffer every day."

Otis waited for Terrell to continue.

"You know how it feels to be taught to hate yourself? My father and Bishop did what they thought was right; what they thought would help me. And maybe they were right in doing so- -"

Otis huffed in disbelief.

"I don't know," Terrell defended. "All I can say is while they thought they ended my misery, they only deepened it."

"Man, wha'chou talkin' about? You sittin' up here an accountant, a nice home... wife and kids..."

"Is that what it is?"

Otis shook his head. "Nah, man. It ain't about having a wife and kids. I don't want that. But I could've had a family, my own type of family."

"You have a family."

Otis turned his head away. "You know what I'm talking about. My whole life was disrupted. I was a kid and I went through all that shit." He stopped and shook his head. "It ain't about a home, or a wife and kids. But I do need somebody in my life... I can't even trust anybody anymore. That's what I'm talkin' about, see. So you need to talk about that."

"And we can, man." Terrell learned forward and raised his hands. Then he sat back as the server brought their drinks and appetizers to the table.

They thanked the young lady and she smiled and left them to their conversation.

"We can talk about you," Terrell continued. "But we have to talk about me too. We've been joined at the hip man. We can't talk about one without talking about the other."

Otis reached over and took a few appetizers off the plate.

"Mushrooms. Why did you get mushrooms?"

"Because I get tired of eating chicken wings."

"Wing dings."

"Chicken wings," Terrell stressed. "Stuffed mushrooms are good. Try something different for a change."

Terrell continued. "Every time I see myself in the mirror I'm reminded I can't love myself." He stirred his cocktail. "The people around me; my co-workers, members of my church- - my family, they all remind me that I'm not supposed to love who I really am."

"Put 'em in check when they come at you wrong," Otis said while chewing a mushroom.

"They never come at me. It's the language, the attitudes- - the expectations."

"The jokes."

"The jokes, the comments," Terrell agreed. "And even then I try to come to our aid, but it's in a detached manner. You know, like, 'well they're human too.' And shit like that."

Otis reached over and put some mushrooms onto Terrell's plate.

Terrell took a drink.

"Your wife know?" Otis asked.

Terrell nodded. "Yeah. I told her."

"That was dumb."

"I thought it was over. That I had a new life."

"That you had been saved."

Terrell whispered, "Yeah."

Otis chuckled. "I never believed that shit. Like somebody as powerful as God lost you. 'Oops! I lost him. Damn!"

"We lose ourselves."

"Oh. So we're that powerful that we can just stray off from a course that's been runnin' this universe for trillions of years. Right." Otis laughed and took a drink. "Maybe the course we travel *is* the way it's meant to be."

"I don't know." Terrell took a large gulp of his cocktail. He speared a mushroom and put it in his mouth. "My wife, man, Karen. She knows and she can't stand it."

"Why? You ain't doin' nothin', are you?"

Terrell shook his head. "No. It's just the fact that she knows." He motioned for another round of drinks. "And you, she can't stand the very idea of you."

"Did you tell her all this before you got married?"

"Yeah," Terrell said.

The second round was placed on the table.

"Then I don't know what you got to worry about," Otis continued. "I mean, you been straightforward and you haven't messed around on her, so, I mean, you know…" he raised his hands and hunched his shoulders.

"Look, I walk around with secret feelings. I'm afraid to love myself; I got a wife who I love, but who loves me and despises me at the same time; and two kids who soon will be able to pick up on all the discord. And I don't have anybody to turn to. Sometimes it doesn't feel as if God is even on my side." He shook his head with a faint smile. " And you say I don't have anything to worry about..." Terrell scoffed as he put his glass to his mouth.

Otis was silent. He sipped a bit of his drink and ate a few portions. "Terrell," he finally spoke, "You know, I'm not much on religion, never have been; but I'm big on God. I meditate on Him and I listen to Him all the time. And one thing I've learned is that I don't know who God is. I mean, like I hear all kinds of descriptions, but ain't nobody sure... for a fact, y'know, and that drives some people crazy, but not me." He lightly poked at his food. "But I guess that's where religion comes in, huh? It makes people *think* they know." He chuckled and shook his head. "You know how man is. Always feel like he *got to know* in order to accept. But I'm cool with all that. I don't feel like I have to understand God to accept Him. So what I'm sayin' is relax with this God thing and don't ever feel like He ain't on your side, man."

"But I don't want to do wrong..."

"Me neither. And you know what keeps me from wantin' to go out and do crazy shit?"

Terrell shook his head.

"Peace. When I'm at peace man, I feel the love." He paused as he listened to his words. "I guess that's why I came back here."

Terrell looked at Otis and saw the depth of his words illuminate in his eyes, his very face.

"See, I don't have to struggle for reason. It's called faith," Otis continued. "Bishop should've taught you that by now."

"He probably doesn't even know himself," Terrell said. "And I'm sure my father didn't."

"Didn't? Oh, your father died?"

"Three years ago."

"I'm sorry."

"Thank you."

They ate a while in silence while their words and thoughts settled. Then Otis looked over at Terrell.

"Terrell. I got somethin' I want to tell you..."

The night before, they hugged; but on this night, they embraced. Two men. Inseparable. Forever connected. Forever joined at the hip.

"It was good to see you again," Terrell said, his arms around Otis' back.

"I'm glad I came."

They unfurled their arms from around each other and stood in the dark, lighted by the street lamps.

"When will you be back?" Terrell looked up at Otis.

"Soon, I hope. I'll be in and out pretty often. I promised my parents I would. It's gonna be kinda expensive but I just have to start figurin' travelin' into my budget."

"You owe it to them."

"Yeah. I know."

"Will I see you?"

Otis hesitated before he spoke. "You got a special situation goin' on there. I don't wanna cause any disturbance in your life."

"You won't."

He looked skeptically at Terrell. "We'll work on it."

"You have my address."

"Yeah. But Terrell, man..." Otis slowly shook his head.

"We'll work on it." This time it was Terrell.

"Yeah. We'll work on it," Otis grinned. Then he put his large hand on Terrell's shoulder. "Can you make it home okay?"

Terrell smiled. "I can hold my liquor now."

"Be cool." Otis spoke and embraced Terrell once again.

"Yeah. You too."

Otis walked to his car and unlocked the door.

Terrell stood for a second then did the same.

As Otis pulled out of the driveway he stopped and leaned out the window.

"The mushrooms were the bomb."

Terrell smiled.

"Forever," Otis called out.

"Forever," Terrell answered as Otis drove away.

He watched as Otis' car headed down the street, its tail lights winking twice before disappearing into the stream of traffic. He continued to sit in his car; there was no effort to move, only to sit and measure the silence that had fallen once Otis left. They had finally spoken; and through the pain there still was love. He thought about how much the two of them had gone through and the lack of hatred for those who had hurt them. That night he had become convinced that they *had* been hurt; and even though he would always love his father, he was able to speak to him in his heart, to the grave, to wherever he was, and he was able to tell him that he had been wrong.

But Bishop Abrams would have to know now. Even more, he would have to face what Terrell now knew, of the story Otis had told.

The men. Sometimes two. Sometimes four. Sometimes too many to recall, living secret lives. The sex. The men with no names. Some barely men. Bishop knew and would have to bear witness to this knowledge.

Terrell shook his head and started the car. In spite of what Otis had told him and what he had seen, it was still overwhelming.

He began to drive.

How could Bishop have been part of the circle of men yet bring such ruin to he and Otis' lives? He didn't want it to be true, but it had to be or else Otis would not have known about Stanton and his connection to the circle of men; some now upstanding men, righteous men. Businessmen, educators, public officials.

Their names replayed time and again in Terrell's head. Names of celebrated black men.

Chapter XXVI

He didn't know where he was going that night. The city was an open map.
He drove. Avondale, Bond Hill, Evanston, Cumminsville.

It wasn't until he drove through Winton Terrace that he came to rest.
Someone had called out to him and he sat until the man came to the car. It was
Derrick who he had met at The Phoenix.

"What's up man?" Derrick grinned as he leaned in the window of the
passenger side.

"Nothing," Terrell answered. "Just out."

"You headin' down the way?"

"Yeah," Terrell suddenly said. "Hop in."

"Wha' 'chou doin' out this way?"

Terrell looked over at him. "Can't a brother drive around?"

"Yeah." Derrick laughed. He was just happy to get a ride. "Put some music on."

"I don't think you'll like the music I have."

"Like what?"

"It's different."

"I'm open to shit. They black?"

"Yeah. But- -"

"Just put 'em on." Derrick was becoming as anxious as a child on Christmas morning.

Terrell pushed the button and the ethereal music of Milton Nascimento came forth.

"He black?"

"Yeah. He's from Brazil."

He listened for a while. "That sound pretty smooth. But let's turn on the radio. The Wiz. How do I turn it on?" He was peering forward and aiming his finger at the lighted stereo face.

"Just push that button to the right."

Derrick pushed the buttons until hip hop music jumped from the speakers. "Yeah," he said as he bobbed his head and called to friends on the street.

"You gonna buy me a drink when we git down to The Phoenix?" he asked.

"I really wasn't going to The Phoenix. I was just driving around."

Derrick gave a sly look. "You out lookin' for somethin'?"

"No. Just out. It's a nice night and I just thought I'd spend some time out."

"Then let's spend it together. We can hang out together," Derrick said.

"Well... I really need to spend some time alone."

"C'mon, man." Derrick raised his hand, while the other hung outside the car window. "You said so yo' self it's a nice night. We can git somethin' to drink, hang out and, you know whatever."

Terrell looked at him and laughed. "And whatever, huh?"

Derrick gave a seductive stare. "Yeah. Whatever," he repeated in a lower more serious tone. "C'mon." The lights of the dashboard reflected off his dark skin. He softly curled his bottom lip between his teeth creating a white ellipse against his face.

"I guess I could use a drink," Terrell sighed.

They drove around for a while, then, at the coaxing of Derrick, they pulled up in front of a bar in The Basin area.

"What bar is this?" Terrell asked as he leaned to look through the passenger window.

"Queen Ann. We can do The Phoenix later."

Terrell looked up and down Central Avenue at the many cars that were parked along the street gleaming under street lights and from the lights of the bar. One spot along the street seemed to have been reserved for motorcycles. A battalion of them, some sleek ninja racers, some Harleys, leaned in diagonals in front of the curb.

There was a lot of activity outside Queen Ann. People strolled in and out of the bar while others leaned against the cars or sat on the sleek bikes.

From where Terrell sat the bar seemed packed to the walls and the voices of the patrons, laughter and calls, rolled out onto the street with the roar of the music.

"Looks like a busy place." Terrell's eyes moved up and down the avenue.

"It is. You ain't never been here before?"

Terrell shook his head. "No."

"Then come on." Derrick slapped Terrell's thigh.

Queen Ann was even more crowded than it appeared.

"This is too crowded." Terrell stopped at the door.

"No it ain't. If we head on to the back, we'll find a spot."

Derrick stepped in and motioned for Terrell to follow.

A man came up behind Terrell. "You goin' in?"

Terrell stepped forward. He snaked his way through the crowd, following Derrick's lead, until they made it to the back of the bar.

"Told you." Derrick grinned triumphantly. "And the music ain't as loud back here either."

"I guess all the bodies absorb a lot of the music up front near the speakers," Terrell theorized.

"Yeah... Wha'chou drinkin'?" he quickly asked.

"C.C. and Seven."

Derrick stuck out his palm.

Terrell gave him a few dollars and he began his way through the crowd.

Looking around, Terrell found a space along a wall and took it. He surveyed the bar and its patrons, comparing both to The Phoenix. Unlike The Phoenix, Queen Ann was brightly lit. There were no indiscernible lights that gave off red hues, and the walls were painted black. But in spite of its bland appearance the bar was electric.

He noticed that the patrons there were a bit above the patrons at The Phoenix; by their dress and manners he figured they were probably mostly employed in lower level government jobs: clerks, supervisors, maintenance, and that they were brothers and sisters who chose to remain in the city as opposed to moving out to the suburbs. They were home folk. They were where he sometimes longed to be.

The crowd continued to grow though a steady movement of people to and from the bar seemed to regulate the swell.

He saw Derrick standing at the bar waiting to be served; it would take a while since there were only two bartenders, but Derrick was patient. He was even engaged in conversation with another guy as they waited.

Terrell thought how attractive Derrick was. The first day they'd met at The Phoenix he had thought so. However tonight there were a lot of attractive men at Queen Ann as well.

Derrick finally got the drinks and wound his way back to where Terrell stood.

"Here you go," he said as he handed Terrell his drink and some change. "I tipped the bartender," he said.

Terrell put the rest of the money in his pocket. "Man, this place is crowded."

"Jumpin' ain't it?" Derrick grinned.

"Oh. This is your stomping ground."

"I come here a lot. I grew up around the corner on Baymiller."

"Then you know a lot of the people here."

"They black. Yeah. They my peeps."

Terrell nodded his head and sipped his drink.

"Where you live?" Derrick asked.

"Mason."

"Mason? Oh that's out there past Tri-County, ain't it?"

"Yeah. Kinda."

"That's way out there. But you grew up out there didn't you? Lincoln Heights."

"Lincoln Heights isn't that far, but almost."

"That's what I thought. So you just come downtown to hang out." Derrick continued.

"No. I work downtown; and I go to First Savior, over on John Street."

"Y'all got any openin's where you work? I need a job man. I gotta git my own place. My sister's drivin' me crazy."

"You live at home?"

"Nah, with my sister an' her kids. Man they wild. I was livin' with my girl but she put me out."

"So you do need a job."

"Yeah."

"Well, I'll tell you, I work at an accounting firm, and unfortunately they don't do much hiring unless you do office work."

Derrick shook his head. "Nah, man, I don't know how to do none 'a that."

"Why don't you go on down to the employment office? See what they have," Terrell offered.

Derrick nodded his head. "Yeah." Suddenly he spotted someone. "'ey. That's my cat. We was in the joint together. Hold on," he said to Terrell and he rushed away.

Terrell smiled as he watched Derrick's retreat. Then he sipped his drink and settled back against the wall.

There were more men in the bar than women, and he noticed that most of them were kind of large, at least six feet, and most of them had large shoulders and chests. They tended to have upper arms the size of softballs and tree trunk forearms that ended with hands like black rock. He had noticed earlier that Otis had that same appearance. He thought about his own physique, which was only average. 'What a little physical work will do' he thought to himself.

He could imagine Stanton coming to Queen Ann's. He even imagined that twenty years ago Stanton's physique probably resembled many of the men he saw that night.

His mind drifted back to Bishop Abrams, but he quickly pushed the thoughts away.

He went to the bar for another drink. Derrick was standing with a couple of guys at a video game nearby.

"Want another one?" he asked Derrick.

"Yeah."

He bought the drinks and handed one to Derrick.

"Thanks," Derrick said before turning his attention back to the video game. It was his turn up.

Terrell stood by and watched as Derrick and two other men challenged each other.

In between turns, Derrick introduced him to one of the men. " 'ey, this is Lawrence. Lawrence, Terrell. Me an' Lawrence go way back." He and Lawrence laughed.

Up front, near the entrance a husky man in tight white jeans and vest shimmied to the music, his arms raised in the air. He was definitely gay, Terrell thought to himself; and so were his friends who sat at the table in front of which he danced. None of the other patrons seemed phased by the group of gay men. It was just like at The Phoenix. He slowly looked around and noticed a few more men and women whom he felt were undecidely gay; a few of them even socialized with some of the heterosexual patrons.

He turned his attention back to the game that was ending; Derrick had lost.

" 'ey, I'm gonna step outside with Lawrence for a minute," Derrick said as he handed Terrell his drink and headed for the door.

Another game was about to begin; the victor was feeling especially cocky.

"Wanna play?" he asked Terrell; his red tee spanned his boulder like shoulders and came down to a slightly protruding belly.

"I'll pass."

A man next to Terrell challenged. "I'll play you." He was a tall guy, lean and with a golden colored complexion. He spoke in a very deep voice as he moved to the video game. "I got you on this one."

"A'ight," the victor said. And the game was on.

Terrell stood by, holding his and Derrick's drinks and watched the game. It was video bowling. He enjoyed the intensity on the men's faces, their expressions heightened by the light of the screen; and their hands, large and solid, as they rolled the pilot ball on the machine, before sending it spinning. The hands of the victor were large and dark brown, like the color of a coconut; while the hands of the other man, the challenger, were abnormally large, even for a guy of his stature, and they were mapped with enormous veins that ran up large forearms.

The two men went at it, each one taking his turn.

"See, I'm gonna make him think he got it." The challenger spoke low and to the side to Terrell. "Strategy, huh?"

Terrell smiled.

The man nodded then stepped back up to the machine.

Terrell took another drink from his glass, then looked towards the door for Derrick, but he didn't see him,.

He set Derrick's drink on a ledge along the wall, then continued to watch the game.

Shortly, Derrick returned. "Where's my drink?"

"Right here." Terrell reached back and retrieved it.

" 'ey", Derrick said before taking a sip. "Can you loan me a few bucks? Me'n Lawrence gonna go git some bud."

"I don't want to give you money for drugs."

"It ain't drugs. It's bud."

"And you said a loan. You don't have a job, remember?"

"Just ten dollars, man."

Terrell noticed Derrick's friend standing near the door.

"I ain't got it man," Terrell drawled in the manner he heard on the streets to ensure the effect of his reply.

"Okay, five. I know you got five."

Terrell relented. "Here, man."

Derrick broke into a smile. "Thanks. I'll be right back."

"You shouldn'ta loaned 'im nothin'," the victor remarked as he stood beside the machine. "Some of these niggas just go aroun' playin' folks. Need to git a job."

"Hell, yeah," the challenger agreed as he lined with his shot.

"It was just five," Terrell said.

"It's the principle though." The victor was standing with his arms crossed in front of his chest. "I work. You work. He can work."

Terrell nodded his head. "I know."

"That shit gits old. And he too old too," the challenger added before letting the ball fly. He stood up and grinned at his score, then he stepped back over to where Terrell stood. "He look like he 'bout my age. I work."

Terrell had no reply.

The game was over. The victor had won again.

"I guess my plan didn't work," the challenger laughed as he went to the bar.

"Nope, I guess not," Terrell laughed. "But it was a good idea." He finished his drink and set the empty glass on the bar, then headed back to take a piss.

The restroom had two toilets, one for sitting and one urinal; the urinal was a long trough. It surprised Terrell to see one in the bar. He'd seen plenty of them when he traveled Europe but it seemed so out of character for this little hole in the wall.

As he stood there he imagined a brother coming in and standing beside him to take a piss also. He wondered if he would keep his eyes straight ahead or would he be tempted to peek? He laughed at the possibilities, washed his hands and left the restroom.

It was ten 'till one and still, Derrick hadn't returned. Terrell was getting tired and was ready to go. He noticed the crowd had thinned, mostly the women had gone; only a few remained. Other than that there were still more men standing around laughing and talking, but even their numbers had lessened.

He went back up to the bar for one last drink. If Derrick hadn't returned by the time he finished his drink, then too bad. As he went to an empty table he wondered why he always felt a need to accommodate people. After all there was no real need to wait for Derrick.

As he palmed his glass he thought that surely Karen would have called tonight. But it didn't matter; he would call her tomorrow.

One eighteen. He looked towards the door and still Derrick hadn't come through. Too bad. He'll just have to find another way home, Terrell thought before shaking his head with a wry smile; shit, he probably wasn't going to go

back home anyway. *'We can git somethin' t'drink, hang out an', y'know,*
whatever.' Terrell chuckled softly then stood to leave.

He walked down the street past the night owls, some of whom eyed him as
if he was an oddity.

When he got to his car he looked one more time for Derrick, then he got in
and drove off.

A few blocks away as he was about to turn a corner he saw a lone figure
cross under the light of a street lamp as it made its way to the other side of
Baymiller Street. It was a man; and he walked on unsteady legs with his head
slightly down.

Terrell realized by the man's height, wide shoulders and bowed legs that it
must be the man he'd met in the bar; the challenger. He was sure of it. The
walking shorts and the light colored Hawaiian print shirt were the same. He
appeared to be a bit high.

Terrell pulled alongside the man. " 'ey. How far you goin'?"

The Challenger looked at him for a moment as he tried to discern Terrell's
face. Then he broke into a grin, " 'sup man?"

"Obviously you need a ride. C'mon."

The Challenger climbed into the car and settled back hard in the seat.

"Thanks." He let out a heavy sigh and leaned his head back against the
headrest.

"How far you goin'?" Terrell repeated.

"Covington."

"You were going to walk all the way to Covington?" Terrell asked as he
pulled off.

The Challenger raised his head and looked at Terrell with a smile. "Yeah. I walk everywhere. I don't have a car," he said as he laid his head back again. "I see y' boy never showed."

"Nah…"

"You shouldn'ta expected him to. By the way, my name's Walt." He stuck his hand out.

"Walt. My name's Terrell."

They shook hands.

"I like The Challenger better," Terrell grinned.

The man looked over at Terrell, "The Challenger?"

"Yeah. That's what I called you in the bar. You know, the video game…"

Walt smiled, "The Challenger. I kinda like that."

The streets were quiet, but not empty. There were people hanging out, walking around, but to where Terrell couldn't imagine.

"You might see y'boy out here," Walt said as they drove down Findlay Street. "A lotta shady shit goes on here."

Soon they were crossing The Roebling Suspension Bridge.

"Mind stoppin' by White Castle?" Walt asked. "I'm starvin'."

"Sure." Terrell pulled into the driveway of the restaurant feeling a sense of benevolence. It was his duty and it had become his way of life, helping people.

"Want somethin'?" Walt asked as they drove up to the drive-through.

"Yeah. Thanks," Terrell replied.

They got their orders and headed on to where Walt lived. They pulled up to the apartment building and Walt started to get out of the car when he turned to Terrell.

"Wanna come on up?"

Terrell shook his head. "Nah. It's after two. I should be getting on home."

Walt laughed. "Man you act like two o'clock is so late."

Terrell thought a second. Maybe Walt was right, maybe two o'clock shouldn't be out of the question. After all, from what he'd learned over the past few weeks little seemed out of the question. Besides, there was something alluring about the man in his car; spending a little more time in his presence would be satisfying. *Just one run at life.* "Okay. I guess these White Castles'll be cold by the time I get home anyway."

"Yeah. I got somethin' to drink."

"That's enough for me with drinks," Terrell replied as they entered the building.

"Excuse my place. I didn't have a chance to clean up."

Terrell stood behind him as he unlocked the door. His back and shoulders were wide; his shirt hung from his shoulders like drapes. He clicked on the lights as they entered the apartment.

"Man, this isn't so junky," Terrell said.

"I usually straighten up a bit, but I came in from work and took a nap; man, I was tired. Have a seat."

Terrell sat in a chair.

"Sure you don't want anything to drink? I got some gin and some scotch. I gotta fill up tomorrow." He spoke while unbuttoning his shirt.

Terrell watched the shirt part, exposing a chiseled body. A slight current coursed through him. He steadied himself as he spoke. He felt foolish, somewhat juvenile feeling the way he did. "You mean today," he corrected, "and nah, no more alcohol for me."

"Juice? Water or somethin'?" Walt walked over and turned on a fan.

"Water."

"I'm surprised you didn't order a drink with yo' food," Walt called from the kitchen.

"I knew I had something at home."

Walt returned with a glass of ice water and a glass of gin and juice.

"That's gonna be kinda clumsy with you sittin' in that chair," he noted. "You can use my coffee table. I ain't no prude."

They spread their food and drinks on the table.

Walt picked up the television remote and turned on the T.V.

Terrell heard the soft click as it came on. "This is a nice apartment, man," he said as he turned his head. "Nice wood work. I always did like older buildings."

"Thanks." Walt put a load of fries into his mouth.

"The fireplace work?" Terrell picked up a burger.

"Nah. I wish it did though, that would be nice for winter."

"It gets cold in here?"

"No, not really. I just think it would be cool to have one goin' while there's snow on the ground."

"Yeah. How long you been here?" The question was posed for more than just conversation. Terrell knew he would never allow himself to get physically close to Walt, but through personal conversation he could live a moment of intimacy with him.

" 'bout a year and three months. It's closer to my job. I used to live in College Hill."

"Where do you work?"

"The airport."

"Oh. I hear they pay pretty good."

"Yeah, they do, but I've only actually been workin' for 'em for 'bout a year and a half. Up 'til then I was a temp."

"That's always a good way of getting your foot in the door. What do you do?"

"I work the runway."

Terrell glanced at his fore arms and hands. They were large and veined like brown marble. He took another bite from a burger. The moment was going well.

"I don't know what this shit is," Walt said as he clicked through the channels of the T.V. "I gotta git a VCR, DVD player or somethin'. Even cable is smack."

"You can get those dirt cheap now, you know." Terrell drank from his glass of ice water. He was beginning to feel comfortable now as he enjoyed the interplay.

"I know," Walt said as he continued to jump through the channels. Then, "I ain't never seen you at Queen Ann before." He spoke with his eyes on the T.V. screen, his hand still working the remote.

"That was my first time there."

"Y'boy brought you down? I see him all the time. He one a'dem niggas you see everywhere."

"I can imagine."

Walt paused to look at a program he'd found. "I guess this is better than nothin'."

His words seemed to signal he was about to settle back and watch the show. Terrell now began to feel intrusive. He looked at his watch. "It's going on three. I'd better get on home."

"Three forty-five, to be exact," Walt said, pointing to a clock on the mantle. Then he continued. "You know, you don't seem like the type that would hang with somebody like y'boy there." He was leaning forward with his forearms resting on his knees.

It was as if Walt was trying to delay him from leaving which caused Terrell to become a bit concerned. Yet at the same time the portentous air piqued his interest.

"I know. We just met like last week or so, at The Phoenix. And I ran into him tonight and he asked me to give him a ride."

"And from there you decided to hang with him." Walt had a fragment of a smile on his face. "You need to watch that." Then he picked up his drink and took a swallow before settling back against the sofa. "The Challenger," he grinned.

Terrell gave a quick smile.

Walt searched Terrell's face for a second. "So what's the real reason you hung out with that nigga? And the reason you gave me a lift?" His eyes twinkled mischievously.

Terrell looked questioningly at him. "I don't know, just..." His voice trailed. Suddenly he felt like a child caught in a wrongful act.

Walt laughed suddenly and slapped his large hand on Terrell's thigh. "It's okay man, you ain't gotta answer." Then he folded his hands across his lap, let out a chuckle, and began watching the T.V.

The moment had changed and Terrell knew it. He knew that Walt was baiting him, and he was also aware that he was willing to become the prey.

Terrell watched him. They became silent. He watched Walt's large hands folded at his lap and the hard ripples of his stomach slowly rising and falling with his breath, breath sweet from alcohol and the way the shirt fell from his chest, the chest, like polished stone, hard and smooth. He wanted to leave but he couldn't; all the years and feelings in wait now held him hostage to the moment. He felt a fear come over him. Inside his head he called Karen's name. She had always been there to quell any errant feelings that might arise. But now she was nowhere around; even the thought of her now was no match for the presence of the man who sat next to him. With a soft breath he let out a final plea, "Christ..." before succumbing to the moment. Slowly he raised his hand towards Walt's body. He saw the shadowed smile across the man's face as he recognized triumph.

Terrell hated Walt for the control he held over him, but now he would do nothing to break the control. He moved his hand to the firm stomach and gently strode the ripples there.

Walt didn't move; he smiled and allowed Terrell to continue.

Nervously, Terrell moved his hand up Walt's stomach to his chest and rubbed the hard pecs.

Walt raised up slightly and removed his shirt, then sat back once again.

"You like that, huh?" he grinned as he looked at Terrell.

Terrell nodded slowly, "Yeah," he whispered.

Walt removed his hands from his lap, laid his head back against the sofa and closed his eyes.

Terrell watched him, again realizing the control he, Walt, had over him, and took advantage of the weakness he felt within himself. It felt good, the weakness, like a loosening of liquid flowing, once free after many years.

His hands went down to Walt's belt and rubbed at the buckle, unsure of the passage. But Walt's hands guided them as they unloosened the leather and opened the fly exposing stark white boxers. Again, his hands paused and he rubbed just above the waistband of the underwear.

Walt reached over and began unbuttoning Terrell's shirt until he had removed it. Then he lifted himself and allowed Terrell to slide his underwear down his lean hips.

Terrell began to breath deeper as the boxers slowly moved past the thick bush of black, along the large dick that lay peacefully between his legs. All the while a musky scent rose to his nostrils.

Walt used one foot against the other to remove his loafers; he raised his legs so Terrell could slide his shorts and underwear over his feet.

"Oh God," Terrell whispered.

"It's okay," Walt whispered, "It's cool."

Dawn rimmed the edge of the city as Terrell headed home. He raced against the coming light because he knew soon the sun would look him in the face and ask what he had done.

Chapter XXVII

"The way I figure it, God knew I was gonna have these feelings."

"Why do you say that Brother Mitchell?"

"Because you said He's all knowing."

"He is."

"Then He knew."

"But He doesn't accept those ways. Out of His love for us He gave us free will, the freedom to make choices."

"Is it really freedom and out of love?"

"Yes. Why do you ask?"

"Because I can be punished for my choices."

"You punish yourself. You see, that road in life that you've been taking can only lead to pain and despair."

"But me and Otis feel good when we're together. We laugh and talk. We have a good time. He's the only person I've met who understands me."

"You're only seventeen. You have a lot to learn about life."

"Bishop? You know- - I didn't choose to be this way."
"I know, I know. But you can choose not to be."

* * * *

All his life he'd chosen not to be the way he was; and though he had grown to no longer fear God, he did feel as if he had fallen into that state of despair the bishop had spoken of. Yet, he knew the despair was not so much over his relationship with God, he had come to know a much bigger God, but it was over the end of his life as he knew it. The life he had come to know had been a life of salvaged loved pulled from the wishes of others, but not one borne out of love of himself. Yet it was a complimenting love because it had allowed him to care for his wife and kids who had become the center of his life, and this, his love of his family, had been all he felt he needed in this worldly life.

But the previous night threatened to change all that. In just one hour he had gone to a state from which he feared he might never return. It was supposed to be over, his love of men. How could this have happened?

The guilt he felt burned like a fever in his head and the bed, the bed he
shared with his wife, seemed to engulf him and pull him as deep as his shame
downward to a place from which he had fled so many years ago. No. There could
be no other life. Those were the thoughts that crowded his head that afternoon as
he lie in bed. He thought of the clandestine way in which Stanton and his bunch
lived their lives, of the lives full of deception. That was despair.

But then there was Otis whose struggle was not with his identity rather than
forgiveness. Was that despair?

There was so much to think about, but his mind was too tired. He had put
himself through so much. He stretched under the sheets and closed his eyes once
again, trying to answer the guilt he felt; but what could he say to ease its pang?
He realized there were no words to say because guilt never demands appeasement,
only atonement. But there in his bed, in the early noonday sun, a realization began
to take place and that was the understanding that he might never attain atonement.
He might never do so because along with the guilt there was a sense of pleasure, a
pleasure as heavy as Walt's weight upon him the night before and deep as his
penetration. It was a pleasure that had sought release for so long and that now
peered from the ugly cocoon to which it had been sentenced. So no matter how
hard he wished for atonement, he knew it could never be.

Finally he got out of bed. He knew what he had to do.

The sound of a television could be heard as Terrell stepped up on the porch, the full weight of his body bearing down with each step.

The sun glared off everything round him: cars, houses, even the lawn radiated an unremitting heat.

He rang the doorbell.

"What's up!" Arthur greeted. He opened the screen door and let Terrell in.

"Just in the neighborhood. Thought I'd stop by. Is it okay?"

"Yeah. I wasn't doin' nothin' special."

An old man sat in front of a television. He was dressed in a crisp white shirt with the collar open and a brown suit.

"This is my father. Daddy, this is Terrell."

His father smiled and waved.

"Hi Mr. Thomas," Terrell said.

"Gettin' kinda cold out there, ain't it?" the old man said.

Arthur shook his head. "Daddy, I keep tellin' you it's summer."

The old man smiled.

Arthur pulled the dishtowel he had on his shoulder into his hand. "Want somethin' to drink? Got some lemonade."

"Yeah, that sounds good."

"C'mon into the kitchen." He looked again at Terrell, "Or maybe some coffee. Want some coffee?"

"Lemonade's fine. Too hot for coffee."

"So what's up?" Arthur asked again as he sat across the kitchen table from Terrell.

"Nothing much. Just running a few errands, getting some things done before heading down to Atlanta."

"When you leavin'?"

"Monday."

"That's cool," Arthur nodded.

"Yeah. I've been away from my family too long now."

"You got family down there?"

"Don't most black folks?" Terrell smiled. "But I'm talking about my wife and kids."

"Oh. How long have they been down there?"

"A few weeks. A few weeks too long."

"Yeah I guess you better haul ass."

"You don't seem too surprised that I have a wife and kids."

Arthur pointed to Terrell's hand, "The ring, man. Besides, most men I know our age either have a wife or had one; and they definitely got kids."

"What about you?"

"One. A girl."

"How old is she?"

"Twenty-four."

"Man. How old were you?"

"Young."

"I got two. Kenya and Abassi. Eight and five." He took a drink and set the glass back on the table keeping his hand around its base.

"I bet they're cute kids."

"They are," Terrell said before receding into silence.

"So how'd it go with your friend? Kick over good times?" Arthur asked, breaking the pause.

"It went okay. Actually, better than I expected."

"What do you mean?"

Terrell smiled lightly. "We just had some things we had to get out of the way."

"And y'all did that."

"Yeah."

"Well, that's good."

"Can we step outside? I think I need a little air."

"Yeah. Or I can turn on the A/C."

"I just need to go outside for a bit."

"Okay."

Arthur went into the living room to let his father know where he would be. He and Terrell then went out to a table and chairs that sat under a large elm tree. They sat in silence for a while under the cool shadow of the tree.

"You and him hang out pretty late? You and your friend?" Arthur finally spoke.

"Nah. We just had dinner and talked a bit. Took a little walk." Then he broke into a grin. "Ran into Derrick last night."

"Derrick?"

"Yeah, you know- -"

"Yeah, I know who he is."

"He asked me for a ride and we ended up hanging out for most of the night."

"Where'd you go?"

"Queen Ann's. That's a nice place."

"It's okay. Derrick ain't no good, you know."

Terrell smiled, "Yeah, I know... that's what they told me last night."

"Who?"

"Some of the brothas at the bar. But it's cool."

He continued to smile unconsciously. "Yeah, I had a nice time."

He looked at Arthur. "You close to your daughter?"

"Yeah, we pretty close."

"That's good. It's good to be close to your kids. They become your best friend in the long run. Even when all else goes bad."

Arthur nodded his head.

"Does she know you're gay?" Terrell asked.

"Yeah."

"How did she take it when she found out?"

"She was cool with it."

"That's because she loves you," he said, pointing a finger.

"Well, yeah, I guess so." Arthur fanned at a bug.

"You have to experience love to know the depth of your soul."

"You sure you don't want any coffee?"

Terrell laughed. "No. I'm fine. Really. Just going over some things in my mind."

Arthur took a drink, peering over at Terrell.

"And she understands you, doesn't she? Your daughter." Terrell continued.

"I don't know about all that. I don't know if she's supposed to understand me, at least not all the way. Like I don't understand everything about her. But we respect each other."

Terrell nodded his head and sipped the lemonade. "She respects you for who you are..." he said as he looked down at the ice cubes that were now diminishing in the heat. "You don't know how lucky you are."

"C'mon man, you got what a lot of brothas wish they had. A wife and kids and a nice home. That comparin' yourself to other people is gonna fuck you up if you don't watch it."

"Yeah, well... Seen y'boys lately?"
"Who?"

"Jerry and them."

"The other day."

"He's your friend, isn't he?"

"What do you mean by 'friend'? If you mean lover, no. I don't have one."

"No, I meant buddy. But," he shrugged, "I don't know if I would put much of a friendship in those guys who were at Jerry's house anyway."

"Now there you go again."

"No, all I'm saying is- -"

"They don't have any morals. That's what you're sayin'."

"No..."

"Nobody's perfect, man."

"And I don't expect everybody to be perfect."

"Anyway, yeah, some of those guys are friends of mine. Only one of 'em, Clyde, is real close; but they're all friends." Then he raised his brow and shook his head, "But Terrell, man, you need to get out of that box."

"Yeah, I guess you're right." He looked around the yard for a moment before checking his watch. "Well, I guess I better get goin'."

Arthur shook his head, "A'ight."

As they arrived at the car Terrell turned to Arthur. "Do you know Bishop Abrams?"

Arthur hesitated. "Yeah."

Terrell shook his head. When he first arrived at Arthur's place, and all during the drive there, he had not been sure why he needed to stop by. It was as if talking with Arthur was a natural prerequisite to the final matter at hand. Now, as he asked the question, he understood his decision. He sought affirmation.

"I'll talk with you." He got in his car and pulled off.

~~~~

Deacon Hansberry smiled and waved an arthritic hand as Terrell entered the church. He was preparing for his male chorus rehearsal.

"Hi Brother Mitchell. You finally decided to join the male chorus?"

"No sir. I came to talk with Bishop."

"He in there," Deacon Hansberry said as he turned his head towards the office.

"Thanks."

"Mm hm. So when you gonna join us?" He had always pestered Terrell to join the chorus, but Terrell always turned him down.

"One day, Deacon Hansberry," Terrell smiled.

"We'll be waitin'," the old man said.

"Yessir."

He made his way down the hall towards the office. From the sanctuary he could hear Deacon Hansberry singing to himself as he continued to prepare for the rehearsal. It was an old hymn, 'His Eye Is On The Sparrow'. Terrell had always liked that song. His father used to sing it when he was in the male chorus. He would stand straight as a fence then rock back and forth, hitting the knuckles of one hand into the palm of the other as he raised his voice to God. The congregation would respond with "sang Deacon Mitchell," and "Yesss!"

Terrell smiled as he remembered watching his father, his eyes looking out over the heads of the congregation to that land he hoped to one day see; and he would feel great pride for the man who, at home, showed little compassion.

Finally, standing at the gleaming oak door of the office, Terrell knocked lightly. He heard the bishop answer, "Come on in", blind faith to whomever might walk through the door. When he saw Terrell, his face opened into a smile, "Brother Mitchell, come in, come in."

Terrell stepped in and closed the door.

"What can I do for you?" the bishop asked as he leaned back in his chair.

"I just need to talk with you about some things." Terrell sat leaning slightly forward.

"Oh. Okay. Everything's going okay with the project, isn't it?"

"Yessir. Yes it is." Terrell clasped his hands, "Bishop, Otis is back."

Bishop Abrams furrowed his brow. "Otis?"

"Yessir."

"I'm sorry, I don't know- -"

"The guy we sent to prison."

Bishop Abrams sat erect. "Oh. I thought he had been back."

"No sir. He's been living in New York. He never returned until now."

"There's not a problem is there?"

"He and I have been talking- -"

"You 're not seeing him again, are you?"

"No sir. It's just that he presented a lot of things to me, and I feel I need to share them with you."

The bishop sat back and picked up a pen that he began slowly turning end to end between his fingers. "Share with me," he repeated.

"Yes sir."

Slowly Bishop Abrams' face took on a rigid expression. "Brother Mitchell, there's nothing to 'share' about that matter. Now there may be things to discuss, but nothing to 'share'."

"No Bishop. There are things I want to share with you." He stared into Bishop Abrams' eyes. "And I think you need to hear me out."

Bishop Abrams set the pen down and folded his hands across his belly. "Go on."

"Bishop, I'm not sure why I'm here. I don't even know if any of this will matter, but, well, you always said that our conscience is a gift from God to help us know right from wrong. And I believe that."

"Brother Mitchell- -"

"Bishop, please, I need to finish this. I really do." Terrell raised his hand slightly as in a testimony. "For years now, I've tried to turn away from my conscience by telling myself that what we did was right, was God's work, but... Bishop, what we did was wrong." He licked his lips. "You know, I was sitting there looking at Otis yesterday. A good man, beautiful person... I know that... and I allowed you and Daddy to just take him down like he was a nobody."

Bishop Abrams didn't respond. He sat with a calm, patient expression.

Terrell continued. "The two of you never even took the time to know him. And you, you had never seen him until the arraignment. How could you pass judgment, pass sentence on someone you didn't even know?" Terrell looked at the bishop and shook his head.

"Because I knew the sin. I knew the crime." The bishop's expression was still calm. "I didn't take Otis down, he took himself down."

Terrell gave a snort. "It's so simple to look at it that way, isn't it? Bishop, you hurt a child."

"He was eighteen."

"A child, Bishop, barely an adult."

Bishop Abrams sat up and pointed at Terrell. "No. You were the child. He was a man who took advantage of you." His voice was becoming tense. "And your father came to me like any loving parent would to put a stop to it."

"He's only seven months older than me. You and Daddy had tried to put a stop to our relationship before he was eighteen." Terrell stared coldly at the bishop. "This wouldn't have happened if Otis had been a girl, would it? It wasn't a matter of age, it was to stop something the two of you hated. You both hated that me and Otis were in love."

"I did not hate anything or anyone, Brother Mitchell. I sought to stop an infraction against God."

"So you ruined the life of an innocent child..."

"He was not a child and he was not innocent. Neither of you were." The bishop raised his voice. "Children don't do what he did."

A sound, like a door opening came from the sanctuary causing the bishop to lower his voice. "What you two were doing was not love. It was something that went against God's law, all natural law, and I stopped it!" he spat in a whisper. "Now I want you to stop this!"

"Natural. And when did you become God? Who gave you the wisdom to determine nature?"

The bishop looked at Terrell for a second, then slowly shook his head. "Terrell, I wouldn't have expected all of this from you. Why are you doing this? You have a life. You have a good life. You wouldn't have all that if we hadn't intervened." He took a moment and measured his effect on Terrell who sat without saying a word. "Are you going to tell me you're not happy with your life?"

Terrell looked away, then turned back to the bishop. "Yes. Yes, I am happy with my life, and I love my family. But Bishop, do you know how it feels to have everything and then to realize that there's a part of you you can never touch, to realize you can never be who you really are?"

"Terrell, stop it. Don't give me that pop psychology stuff. We all have secret desires, but we don't have to explore them."

"I'm not talking about desires. I'm talking about who I am."

"It doesn't change a thing, Brother Mitchell. Either you're going to abide by God's laws or you're not. Now if you want to throw away all you've gained for a corrupt life, then you go ahead. I've done all I can do." He stood up. "Now I'll see you to the door."

Terrell looked up at him. "I know why Daddy did what he did, but what did you get out of it?"

By now the bishop had crossed over to where Terrell sat. "I saved you from doing something you shouldn't do. Now I think we need to end this conversation."

Terrell stood and walked towards the door with the bishop behind him. "Or were you trying to save yourself?" He spoke with his back to the bishop.

"What? Just leave, Terrell."

Terrell turned at the door. "I know about the circle of men, Bishop; the parties and all..."

The bishop blinked a few times. "What? What're you talking about?"

The chords of a piano were heard from outside the office.

Terrell started to open the door when the bishop spoke.

"Who told you that?"

"It's known," Terrell answered as he turned to face the bishop.
Bishop Abrams stood silent, his mouth agape, eyes staring in disbelief.
Suddenly the eyes came back to life. "That was long ago. We were
younger then, foolish. It was personal and no harm was done."

"I know of one boy who was involved, Bishop. He was seventeen years
old, just like Otis was seventeen."

"I never did anything like that. Some of them may have, and to my
knowledge that never happened, but for sure I never would have done such a
thing. And I resent such a statement coming from your mouth."

"I know of at least one, Bishop," Terrell repeated.

Bishop Abrams stared at Terrell, his hazel eyes burning with anger. "How
dare you come in here and accuse me of something like that. What I did before I
found the Lord has been forgiven." He raised his hand and shook a finger at
Terrell "And you just remember who saved you too."

Terrell stood and looked quietly at the bishop. Then, "Bishop, I happen to
know that you've visited the circle a few more times after that."

"That's a lie. Get out!"

Terrell put his hand on the doorknob. "So you do know how it feels." Then
he opened the door. The sounds of the chorus rose through the air as he walked
through the sanctuary of the church.

Chapter XXVIII

"So I guess we can call that The Last Supper," Antonio remarked as
he and his father left Courtney's apartment.

Otis shook his head. "No we can't. Because The Last Supper was
for somebody who knew he was about to die. You don't have any plans I
don't know about, do you?"

Antonio gave a quick laugh and looked out the side window of the
car as they pulled out of the driveway. The night was warm and alive, a
night he found ironic for one of the last times he would see his father for a
while. He was experiencing emotions that night that he didn't want to feel,
like love and loss, since they were feelings he had always associated with
weakness; but sitting beside his father, a man he had always been told was a
strong and sensitive man, he was able to negotiate his discomfort and to
speak freely about how he felt.

"Well it's almost like that."

"C'mon now Antonio, you ain't about to die and neither am I. If anything it's the beginning of a new life. At least that's the way I see it." Otis turned onto the main road. "You met the aunt you never new you had, tonight didn't you?"

"Yeah." Antonio smiled softly. To think that Courtney, the girl he used to chunk rocks at when they were young, was his aunt was still hard to believe.

Nonetheless he had extended an olive branch to her that evening when they had gone to her apartment for dinner. He had expected to at least hear some comments from her about how she used to hate him when they were younger (something that would have left him with a secret feeling of success) but was relieved to find her a gracious host as she entertained he and his father for the night.

The evening spent at Courtney's place left him wondering how his mother could have allowed him to go for so many years without knowing that the people next door was his family too? And that was all they had ever been to him, the people next door who had the tall skinny girl who he liked to harass.

Keeping him ignorant was probably just another part of her attempt to keep him safe in her fucked up world of make believe. That was what he thought now as he rode in the car and felt the night air rush against his face.

Otis continued, "Besides, I told you I would never disappear on you again, didn't I?"

Antonio gave no reply; he simply looked out the window. After a while he spoke.

"You think Courtney and your moms can change your ol' man's

feelin's about me?"

"Aw yeah. It might take a little time but he'll come around."

"Mmh. It really don't matter no way." He spoke as he fingered a vent on the dashboard, closing and opening the slats.

But he had only spoken a half truth when he had said it didn't matter because a part of him did want to be accepted by his father's family; any family because it would mean that he did have a history that extended beyond the stifling, solitary world of his mother.

Yet at the same time he was reluctant to accept anyone who had not been a part of that world; and that was one of the things that had always kept him from forming substantial relationships.

But deeper than all else, was his feelings of inadequacy. He had never felt he fitted into anyone's life but his mother's, the life he despised. He had come to feel like he simply didn't belong to anyone or anything. A freak. So he had convinced himself that all this talk about his new family was something being postulated more out of his father's guilt and romantic longings than anything else. But he was willing to give it a try.

"Well I hope you change your mind, man, because those are your people whether you like it or not," Otis continued as he turned for a quick second to look at his son. "And besides, while I'm away, they'll be your main connection to me."

Antonio nodded his head. "I guess you got a point there."

They came to a stop at a light. Across the street there was a convenient store that blazed in the night, and all along the front in the parking lot were young men anxiously eyeing passing cars. Most of them were about Antonio's age and they moved like dark specters against the storefront.

Otis noticed Antonio looking at them as if he had knowledge of their methods, as if he was assessing their skills. This prompted Otis' concern.

"So what're you gonna do while I'm up in New York?" he asked.

"Work, I guess. To save me some money to come up there."

"Well you know I got you covered on that."

"Then why don't you just take me with you?" Antonio didn't look his father's way as he asked the question because he wasn't sure if he was ready for the reply.

Otis hesitated for a moment before he answered. "There are some things we have to look at."

Antonio turned his head back to the streets.

"We'll talk," Otis promised.

Suddenly Antonio turned to him. "Why were you in the joint?" He tried to pose the question in as non-obtrusive a manner as possible since he figured the subject he was broaching was a sensitive one, but he had to learn his father before he left. Maybe for good.

He never knew for sure that his father had been in prison; his mother had never told him why Otis was away. She only held him in sway with the promise that he would someday return. And it was this promise, this magical trust, that sustained him through all the bleak times in his life. And now that Otis had returned Antonio felt he deserved just a little bit of that magic, so being told to hold on a little longer wasn't what he wanted to hear.

It wasn't until he had become older and had begun to learn the ways of the world that he figured the magus for whom he waited might just have been in lock up.

Again, Otis was slow to respond. Then, "I was wondering when we would get to that."

"Was that one of the things you wanted to talk to me about?"

"Yeah," Otis answered.

"Oh. So what happened?"

"I was accused of something I didn't do."

"What?"

Otis didn't answer him.

"So you were set up?"

"Yeah. They set me up."

Antonio was now looking into his father's face trying to glean the story from his expression. "How?"

Otis nervously licked his lips as he searched for the words he wanted to say, but he wasn't sure of the words, how to let his son know that he was gay. In spite of Antonio's thinking that his father was about to leave him for good, it was he, Otis, who now worried about how not to lose him.

His hands tightened on the steering wheel. "Look, I- - really- - I'm not into this right now."

Antonio continued looking at him.

"But I was innocent. That's what matters," Otis contended.

"I believe you. It's just so fucked up that all that happened to you."

Otis nodded. "It was."

Slowly, a mischievous smile came across Antonio's face. "You know, we can always just keep drivin' and lose this place." He half kidded to ease the pain he saw in his father's face. It worked.

"Okay. We can do that for a little while, until it's time for you to go back to your place."

Antonio continued to smile. "If it'll give us more time together then that's cool."

Chapter XXIX

"You have to talk to him Terrell. I don't know what you said to him yesterday, but you upset him. He's too old for this, man."

"I didn't say anything that wasn't true Stanton, and he knows it." Terrell pushed the dish cloth across the counter top and swept vagrant crumbs into his hand as he finished cleaning the kitchen; it was part of his final chores around the house before he left for Atlanta.

"But it's not about that anymore." Stanton's voice came over the intercom in a plea.

"How can you say it's not about truth Stanton? That's exactly what's it about."

"But the truth's been told, Terrell. We all know the truth, so it's not about that anymore."

Terrell dried his hands on the dishtowel. "Then what is it about?"

"It's about a life's story. It's about a man who made some mistakes but who did much more good than his... crime."

Terrell listened as he put the receiver to his ear.

"Look, just come by and talk to him. He's been a friend to both you and me. You know that. Don't let it end like this. Just come by and talk with him."

He would not have taken Stanton up on his request, would have gone straight to Atlanta had it not been for Arthur, fair and just Arthur, who had told him it was only right that he should give the bishop a chance to tell his story. Even if he ended it with 'so fuck you', it would be worth hearing in order that he, Terrell, could shape a more accurate opinion of the situation. That is what Arthur had said in so many words when Terrell had called him after hanging up from Stanton.

But Arthur's suggestion served only as an added incentive to his going to Stanton's home to meet with Bishop Abrams. The other one, the one that drove him with intensity, was a need for validation. Twenty years ago the old man had taken away from him the most cherished gift a person could own, self worth, and now Terrell felt it was up to him to take it back, even if he had to wrench it from the old man's crooked fingers.

That night he drove up Prospect Hill, rising to the north of the downtown skyline, where he pulled up in front of Stanton's brownstone. The bishop was already there; his car was parked across the street.

Terrell didn't hesitate one minute. He immediately got out of his car and walked up the stairs to the front door. He heard the sound of heavy footsteps walk across the floor and when the door was opened, he was met by Stanton and a large bouvier.

Stanton greeted him in a cautious tone, "Come on in."

Terrell stepped in and the dog sniffed at his leg and feet.

"He won't bite. Come on in," Stanton repeated. "Bishop's in the living room." Stanton then led the large dog away by the collar to a room and closed the door, putting the dog away.

The bishop was sitting in a chair near a corner of the room. He sat with his hands folded in his lap. By the expression on his face, a weakened, sallow look that held eyes darkened by exhaustion, Terrell could see that the hands were clasped more out of nervousness than the confidence he was used to seeing in the man.

A rush of sorrow came over him as he beheld the bishop; stars are sometimes at their saddest when they are diminished. But he knew he had to stand fast. His well-being depend on it. He spoke to the bishop. He couldn't summon the respect to greet him. The bishop returned a greeting, his tone guarded.

"Why don't you take a seat here." Stanton gestured towards a chair. He then seated himself on the sofa. He leaned forward, "Look- -" he started to speak but was interrupted by Bishop Abrams.

"Brother Mitchell, I was telling the truth the other day. I haven't been involved in any of those activities since I got my calling. Mother Abrams has been the only person in my life since then."

"He's telling the truth Terrell," Stanton added as Terrell settled into the large chair.

"But the others are," Terrell said. "The others are involved in *those* activities and they're all your friends. Do you ever tell them they're wrong?"

"I don't have anything to do with what they do," the bishop defended.

"They're your friends."

"Who live their own lives."

"You have something to do with their lives though. You know that. You have a say in the life of anyone who gets close to you. You've helped Stanton get contracts and you helped Congressman West get elected; you confer with and advise your friends all the time, and they're all a part of this."

Stanton looked at Bishop with concern.

"Yeah, I know all about Congressman West, and all the others too," Terrell admitted.

"Who told you that?" Stanton spoke after turning back to Terrell. "Arthur?"

"No," Terrell replied before turning back to the bishop, "So what do you tell them when you're sitting in one room pretending like you don't know what's going on in the next one?" Terrell shook his head as he continued. "Bishop, I know you continued to show up to these 'soirees'," he swept the back of his hand through the air. "My source can vouch for it because he was once one of the young men."

At first the bishop was at a loss for words. Finally, he quietly spoke. "Your 'source' never saw me in any of the rooms."

"Just who is this source of yours anyway?" Stanton questioned, giving his full attention to Terrell as suddenly his concern for the bishop had become secondary. He continued, "I hear your old friend is back in town. Is it him? Because if it is, I don't even know him."

"No it's not him; it's a friend of his," Terrell replied. "Do you think the guys you've had don't talk? Do you think they're just pieces of meat for your pleasure?"

Stanton raised both of his hands and spoke, while creating slight chopping strokes to emphasize his words. "Terrell, now you know you can cause a lot of damage with what you're saying don't you?" He spoke, measuring each of his words as well as Terrell's reaction. "There are a lot of important people... good people who have given a lot for us. I mean they are people who have done more for you than you could ever know."

Terrell shook his head. "Stanton, man if I know, then that means the word's out- - somewhere you and all those 'good people' are known for more than your public deeds. How long did you think you could get away with all this?"

Suddenly Stanton made a vain attempt at calling Terrell's hand. "So we all messed around. We were all adults. Ain't nobody's business but ours."

"How do you know all the guys you had were adults? From what it seems you all come pretty close to crossing the line. Even I saw that when I was at Jerry's house. And I'm sure if someone decided to dig deep enough they would find that you crossed the line once or twice, maybe many times. None of you ever took time to find out because you were so busy taking care of *your* business. So you see, I don't have to say anything at all."

The room fell silent as if the cold shadow of Death had crossed it. From the other room Terrell could hear the dog sniffing at the door.

Now the three men sat with their eyes on the thing that had entered the room. This thing, amorphous and without name lay still before them, yet was so relevant that none of them could take their eyes off it. It was the thing that held each of the men's deepest concern within it: fear, guilt and the danger of matters unresolved. It was the thing that had brought them together that night and it was the thing that held them there.

Quietly, Terrell finally spoke. "It was the men, bishop. It was all the men who came through here that kept you coming back. Whether you touched them or not, just the fact that they were here kept you returning." He looked at Bishop

Abrams. "You're playing a game Bishop. And you're hurting people in the process."

Bishop Abrams lowered his head and rubbed his hand through his hair. "Terrell, I didn't hurt those guys." He looked at Terrell. "Never once, in years, did I even touch any of them. And yes, I admit to complicity, but you must know that I, never, engaged in their behavior."

"But you were still with us John," Stanton clipped. He called the bishop by his first name, no title as he was becoming offended by the bishop's attempt to separate himself from the circle.

Bishop Abrams gave a dismissive glance towards him and turned away.

Terrell continued. "You've hurt people in ways you don't seem to understand, or either refuse to understand." He watched the elder man for a second in the hope of catching at least a glimpse of humility, but there was none.

"How may people have you hurt by convincing them, no, coercing them," Terrell raised a finger stiffly into the air and shook his head, "into being someone other than who they really are?"

Bishop Abrams leaned forward. "None Brother Mitchell, and you know why? Because being homosexual is not who they really are."

"You don't believe that, Bishop, you know you don't. In your heart you know that's not true. You know that the way you feel wasn't your choice, so why do you feed into that lie?"

The bishop clenched his fists tightly in his lap, "Because I believe we have the capacity to turn to our higher selves. To overcome our faults, to- -"

"Oh John. Man, please." Stanton had had enough. "You know, I asked Terrell to come here to iron out this whole matter, but," he shook his head and stood up, "this denial stuff has to stop. Terrell's right, and you know it. Hell, all of us here know it. So why don't you just stop it."

The bishop slumped a bit, the weight of truth ringing his shoulders. He spoke in a soft voice. "Terrell. I just didn't want you to become like me. I just couldn't stand by and..." He slowly shook his head.

At that moment a car pulled up in front of the house. Stanton looked towards the window but not recognizing the car, continued the conversation. "Look, while I don't agree with Terrell that anybody who hung around us was under age, what he's talking about now, the hurt, is something entirely different."

The doorbell rang, cutting short Stanton's thoughts. The dog pawed at the door of the other room.

Stanton went to the door and looked out. "What's he want?" he mumbled as he opened the door. He stood as if to deny the person entrance but the man stepped inside anyway, brushing past Stanton. Terrell immediately recognized the man as being the same young man he'd seen at Jerry's house getting his dick sucked.

"You didn't give me all my money," the young man said.

Stanton shot out his arm to block the young man from coming further into the house. "I gave you..." Stanton started gruffly, then looking back at Terrell, he lowered his voice and spoke in a restrained manner. "I gave you what I always give you."

"I told you I needed more that night."

"You didn't *do* any more that night," Stanton smirked.

"Man, you gon' gimme my money." The young man spoke as he pushed Stanton's arm away.

Stanton grabbed the young man by the shoulder and slammed him against the wall.

Terrell and the bishop jumped to their feet. In the other room the large dog barked ferociously and shook the door with such force that Terrell thought it would break into.

"You need to leave," Stanton snarled as he held the young man against the wall.

Bishop Abrams called out, "Stanton! Stop it!"

Terrell stood speechless. Every word that could have come from his mouth was frozen somewhere in his head.

The young man's wiry frame was pressed hard against the wall by Stanton's large arms, but his anger had swelled to the point that he was willing to take the older man on. Suddenly, with great force, he propelled himself from the wall and he and Stanton went crashing into a table and lamp that sat along the adjacent wall.

Now the dog was almost through the door. Veins of light escaped as the door began to separate from the doorjamb. Someone was going to die this night. Terrell just knew it.

Father, is this payment for my sins?

Bishop Abrams rushed to the two men who had fallen to the floor. "Stanton, stop it!" Then he called to the dog, "Titus! Down! Lay down! Now!"

The dog seemed to recognize the bishop's voice and the door ceased to shake and the bark dwindled to a confused whine.

"Help me!" the bishop called to Terrell.

But just as Terrell was about to help the bishop separate the two men, another man charged through the doorway. It was the driver of the car in which the young man had arrived, and having witnessed the melee through the open door, he rushed to the aid of the young man. He threw Bishop Abrams out the way, pulled the young man from Stanton, and then, with all his might, lifted Stanton and pinned him to the very wall to which the young man had been held.

Terrell's breathing stopped as he looked on. Finally, exhaling a rush of air, he called the man's name. "Otis!"

But Otis didn't hear him. "Don't ever touch my son like that! You hear me!" He yelled in rage as he jammed Stanton against the wall.

"Otis!" Terrell called his name again.

This time Otis heard him. He turned and looked at Terrell. A stunned look had replaced the mask of rage on his face. "Terrell!?"

Stanton made an effort to swing at him, but Otis extended his arms and slammed him hard once again against the wall causing Stanton to momentarily lose his breath.

Terrell rushed over to where they were. "We have to make sense of all this. That's why I came here. We have to make sense of all this." He was waving his hands as if by doing so, he could dispel all the tragedy that had gathered in the room. Then he looked at Stanton who, though pinned against the wall, still attempted to fight back. "Stanton, stop it. It's over." He directed his words in an even tone. "Stop it. We have to stop this."

After a while the anger in Stanton began to subside, his body loosening. This caused Otis to begin to calm as well. He relaxed the muscles that had strained his arms and cautiously loosened his hold. Behind them Bishop Abrams lay crumpled on the floor.

"You okay?" Terrell asked.

"Y- - yes. I'm okay," he answered weakly.

Antonio stood to the side. His eyes were wide with confusion. "...Daddy?"

Terrell looked at Antonio and upon hearing him call his father, shook his head, "Oh my God."

Otis tuned to Terrell. "What the fuck is going on here?"

Stanton struggled to regain his composure as over in the corner Bishop Abrams tried to get up.

"What the fuck is goin' on here!" Otis yelled again as he turned to his son who could only shake his head.

Terrell went over to help the bishop. "Bishop, you sure you okay?"

Suddenly. Those words. The man. The awareness cut through Otis like a sharp blade opening all the years and all the memories. "Bishop?" he asked as he turned back to Terrell. Now it was he who stiffened, his face stone hard and with eyes like flame, as he walked towards the bishop.

The broken glass of the lamp splintered and popped underneath his shoes with each step he took.

"Bishop, you know me?" He spoke menacingly. He wanted the old man to feel fear before he killed him. Killing him without seeing his legs shake or piss run down his leg would not be enough. He asked again as he came closer, "You know me?"

Terrell stood in front of the bishop. "Otis. Don't!" He could feel Bishop Abrams' body tremor against his back. "You have a life now Otis. Leave it alone. You got your life back."

Stanton started to move towards Otis to stop him but thought better of it, so he looked at Terrell in hope of him reaching the tall muscular man who had fire in his eyes and the cold of death in his mouth.

"Otis." Terrell was almost pleading now.

Suddenly, from the doorway Antonio called out.

"Daddy! No!"

Otis slowed a bit but continued his focus on the bishop.

"Man I don't wanna lose you again," Antonio said as he began to cry, "I don't - - wanna lose you again."

The sound of his tears stopped Otis. "You ain't gonna lose me." He spoke while still looking at the bishop. Then he turned to his son. "You ain't gonna lose me." And he walked over and took his son's head and held it to his shoulder.

Terrell felt Bishop Abrams go limp, his body releasing the fear. He helped the bishop into the living room where he sat him down. He looked back into the foyer where Otis stood with his arm around Antonio's shoulders continuing to console him, while Stanton stood back with a look of humility.

Bishop Abrams dropped his head and began to cry in a soft whisper. "I'm sorry. I'm sorry."

Terrell walked away from him and back into the foyer. "Stanton, we're leaving."

Stanton nodded.

"Let's go," he said as he put his hand on Otis and Antonio's shoulders.

In the distance he heard sirens coming towards the house. He knew Stanton would dismiss the police without any charges being pressed, so he turned to Otis and Antonio. "We have to talk." Then they got in their cars and drove away.

Chapter XXX

Otis walked further into the living room, away from the dining area where his family sat, so he could hear Emory better.

"Yeah. United flight one-eleven. It should arrive around noon."

"It's a good thing you're flying into Newark because that's my lunch break," Emory warned.

"Of course I'm flyin' into Newark. Why would I go way out to Kennedy?"

"You know how you can be. You can do some pretty strange shit."

Otis laughed. "I know. But those days are over."

"I hope so."

"Yeah, well…"

"That it?"

"... Yeah."

"See ya tomorrow."

"Tomorrow."

He hung up the phone.

"Tell your friend not to interrupt your going away dinner." It was Dana, as usual, issuing a reprimand to him as he returned to the dining room.

His mother looked at him, then turned to Dana. "This ain't no goin' away dinner, it's a comin' home dinner."

"Here here, granma," Jamil said. He then raised his glass for a toast.

"Here's to Uncle Otis' homecoming."

Everyone raised their glasses.

Later that night as he was packing, someone knocked on his bedroom door.

"Come on in," he called as he folded a pair of slacks.

"It's just me," Munny said as she stuck her head in the room.

"Come on in."

"I made a cake for you to take back." She stepped into the room carrying a marvelous white cake.

"Awww. Thanks."

She smiled as she placed the cake on the bureau and covered it with a plastic cover. "I hope your friend likes it."

"Friend?" He was caught off guard by her assumption, but accepted her comment as a step towards her accepting his life. "I'm sure he will. He loves good food."

"So he eats a lot like you."

"Yep," Otis laughed.

Munny walked over to the bed, where Otis stood, and began helping him pack. "So everything's okay with you? Your job and all?"

"Yeah. Emory worked everything out for me. I just have to make certain commitments when I get back. They already have it in writin' for me to sign."

"That's good, because it would be crazy for you to throw all that away. Especially with what you been through. Everything should be of real importance to you."

"I know. And I knew that then; but it was like, suddenly nothin' mattered anymore. It was like, I just had to go."

"I guess it was time to go."

"Yeah."

"I can understand that." She picked up a shirt and flapped it to shake out the wrinkles. "Sometimes we have to just let things flow. I always said," she lay the shirt flat across the bed, "that we all got our own course to travel. You were just following yours."

"Yeah, but I almost fucked everything up."

"Maybe, maybe not."

"Oh, I almost fucked it up," Otis said, nodding his head. "Thank God Emory helped me out."

"You know what Mama always said, 'Everything has its place and time.' You were where you were supposed to be and Emory was where he was supposed to be."

"All the actors in place, huh?"

She smiled. "Now remember that so you can know your cue next time."

Otis widened his eyes. This was not the Munny he was used to. "Yes ma'am."

Munny blushed and continued with the packing.

"How 'bout yourself. You okay?" Otis asked.

She didn't look up; she went about her task. "Oh yeah."

"Ford must be treatin' you alright. You been there, how long?"

"Going on seventeen years. It's a good place to work. I'm just surprised

I've never been laid off during the downturns."

"That is good."

"I figure it's because I'm a woman; you know, they have to keep a certain number of us there to make it look good."

"Or maybe you're just a good worker. Remember? Let it flow." He wanted to say more, to ask more about her. How was her life? She was the quiet one, the one that stirred the least; yet he watched her moving about his room with such calm that he realized that whoever she is, she is at peace. There was no feel of remorse about her, no sense of pain or anger. Yes she stirred the least, but the waves encountered from her touch reached far. He would have to return to learn more. Yes he would return.

They finished packing and Munny turned to him. "Wake me before you leave tomorrow."

"I will."

She hugged him and disappeared from the room.

He sat for a while and looked at the luggage on the bed. The house had become quiet as everyone had left or had turned in for the night. He would have gone to bed as well, but he knew he wouldn't be able to sleep. He was still weakened by the scene from the other night, not over encountering the bishop, he had seen just how insignificant he had become, but from discovering the life his son had been leading.

That night, on the way back to Antonio's apartment, he had told his son of the events that had led up to his leaving Cincinnati. Then he had turned to him and had asked "why?" Why had he chosen to live the life of a hustler?

At first Antonio had no answer, he had shaken his head and hunched his shoulders before turning away. Then, with his face still turned from his father, he said, "It makes me feel like I'm somebody."

His voice had been so small that night, but now it rang in Otis' ears as he sat on his bed. He knew he would have to do something before he left the next day.

Epilogue

The last of the bags were in the car. Terrell took one last look around the house to make sure everything was secure.

He had decided to leave for Atlanta a day earlier; the kids were ecstatic over the news and Karen had seemed satisfied yet concerned.

He understood her concern because he shared it.

His plane would be leaving in about three and a half hours and he would be on it. It would be the first step on a long journey the outcome of which neither he or Karen could be certain.

As he moved through the rooms checking for lights left on, or open windows he felt sure of one thing, and that was the love he held for himself. It had been taken away from him once before, this love, but now he had taken it back. And he knew that, no matter the outcome, the love he now held was large enough to accommodate anyone, even those who might not be able to accept him.

He had decided he would never tell anyone about Bishop and the circle of men; even Sister Abrams had placed a call, her secrets were just as dark. The congressman and his wife... Karen nor anyone else must ever know, at least from his mouth. He had agreed to keep their secret; it was easier that way. After all, the events that were now unfolding in his own life would most likely consume more than enough of his time and energy. He had too much to do than to involve himself with the lives of others.

His rounds completed he walked through the living room where he stopped at the phone. He picked it up and erased all the messages and cleared the display. Then he hung up the phone and walked out to the car.

Otis adjusted his seat at the request of the stewardess as the plane began its descent. He had taken a trip to the past and was now returning home. He thought about the people he left back in Cincinnati: his family, friends and loves. They all formed a collective conscious that would forever serve as part of the stream of his life.

And the past. He now realized that the past was not to be revisited for the sake of retribution nor redemption. That could never be. Rather, it served as a milepost for the seasons to come; and now that he understood all this, he would forever be grateful.

He looked over at Antonio who peered out the window of the plane. There was a life to be lived for the both of them.

The plane rounded and readied for its descent, and, looking out the window past his son, he took in the grotesque beauty of New York City and smiled as the plane touched down on the runway.

The End

04 07

Printed in the United States
72558LV00004B/220

9 781411 631977